••○ Praise for The Ic

"An icy adventure with a warm heart, *The Ice Sea Pirates* is a fantastical celebration of the precious power of love." Kiran Millwood Hargrave, author of *The Girl of Ink and Stars*

"Philosophical, breathtakingly beautiful and unwaveringly kind, *The Ice Sea Pirates* is a wild adventure with a huge heart. If brave Siri ran the world, it would be a much kinder place ... a beautiful book singing with hope and justice." Sarah Driver, author of *The Huntress*

"If you love a rollicking adventure where the unexpected makes you stop and think, you'll love *The Ice Sea Pirates.* ... a hypnotising read-alone for confident middle graders or a perfect bed-time story for any age." *Kids' Book Review*

"non-stop action and page-turning excitement" *The Sapling*

"The joy of this narrative is in the telling ... a dramatic and atmospheric story." *The Source*

"What I really, really loved about this book is that Siri's journey involves encounters with massively complex characters ..." *Radio New Zealand*

"Frida Nilsson's epic adventure is a modern classic ... It's impossible to put down." *SvD Swedish Daily News*

"With her fantastic imagination and strong storytelling, [Nilsson] has us on tenterhooks until the very last page. This is the magic of reading at its strongest." *Ulrika Larsson*

The Ice Sea Pirates

The Ice Sea Pirates

Frida Nilsson

Illustrated by David Barrow
Translated by Peter Graves

GECKO PRESS

UK edition first published in 2018 by Gecko Press
PO Box 9335, Wellington 6141, New Zealand
info@geckopress.com

Distributed in the United States and Canada by Lerner Publishing Group,
lernerbooks.com
Distributed in the United Kingdom by Bounce Sales and Marketing,
bouncemarketing.co.uk
Distributed in Australia by Scholastic Australia, scholastic.com.au
Distributed in New Zealand by Upstart Distribution, upstartpress.co.nz

The cost of this translation was defrayed by a subsidy from the Swedish Arts
Council, gratefully acknowledged.

Edited by Penelope Todd
Cover design by Ness Wood
Design and typesetting by Vida & Luke Kelly, New Zealand
Printed and bound by CPI Group (UK) Ltd, Croydon, CR0 4YY

ISBN paperback: 978-1-776572-00-7 (UK)
ISBN hardback: 978-1-776571-45-1 (USA)
ISBN paperback: 978-1-776571-46-8
Ebook available

For more curiously good books, visit geckopress.com

Contents

Map of the Ice Sea   10

1. Miki   13

2. Iron Apple   20

3. The Cormorant that Came Back   29

4. The *Pole Star*   37

5. Sea Parrot for Supper   43

6. A Long Way Out, a Long Way Home   50

7. The Story of Hanna   56

8. A Gun in Bed   63

9. The Wolf Islands   69

10. An Errand with Urstrom   78

11. The Signal   85

12. I Fire a Gun   93

13. Some Are Cut Out to Be Hunters   101

14. A Boat Called *Cuttlefish*   108

15. Wood   116

16. The Child in the Water   124

17.	The Inhabitants of Snowrose	131
18.	Looking for a Boat	138
19.	The Game	144
20.	Leaving	150
21.	A Visit from the Sea	157
22.	Snow	163
23.	The Boy on the Stool	170
24.	The Blanket	176
25.	Blood in the Snow	183
26.	No Finer Fisherman	188
27.	The Shops in Seglen	195
28.	The Seglen Arms	201
29.	Disaster	207
30.	The Man on the Hill	213
31.	Who Found Me on the Ice?	222
32.	The Corpse of *Cuttlefish*	229
33.	Target Shooting	235
34.	Bragder	242
35.	The Mine	250
36.	The Children	257

37. Little Sister 264

38. The Coal Seam 272

39. Captain Whitehead 281

40. Pressure and Heat 289

41. True Dreams 296

42. Dove 304

43. The Right Piece 312

44. The Ring 321

45. A Triple Salute 327

46. Free 334

47. Between Wet Holm and Cat Skerry 343

48. Young Things 349

49. Blue Bay 356

◆ ◆ ◇ ◆ ◆

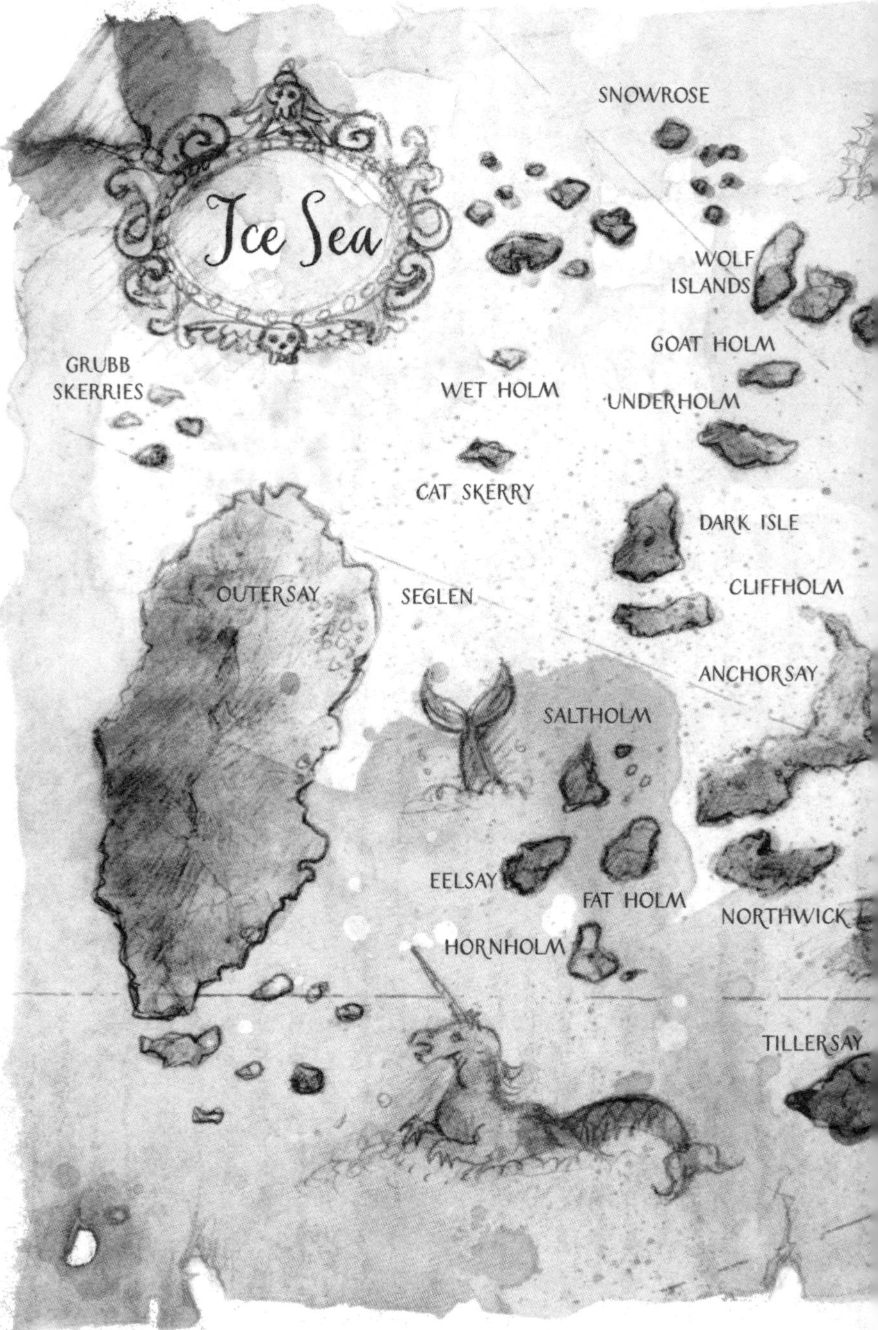

Ice Sea

SNOWROSE

WOLF
ISLANDS

GOAT HOLM

GRUBB
SKERRIES

WET HOLM

UNDERHOLM

CAT SKERRY

DARK ISLE

OUTERSAY

SEGLEN

CLIFFHOLM

ANCHORSAY

SALTHOLM

EELSAY

FAT HOLM

NORTHWICK

HORNHOLM

TILLERSAY

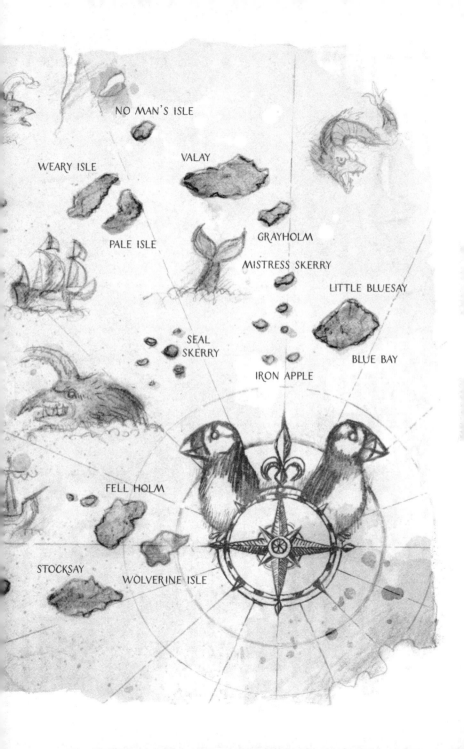

Miki

This story is about the time I went out on the Ice Sea. It was the middle of November, I had just had my tenth birthday, and there were whales resting in our bay. Clouds of spume hung above their shining backs, and a thick mist, white and beautiful, had been blanketing the horizon for days.

In Blue Bay, where I live, winters can be so cold that the air freezes the sails of ships. I found a bird on the ground once, a cormorant that had dropped from the sky when its wings went rigid from cold. It wasn't dead. I carried it home to Dad, who has such a knack with animals that we were able to let the bird go after a couple of days.

Dad has a way with everything in the natural world. There's something on our kitchen wall—a thing most people don't have on their walls. A piece of a mermaid's flipper. Not very big, about the size of the corner of a hankie, a little bit furry and slightly pinkish. When Dad was younger, he caught the mermaid in his net when he was fishing for cod. She was so frightened that she screamed and her flippers whipped back and forth. She obviously thought he wasn't going to release her, but he did, of course.

"Because it's one thing to catch cod and quite another to catch a mermaid," he said. "There are some things we don't do!"

Once she'd calmed down he freed her gently from the net and let her go. But a small piece of flipper had been torn off and lay on the bottom of the boat. That's the piece he mounted on a board and nailed up on our kitchen wall. Miki and I glued pebbles around it.

Miki is my sister and she's the reason I ventured out on the Ice Sea. Because, you see, there are some people who believe there's no difference between catching a cod and catching a mermaid. Or doing even worse things. Where I live, there was a time when pirates roamed the seas. Foul, wicked pirates.

"Tell me about Whitehead," Miki used to say when we were lying on the pull-out sofa and it was time to go to sleep. Dad was in the bedroom snoring so hard the whole house seemed to shake.

"But you won't go to sleep if I do," I answered. "You'll stay awake half the night crying and you'll wake me up. We'll be useless in the morning."

"I promise!" she whispered close to my ear.

"I promise to go to sleep. Please tell me. Please, please, please, nice Siri!"

So I told her anyway. And, as always when I told Miki about Whitehead, I started like this.

"There's a man who treats children as if they're animals. And inside that man, in the place where other people have a soul, there's a space as empty and cold as an ice cave."

"He's the coldest man there is," Miki said. She always wanted to help out with the storytelling and, in fact, she knew the story as well as I did.

"That's right, the coldest man you can possibly imagine," I said. "He's a pirate captain, you see, and his hair is as white as snow. It's so long it reaches his waist, but he wears it up in a bun, the way ladies do."

"Why?"

"Because he doesn't want his hair to freeze and snap off. Anyone who joins Whitehead and serves as one of his pirates becomes rich. Unbelievably rich. Do you know why?"

"Because Whitehead lets his crew keep all the loot for themselves."

"Yes. He lets his pirates share all the gold and silver, all the iron and furs, all the money chests and valuables among themselves. He doesn't want anything. The only thing he wants…" I felt a shudder in my stomach as I always did when I reached this part of the story. "The only thing he wants is children. Small, thin children, the smaller the better. Whenever the pirates get hold of small children they throw them straight into the ship's hold."

"What does the ship look like?"

"It's white, with three masts. On the prow, right at the front, there's a wooden raven's head with a gaping bill. The ship's called the *Snow Raven*."

"But nearly everyone just calls it the *Raven*."

"That's right. And in the *Raven* they sail all the way to Whitehead's island."

"Where's that?"

"Far to the west. As far as you can sail before tumbling over the edge of the world. You know there's a place called Seglen, don't you, Miki?"

"Yes." Miki's voice was hoarse.

"And you know what kind of place it is?"

"It's a village. A big village with paved streets. Pirates go there to drink and brawl and..."

"Well, I'm not exactly sure about the brawling. But I do know that Seglen is not a nice place and that a lot of rough people go there. All kinds of crooks. People who want to make money by stealing it from others. And by far the worst are the ones who come looking for Whitehead so they can work for him. Probably Whitehead's island is somewhere near Seglen."

"What happens to children who are taken to his island? What do they have to do there?"

"Whitehead has a mine," I said. "A great chasm in the earth."

"What kind of mine?" Miki said.

"No one knows. But they *say…*"

"They say it's a diamond mine!"

"Exactly."

"And there are masses of diamonds in the ground. Some as big as apples," Miki said.

"That's what they say, anyway. They also say he has a prison warden—a woman—who guards all the children. That woman…"

"That woman is Whitehead's daughter and she's had all her teeth taken out and diamonds put in instead."

"That's right. And Whitehead drinks his wine from a mug carved from a single diamond. You know how valuable diamonds are, don't you, Miki?"

"Mm."

"You could buy our whole island for a diamond no bigger than a pea."

"But why…why does he need children to work there? Why can't he have grown-ups?" she asked.

"No one really knows," I answered. "But just imagine crawling round in the dark from morning till night. With a pick in your hand and your knees all bloody. Children aren't likely to last long in the mine. Either their backs break from the loads they have to carry or the damp gives them lung disease.

Or the darkness drives them so mad that they…well, they just give up the ghost."

Miki swallowed hard.

"It's the worst thing…" she whispered.

"Yes," I whispered back. "To be kidnapped by pirates and taken to that mine is the worst thing that can happen to a child."

And that's the point in the story where I'd stop telling Miki about Whitehead.

When we were lying in bed, all this seemed no more than a fairy tale. Or something that could only happen to other poor children. Of course, we were terrified of the pirates, but it never ever occurred to us that we might meet them ourselves one day. I would never have believed for a moment that Whitehead would sink his claws into my little sister.

◆ ◆ ◇ ◆ ◆

2

Iron Apple

Now I'm going to tell you about a day at Iron Apple—a day I'll never forget. It sticks in my memory with a sea urchin's grip and I know it will never let go as long as I live.

Miki and I were going to pick berries. As we headed out that morning Dad looked miserable.

"Why can't I come with you?" he asked. He was wearing nothing but his long johns.

"You couldn't manage it," I said. "You know you couldn't. Eat your breakfast and we'll see you at lunchtime."

Dad looked at his slice of bread on the table, with a piece of cold boiled cod on it.

"I'm not hungry," he muttered. "And I don't like you going out on your own like this. It's not right."

"There's no other way," I answered, pulling my cap down over my ears. "We have to have something to eat, don't we?"

He looked at me with his big watery eyes.

"If only I weren't so old," he said. "Then I'd spend all day rowing around at sea, rowing so hard that the waves foamed. And I'd bring home enough berries and eggs and fish to fill your stomachs. And if I met Whitehead's mob I'd smash their darned ship to firewood."

He put his hand to his eyes and wiped away tears.

"Don't worry," I said. "There's a good view from Iron Apple and if we sight the *Raven* we'll jump in our boat and row home. We'll race them."

Miki shuddered. Dad looked at her; he would rather let her stay home. But he didn't say anything: it was much quicker with two of us picking berries.

I reached up and stroked his cheek.

"Little Stick," I said. "Don't worry. We'll be back quicker than you think."

We called Dad Little Stick even though he was big and tall. We did it because he always said that if Miki and I left him, he'd snap in half like a little stick.

Iron Apple is a small island that belongs to us. That's the way things are out here—each family owns several islands where they can hunt and collect food without anyone else interfering. That day Miki and I rowed out in the dinghy on a sea that was gray and smooth. There was a cold, biting dampness in the air, though, and the whole world seemed painted with milk. The mists of November were slowly creeping closer to the shore.

"Tell me about when our parents met," Miki said. She was hanging over the side looking down at the water.

"I've told you a thousand times already."

She turned round. "Just once more then," she asked. "Please, Siri?"

And so I told her the story because I could see she was anxious and it was good to give her something else to think about.

"Dad was out in the boat setting his nets when a sudden storm blew up and he fell into the water. There was no one to help him and the water was so icy that he knew he'd soon die. But then, through the foaming waves, he caught sight of a skerry and swam towards it as fast as he could."

"He could swim in those days, then?"

"Yes, he could. This was a long time ago. Long before you and I were born. He was the strongest man in the whole village."

"But he couldn't climb up, could he?"

"No, the rocks of the skerry were too steep. He'd come to the point of thinking it was hopeless and letting the waves swallow him, when Ma appeared. She lived on the skerry all by herself and was just going fishing."

"With her toes!"

"Yes, with her toes. She always went fishing with her toes. You'd never believe how the fish took the bait! And suddenly she had a bite. It was Dad, who'd caught hold of her little toe, and she pulled him up. He was more than twice as old as her but he stayed on the skerry for seven years. Then I arrived and that's when they moved to the village."

"And then I came."

"Yes, that was a little later, though. And you were so slow. It took you three days and three nights to come out of her tummy once you got going."

Miki poked her finger into the water. The swell washed over her hand and wet the sleeve of her jacket.

"Why did she die?"

"Because she became ill."

"Because of me?"

"No, it wasn't that…she would have died anyway."

That, perhaps, wasn't strictly true. Our mother had almost certainly died because Miki took so long, but no one ever mentioned that, and no one loved Miki any the less because of it. If anyone was glad about Miki's arrival it was our mother. She said it was always nicer to get something you really had to fight for. She only lived for a week after that.

Iron Apple lay wreathed in mist as we approached.

There was no question of a view out to sea—we'd be lucky to see where we were putting our feet.

We each had a basket for berries. Snowberries are white, quite bitter, and ripen late in the year. They can be stored for a long time in a jar of water. If there's any honey around they make a good preserve.

But what made berry picking tricky on Iron Apple were the bogle birds. They weren't so dangerous during the summer since the cock birds were away in other waters and we could collect their eggs for eating. But the cock birds returned in late autumn, and after that the eggs had chicks in them, ready to hatch when winter was at its freezing coldest. Once the eggs have chicks inside, the mother birds go mad if anyone approaches their nests. I actually know a man in Blue Bay who had his ear pecked off, because bogle birds have strong-toothed beaks for chewing stones. They eat stones to make them heavy enough to dive deep for fish. Bogle birds are big and need to eat a great deal: a female weighs at least thirty-five pounds. They have dense, black-speckled plumage, and their enormous webbed feet have claws as well.

The most important way to avoid being pecked is not to look scared, but Miki was useless at that. She was only seven, so it's hardly surprising. But I suppose I was a bit hard on her. When we'd

searched the whole morning and found only a handful of berries I told her to go and see what she could find on the other side of the island.

She looked at me with her gray eyes. She'd lost quite a few front teeth and a new lower tooth poked up like the tip of a small ice floe.

"Can't you come with me?" she said. "I don't want to go so far on my own."

"Don't be childish," I said. "It's not far at all."

She turned round and stared across the rocky island. The wind was rising and it tugged at her thick black hair. She looked as if she was going to cry again.

"Do you need your hand held even for the toilet?" I said. "The sooner you go, the sooner we'll be home!"

She swallowed hard and although she obviously didn't want to, she set off across the rocks. She was wearing her winter boots. They'd been mine too, when I was seven.

After a while I caught sight of white-speckled bushes and hurried over. There were masses of berries! I picked and picked and soon had twice as many in my basket. I ran my fingers through them. There's something special about the feel of berries in a basket, particularly if you've managed to collect lots.

All of a sudden I heard a scream from the other side of the island. At first I just sighed, sure it was

Miki making a fuss about the birds. But then I felt a sort of jolt inside, because there were no more screams. Once she started, Miki usually carried on. All I could hear was the wind, so I picked up my basket and headed in her direction.

"Miki!" I called.

There was no reply. I started running. Bogle birds have strong beaks and I didn't want to take my sister home to Blue Bay minus her ears.

"Miki!" I shouted louder. But there was still no reply, so I hurried over the rocky ground as fast as I could.

When I reached the other side of the island, it was empty. There was no sign of her, or of any birds. The wind had blown away the mist and I was about to shout for the third time when I saw a rowboat. In it sat four men—and Miki! They'd tied a rag around her mouth and one had a grip on her arm. The boat was rowing farther and farther from Iron Apple. The basket fell from my hand and all the berries rolled out. I was going to shout again, but then I caught sight of another boat. A much bigger one. The words stuck in my throat, too frightened to come out. Perhaps because they knew the depths of wickedness that lay anchored there on the drowsy sea. The three masts were as straight as spears, the hull as white and rounded as an egg. The sails flapped impatiently in the wind and on the prow of the ship was an ugly wooden raven's head, its beak gaping wide. It was Whitehead's *Snow Raven*, the ship we were all so afraid of, the ship that Blue Bay people had talked about so often it had been easy to take it for a fairy tale. Oh, if only the *Snow Raven* was no more than a fairy tale!

There were people on deck and some were lowering a rope ladder to the men in the rowboat. They lifted Miki first and then climbed up themselves. They tied the rowboat to the stern of the ship. The wind across Iron Apple was growing stronger and the crew slowly turned the ship and set a course for the horizon. They'd soon be gone, and when that dawned on me, I recovered my voice.

"MIKI! DON'T BE SCARED!"

But Miki was already below decks. A couple of the men turned and saw me standing there. They shouted to the man at the wheel. I assumed they were asking whether they should turn back for me too. The man hesitated before shaking his head and steering out to sea. I wondered whether Whitehead was also there watching me, or in his cabin thinking of the myriads of diamonds his new prisoner would bring him from beneath the earth.

◆ ◆ ◇ ◆ ◆

The Cormorant
that Came Back

Never had I run as fast as I ran that day—my boots hardly seemed to touch the ground. Don't be scared was my only thought, don't be scared, Miki, I'm going for help. When the men and women in the village hear what's happened they'll take their guns, every one of them, and set out to bring you home.

My basket stayed on Iron Apple while I threw myself into the dinghy and started rowing. The wind was against me, but terror flowed into my arms and helped me row hard. The boat flew across the water but, even so, the journey seemed to take an eternity. A horrible, icy eternity that made my stomach churn.

Eventually I neared the bay. A vessel had arrived a couple of days earlier, but a cluster of smaller boats, all low, single-masted and unpainted, were also tied up at the fishing wharf. The Blue Bay fishing boats.

There were a lot of people about. One man was mending a mast and someone else was tarring a hull. A sail was being patched and a catch unloaded. Someone was laughing at a joke and someone else cursing a tangled fishing line. Wherever you looked, men and women in gray clothes were bending over their tasks.

Olav was sitting there, gutting cod. He was a friend of Dad's and they'd often fished together. A gull was eyeing the skin and scraps around Olav's feet. I tied the dinghy and rushed up onto the quay. Olav raised his knife in greeting.

"You seem to be in a hurry," he said with a smile. "Are you being chased by a prawn?"

"I have to get home," was all I managed to say as I ran past him "Dad..."

"Your dad's here!" he called after me.

I turned and Olav pointed over his shoulder with the knife.

"He's struggling with a net."

And so he was, sitting against a shed wall, trying to mend a net. He was stiff, his fingers wouldn't obey him and the net was awkward.

"Dad!" I yelled.

Dad raised his head. He looked happy, as he always did when he saw me or Miki. He said we were the two lighthouses lighting the darkness around him, however black it might be. But when he saw that I was crying, his smile disappeared.

"What's happened?" he asked.

I rushed into his arms.

"They've taken her, Dad! It was my fault!"

He looked at me, anxiety in his big watery eyes.

"What are you talking about? Where's Miki?"

Several men and women nearby had stopped working and were staring in our direction. Olav had moved closer. I was crying—crying so hard that my words were thick and muddled in my mouth.

"We were on Iron Apple. I told her to go to the other side of the island and...and...there was a boat. They took her, took her out to a ship...oh, oh, oh!"

Dad said nothing. He looked at me as if he were a child and I was speaking a language he couldn't understand.

Then Olav, standing with a half-gutted cod in his hand, said, "Who took her, Siri? What kind of ship was it?"

I raised my voice so everyone could hear. "The *Snow Raven*!"

Within seconds every single person on the wharf had fallen silent.

"Whitehead's taken my sister!" I went on. "We have to go after them and get her back!"

They all stared at me with strange, frightened

looks. No one said a thing. No one shouted, "Yes, let's go after the ship!" None of them rushed to fetch their guns.

"Hurry!" I shouted. "They're sailing west from Iron Apple. They'll be at Seal Skerry by now!"

No one moved. They looked away, stared at the ground, muttered to one another, and then someone said, "Anyone going after the *Snow Raven* is as good as dead!"

"That's right. It has sixteen cannon and the crew is only too happy to shoot at anyone who comes near," someone else called out.

"No one can get the better of Whitehead!"

Olav put a fishy hand on my shoulder. "Siri." He looked at me with sorrow in his eyes. "Your sister is gone. People taken by Whitehead no longer exist. That's the way of it."

There was someone, though, prepared to step forward. Fragile as an old boat with its wood rotting and white, but his fists were clenched. My dad.

"I'll go after her!" His voice shook with anger and courage. "I'm not afraid! A sea worm is no better just because he commands a ship! Who dares come with me?"

No one spoke. Several men shook their heads.

"Old fool!" someone whispered. "Fair chance he'll die of old age before Whitehead gets round to killing him."

Dad pretended not to hear. He thrust out his jaw, tucked the tangled net under his arm and walked away. I followed him.

The cottages in our village climb the cliffs. They're built of wood, often driftwood since there are very few trees on our island.

"Do you really think you can do it, Dad?" I asked as we trudged homeward. He walked with a slight limp since an accident when he and some others were out netting sea parrots on the steep cliffs. Dad had fallen quite a way.

"I may be old," he said, "but that doesn't stop me being a father." He hid his face in his hands. "Poor little thing. You know how frightened she always is. I can't bear to think how she'll be feeling." He sniffed and put on a determined face. "At six tomorrow morning the *Pole Star* sails. It will be the last ship to leave Blue Bay before winter and it will call in at Seglen. I'm signing on."

I shuddered. Seglen! That was the dreadful place I'd often told Miki about. The place where pirates, ruffians and rabble clustered as thick as auks on a rock skerry. And Dad meant to go there.

"That's my best chance of finding Miki and bringing her home," he said as he limped along the village street. "Let's get home and do my packing."

By that evening everything stood ready inside the door. A kitbag of warm clothes, a couple of fishcakes wrapped in paper, Dad's winter boots and his gun. He checked it all carefully then nodded.

"Right then. I'm going to get a few hours' sleep. Wake me in time, won't you?"

I nodded. I was always first up in the morning, woken by the fact that the kitchen fire had gone out and the cold was nipping my nose. After stirring the embers with the poker and putting on fresh wood I'd go through to the bedroom and shake Dad awake. That wasn't always easy: I think he would have slept for days on end under the fur covers if he'd been allowed to.

He walked over to the bed with stiff, uneven steps and loosened his braces. As he sat there on the edge of the bed I realized how small he actually was. Like a twig, gray, dry and thin. It would take little more than a touch to snap him.

"Are you crying?" he asked me.

"What if you don't come back?" I said, drying my cheeks. "What if...what if I'm left here all alone?"

He looked down at his feet and chewed on his lip. Then he said: "Remember the bird you found on the ground one winter? With frozen wings?"

I nodded.

"Did you know that I've seen her since then? That she's been back?"

"No." I sat on the bed beside him. "When?"

"She comes sometimes and taps on the window with her beak. Just to say hello. I usually give her a piece of fish. Nothing special really. But what I mean is…well, the things you do leave a trail. Good things leave a good trail, and bad things leave a bad trail. If I don't go for Miki I couldn't live with myself. My trail would be too painful."

He looked me in the eye.

"I've let you and Miki work much harder than you deserve. I've been ashamed of that every single day. And I'm not so stupid that I don't understand how this journey will end. After all, I'll soon be seventy, but I have to go."

He stroked my cheek. Then he lay down to sleep with all his clothes on.

I understood what that meant. He knew he wasn't going to survive. But rather than stay home with a bad conscience, he was going anyway.

But was he giving any thought to me? Was he thinking of my conscience and the trail that would stay forever with me? I was the one who'd told Miki to go to the other side of the island. She'd begged me to go with her and I'd just mocked her. And now Dad was going to his death because of it.

I lay wondering for what felt like an eternity until I finally made my decision. The fire in the hearth was going out. Quiet as a mouse I tiptoed over and threw in four or five sticks. Then I put on my jacket and my winter boots. They were just like the ones I'd had when I was seven—the ones Miki was wearing now.

Don't be scared, Miki, I thought. I'm coming to fetch you.

I emptied Dad's clothes out of the kitbag and put in two pairs of socks and my thick jumper with the collar. Then I shouldered the bag and opened the door. I knew that my chances of getting the better of Whitehead were as small as anyone's, but I certainly didn't intend to die out there on the Ice Sea!

◆ ◆ ◇ ◆ ◆

The *Pole Star*

A whale, quite a small one, had drifted into the bay in its sleep. Its back gleamed in the moonlight. No one in Blue Bay hunts whales because it brings bad luck, so whales would safely gather outside our bay every year when the temperature went down. They'd stay for a few weeks before swimming to warmer waters so far south that no one I knew had ever been there.

The *Pole Star* of Tillersay Island was a two-masted cargo ship that sailed its circular route time after time: Tillersay to Blue Bay, Blue Bay to the Wolf Islands, the Wolf Islands to Seglen, and Seglen back to Tillersay. It was about to make its last trip before winter.

Not many of the crew were in sight as I walked up the swaying gangway. Two sailors were loading barrels, watched by a cat sitting on the quayside.

A tall man with hollow cheeks and a surly

expression caught sight of me. "And where are you going?" he asked, striding over. He wore a fur coat with gleaming buttons and thick gold earrings.

"I'm coming aboard," I said. "I'm coming with you to Seglen."

"Are you, indeed?" He gave me a searching look. "And do you have the money to pay for your journey, by any chance?"

"No, I'm going to work my passage." That's what Dad had intended to do. "I'll do any jobs that need doing on board."

The sailors turned and grinned.

"Is that what you reckon?" The man laughed. "A nice thought, but sadly we've no use for someone who barely reaches the ship's rail. Why do you want to go to Seglen? It's no place for a child."

"I'm going to find Whitehead," I answered. "He's taken my sister and I'm going to take her back."

At that, the man went pale and his eyes grew round and white. The sailors were no longer grinning.

"W-whitehead?" the man said in a hoarse voice. "Are you completely...?"

He fell silent and scanned the dark horizon as if the *Snow Raven* might come dashing over it at any moment. He swallowed hard, then shook his head.

"Go! Get off! You're of no use on the Ice Sea."

"She'd be of some use to me, though," a voice growled. The surly fellow turned round. Behind him stood a big, broad-shouldered man with a bushy red beard and a fat belly.

The surly one raised his eyebrows. "Really?" he said. "How, may I ask, Fredrik?"

Fredrik looked at me. "Can you peel turnips?"

"Yes," I said.

"Can you pluck birds?"

"Yes."

"Gut fish?"

"Yes."

"Cook peas?"

"Yes."

"Pick maggots out of bread?"

I hesitated because bread maggots, well, any maggots, were some of the nastiest things I knew. But I nodded. "Yes."

Fredrik turned back to the surly man. "That's a whole lot of things she can help with, if you ask me. I could do with a hand in the galley, but it's such a squeeze it has to be someone small. This little shrimp is perfect."

The surly fellow clenched his fists. "Are you the captain or am I?" he asked.

Fredrik smiled. "Are you frightened, Urstrom?"

The question enraged the man called Urstrom, but he couldn't come up with an answer. "Pah!" he snorted. "I'd like to know where you get your stupid ideas from."

He walked off. Fredrik beckoned me to follow him. I continued up the gangway with my kitbag and went aboard.

I stood on deck as we cast off, looking back at Blue Bay. Our little village, which I'd never left before except to set out nets, collect eggs or pick berries, lay asleep. Now I was on a journey, off to a faraway place to meet…

The thought stopped there. I didn't dare think about what I'd undertaken, so I thought about Dad instead. Perhaps he was waking up at this very moment and realizing he'd overslept. He'd leap out of bed and see that I'd packed and gone. It would dawn on him what had happened and he'd be desperate.

No, I couldn't bring myself to think about that either. And, since Fredrik was shouting for me, I didn't have to.

"Right, Shrimp! Time for you and me to go to the galley. We need to have breakfast ready within the hour."

The galley really was a tight squeeze. It was a miracle the two of us could fit. There was an immense cauldron hanging on a chain over a brick-lined cavity with the embers of a dying fire in the bottom. Fredrik threw in wood, which soon caught alight on the embers. Next, he ladled a huge quantity of water into the cauldron and I had to try to scoop an enormous quantity of barley into the water.

"There you are." Fredrik sat down on a small stool. "That's how we make porridge for the crew."

We were silent for a while. Fredrik yawned and watched the dancing flames.

"Hmm," I said after a while, "Urstrom…?"

Fredrik's blue eyes looked straight into mine. "Well?"

"Do you think he's very angry? To have me on board, I mean?"

Fredrik smiled and put his feet up on the edge of the fireplace. You could see from his boots that this was a habit—the leather was sooty and scorched.

"Pirates are the greatest danger for anyone sailing a cargo ship," he said. "I wouldn't count on having too many friends on board if I were you."

I didn't answer, but I felt a knot in my stomach. It would be days and days before we reached Seglen. Imagine being disliked by every single member of the crew.

Fredrik smiled again and said: "You have one friend, anyway."

He held out his huge hand and I felt a bit ridiculous shaking it the way grown-ups do, but at the same time I was happy. Something told me that Fredrik was the best person on the *Pole Star* to have as a friend.

◆ ◆ ◇ ◆ ◆

5

Sea Parrot for Supper

Fredrik was not the kind of person anyone ignored, neither captains nor seamen. Of all the crew he'd been on the ship longest, he was huge and beefy, the tallest man on board, and his beard reached his chest.

I was very fond of him. He was kind and nice and made sure I didn't have too much to do. He was forever asking if I needed a rest.

Nor did I have to pick maggots out of the bread.

"It's more filling this way," he said, giving the crew bread with the maggots still in it. I would sit and watch the white critters poking their heads out of the slices. They'd twist and wriggle blindly this way and that. Each time I saw one of the crew take a bite everything went black for a moment.

Fredrik had a gun. He told me he occasionally shot at sea parrots. Sometimes the parrots would settle in the rigging to rest their wings and Fredrik would run for his gun. If he was lucky he'd hit one and it would tumble down dead, landing on the deck with a satisfying thump. Sea parrots tasted good and we both liked them. Well, who doesn't?

Things turned out as Fredrik had said: apart from him, no one wanted me on board. It would bring bad luck, the crew said, and so they were nasty to me.

One day when we'd cleared up after dinner and before we needed to start on supper, Fredrik decided to check his gun—clean the barrel and so on. I took the chance to go outside. Up on deck the wind ruffled my hair. I stood by the ship's rail, watching the swell rise and fall like some enormous creature breathing. I'd already seen several crew members being seasick, but it didn't affect me. I'd lived half my life on the bottom boards of a boat and was used to the movement.

I'd never seen waves this big though. They were so big they made you realize that man-made vessels, however long and however many masts they have, are nothing more than wooden boxes.

"There's the girl who's going to kill Whitehead," I suddenly heard behind me. I turned to see three seamen sitting on the deck. Two were chewing tobacco.

I turned away again and gazed at the sea, but I already knew they weren't going to leave me alone.

"How are you going to do it?" one of them asked.

"Do what?" I kept my back to them.

They stood up and came slouching over to surround me. As if being friendly, one leaned on the rail and looked at me. He had a pimply nose and hair like straw.

"Have you got a gun?" he asked.

"No," I mumbled. I'd left Dad's gun at home. I was actually afraid of it, afraid that it might go off by itself.

"Have you got a knife then?" the pimply seaman asked.

"No," I said again.

The sailor spread his hands: "Well, how are you going to kill him if you haven't even brought a weapon?"

"She'll beat him to death!" said a man with a big forehead and ridiculously twisted moustache.

He grabbed my arm and squeezed as if to see how strong I was. "Lord above, not bad at all! Whitehead will have to watch out!"

The other two laughed and then several men who had overheard joined in.

"Let go of me." I pulled my arm free. "I'm not going to fight."

"But you will!" someone yelled.

An old sailor with a furrowed gray face and beard came over.

"You're going to have to get in shape a bit before you get there," he said, rolling up his sleeves. "Let's see if you can land one on me. A hard one!"

Others moved closer to watch, and I was surrounded now by a whole crowd of seamen laughing and yelling for me to hit him.

"Leave me alone!" I tried to elbow my way through them all, but they pushed me back.

"Well?" said the comedian who'd rolled up his sleeves and behaved as if he was taking the fight seriously. "I want to fight!"

"Fight!" said the others. "Fight! Fight!"

Just to get away from there, I finally launched at the sailor and punched him on the jaw. A pathetic punch, but he put on a show, howled and crumpled as if I'd dislocated his jaw. The other men doubled up with laughter.

I tried to push my way through again, but the sailor jumped back to his feet with a roar and pretended he'd found new strength. He clenched his fists and then lifted me up in a bear hug. I kicked out violently and threw my head back.

"I don't want to!" I snarled. "I won't!"

"Try telling that to Whitehead when he has hold of you!" someone shouted, and once again the others laughed.

The sailor went on roaring, "It's into the sea with you!" in a voice meant to sound like a pirate's.

He carried me over to the rail as I screamed for all I was worth, because I couldn't be sure if it was just an act or if he'd take it into his head to actually throw me in.

Then came the sound of a shot, so close it made your ears ring. The seaman jumped and let me go. I fell to the deck and looked around. There stood Fredrik, gun in hand. He stared long and hard at the sailor, who was now so cowed his mouth hung open.

"D-did you sh-shoot at me?" he said.

"I wouldn't dream of it," Fredrik answered.

Then he walked across the deck and picked up a little bundle of feathers with webbed feet and a pretty beak striped in red, yellow and blue. It dripped blood.

Fredrik looked at me. "Are you coming, Shrimp?"

Still trembling in every bone, I stood and ran over to him. My heart pounded frantically against my ribs. Fredrik put his hand on my shoulder. Then he looked at the sailors shuffling their feet and looking stupid.

"I imagine you all feel like fine fellows now that you've frightened the life out of a child?"

None of the sailors answered at first, then one gave an ingratiating smile and said: "We were just having a bit of a joke. She knew that well enough."

He cleared his throat. "You've always been a good shot, Fredrik. It'll be nice to have a bit of bird for supper."

Fredrik slung his gun onto his shoulder. "You, you vermin, will get nothing but herring for supper. This bird is for those in the galley."

We went down to our quarters. I sat on a stool and felt the shivers leave my arms and legs and my heartbeat slowing down. We helped each other pluck the bird and then Fredrik made a really tasty dish, stuffing it with eggs and raisins before putting it over the fire.

"Why are you so kind?" I asked as we feasted on the juicy meat.

"Kind?" Fredrik said. "Am I really?"

"Yes. Hadn't you noticed?"

Fredrik shrugged.

"I don't know if I'm kind," he muttered. "Well, I suppose I've tried to be kind to you."

"But why?"

"Because…because I think that someone who's going to take on Whitehead is in need of some kindness."

I felt strange when he said that. Dad's friend Olav had owned a goat at one stage and when it grew old and sick Olav knew he had to put it down. He felt so bad about it that for several days he was excessively kind, giving the goat white bread and treats, until he could bring himself to do the deed. I thought about that goat now.

"Have you ever seen him," I asked. "Whitehead?"

Fredrik looked down at his feet. He put a raisin between his front teeth and nibbled. Then he sighed so deeply it was as if all the air hissed out of him.

"I'm going outside for a while." He stood up and left the galley.

◆ ◆ ◇ ◆ ◆

6

A Long Way Out, a Long Way Home

Fredrik didn't talk to me for the rest of that day. A cloud seemed to have settled on him and his eyes looked like smooth gray pebbles washed up by the sea.

I didn't see him during the evening and I was left to do all the work for supper on my own. I managed that no trouble, but it felt bad to have fallen out with Fredrik. I don't suppose we were enemies exactly, but I realized I'd asked him about something I shouldn't have.

After the meal had been served and eaten, it was time for me to do the dishes. I took off my apron and hurried down the steep ladder. Fredrik had tried to train me to go backwards, but I usually went forwards as if it was an ordinary staircase.

It was warm and humid in the cabin. Oil lamps along the walls spread a pleasant yellow light. They were needed, for the night outside the small square windows was pitch-black.

Seven or eight men still sat around the table. They'd been drinking brandy and were getting rowdy. Urstrom was one of them.

I began collecting the wooden platters, mugs and spoons. The waves were the very devil that night, splashing noisily against the hull.

When I reached the men, they quietened. Their eyes followed me as I scraped the platters clean and stacked them.

Then all of a sudden one grabbed my arm and said, "Well, did the bird taste good?"

It was the man Fredrik had earlier called vermin. He was very stocky with hair in a bowl cut. He looked angry—perhaps he thought it unfair of Fredrik to crush him in front of the others.

I mumbled something in reply, freed my arm and went on collecting the dishes. But the stocky fellow raised his voice so everyone could hear.

"Do you think it's right, Captain, for a cargo ship to carry a pirate hunter?" he said.

Urstrom didn't answer, just fidgeted with an earring. He wasn't really the type for gold rings: I suspect he wore them to look more trustworthy, but I thought he looked ridiculous. Like a young ram that hasn't grown into its horns.

"What I mean," the stocky man continued, "is

this: what happens when the pirates capture the girl and find out she came to Seglen in our ship?"

Urstrom took a swig but still said nothing.

"If I were Whitehead," the man continued, "I wouldn't be too pleased with the captain who brought her across the Ice Sea. I'd assume it meant that the captain of the *Pole Star* was declaring himself my enemy. I might pay him a visit, teach him a lesson. Might even send his ship to the bottom!"

"She's just a child," Urstrom said through clenched teeth.

"Yes, a child," the man said. "But she's also the only person, as far as I know, to have taken it upon herself to challenge Whitehead."

There was a short silence. The only sound was the ceaseless crash of waves against the ship's hull as we made our lonely way across the sea. The stocky man had put into words what every man aboard had been thinking. Urstrom perhaps more than all the rest.

"I agree with Ottosen," one of the others said. "We're peaceful merchant seamen. Why put our lives in danger for her sake? Better not to anger Whitehead."

Silence again. Urstrom looked at me. His brow furrowed and you could almost hear his mind grinding away between his ears.

"It's not…it's not…" I said in a weak, dry voice,

"absolutely certain they'll capture me. Is it?"

They all looked at me and not one of them was laughing, but there was no doubt what they were thinking. That the child standing before them was poor and rather simple. At that moment, I believe, most of them actually felt sorry for me.

"I have to do the washing up," I mumbled. I took the stack of dishes and hurried off, as quickly and quietly as a ship's mouse.

That night I lay awake for a long time in my hammock. I cried and cried and couldn't stop. Tears ran into my mouth and made me think of autumn when Miki and I collected driftwood from the beach. In autumn, storms lashed the water from all directions, whipping it to wild foam and the air everywhere tasted of the sea. By the time we got home our lips were wrinkled and salty.

I wasn't crying because the crew of the *Pole Star* was being nasty to me. I could easily put up with that. In many ways they were right. How was a shrimp no higher than the ship's rail to get the better of Whitehead? No one else even dared try, and grown men were scared to death of him. But a fool like me had set sail without a gun or a knife and with no idea how I'd go about it. I lay carefully on my side because it was easy to fall out of the hammock. The ship's timbers creaked and groaned and the crewmen snored. They slept in shifts because they were needed day and night as the ship raced across the waves with its snout towards the Wolf Islands and its rump pointing back at Blue Bay. We'd come a long way now. Some of the sea spiders that climbed aboard were as big as fishcakes. A long way out and a long way home. What could I do?

As I lay crying and wondering, someone shook my shoulder. It made me jump because I thought everyone else was asleep. I turned and saw the outline of someone big, tall and broad-shouldered.

"Will you come with me for a little while?" Fredrik asked.

I sat up, slid from my hammock and pushed my feet into my boots. I was already wearing my jacket because it was cold at night on the *Pole Star*. Fredrik went first, quickly climbing several ladders, and we soon reached the galley.

He said nothing for a while and nor did I. I dried my cheeks and soon the tears had slipped back to their little lair in my belly. Fredrik heated water and then groped deep in a packing case and came up with a jar of honey. A secret jar, of course, just for him! He scooped two large spoonfuls of the precious honey into a mug, topped it up with hot water and offered it to me.

"Don't you want it?" he asked.

"No," I said.

He put the mug to one side. There wasn't much

life left in the fire so he put on more wood and stirred it with the long poker.

"Are you angry with me?" I asked.

He swallowed and stared into the dancing flames. Then he gave another of those heavy sighs, as if all the air was leaving him.

"It's not you I'm angry with," he answered. "It's myself." He looked at his hands resting on his knees, and sat there for some time before saying: "The two of us have more in common than you think. Not just that we can pluck birds and make porridge."

"So?"

"What was your sister's name?" he said. "The one Whitehead took?"

"Miki," I said.

Fredrik nodded.

"Mine was called Hanna."

"How do you mean?" I said.

"The sister Whitehead took from me," Fredrik said. "She was eleven years old."

◆ ◆ ◇ ◆ ◆

The Story of Hanna

It was almost impossible to believe what Fredrik was telling me. That he'd been through the same thing as me. Fredrik—the man with the big red beard and kind blue eyes, the man who was almost always happy, who could peel half a hundredweight of swedes with a smile on his face—like me, had had a sister kidnapped by Whitehead.

"What happened?" I asked.

Fredrik's face turned hard when he started his account, and the more of it he told, the harder his face grew.

Fredrik and Hanna had lived on a fairly large island called Fell Holm. Both had rich red hair that looked like molten gold streaming from beneath their caps. Their mother and father worked in the fish sheds gutting cod, as did most of the other parents. The family ate boiled or fried cod roe for supper almost every night. It does taste really good, but Fredrik said he'd eaten so much cod roe in his time that it stuck in his throat. He was sick of that grainy gray mush and what he liked best in all the world was freshly cooked crab.

This is what happened. When their mother and father had gone to work one morning Fredrik told his sister to get dressed and they'd go down to the small bay where the boats were moored. Since he was two years older, he was the one who decided how they spent their days. Every family on Fell Holm had its own shed down near the boats, where they kept their nets and rods and fyke nets. Not every family had crab pots because there weren't many crabs off Fell Holm and fishing for them was hardly worth the effort. But there was one old fisherman called Seaver who had pots and when his luck was in he'd catch a few crabs.

No one else was around when Fredrik and his sister arrived at the fish sheds and many of the boats had already gone out. They took three crab pots from Seaver's shed, got into their own dinghy and rowed north. Most of the fishermen usually went west or south but Fredrik and Hanna didn't want to bump into any that day. They baited the crab pots with roe sacs they'd brought with them, then lowered the pots into the water.

The thing about crab fishing is this: for a decent chance of a catch the pots should be left out for at least one night. But Fredrik and Hanna couldn't risk keeping Seaver's pots for that long, so after a couple of hours Fredrik decided to see if they'd caught anything.

And what luck! They'd caught seven crabs. Seven! No one on Fell Holm had seen a catch like that for years. Now it was a matter of getting home and eating the lot before the gutting sheds closed. Fredrik took the oars and with strong strokes rowed them over the waves back towards Fell Holm.

Then Hanna suddenly noticed another rowboat approaching. They threw their coats over the pots and made sure no crabs were scrabbling up out of the bilges.

The man called Loa was on his way out to catch sea parrots. He told them that back at the island, Seaver was in a right royal rage. Apparently someone had stolen his crab pots and he intended to wait for the thief to turn up. Loa rowed on his way and, as luck would have it, didn't bother to wonder what Fredrik and Hanna were doing at sea.

Fredrik and Hanna had no idea what to do now. Fell Holm is a steep island with only two sensible places to land. One is the main wharf where the fish sheds are, but there they risked being discovered by their parents. The other was the smaller bay where Seaver was waiting. Fredrik could put up with a thrashing for borrowing the pots but he definitely didn't want to lose the crabs. He had no doubt that Seaver would search their boat and claim the crabs since they'd been caught in his pots. So Fredrik came up with a plan: he'd put Hanna ashore on a skerry with the crabs, then he'd row in to the bay with the pots, admit to Seaver that he'd borrowed them, but say he'd caught nothing. He'd take his thrashing and leave. After that he'd watch Seaver and as soon as he left the huts Fredrik would run back to the boat and row out to fetch Hanna.

At this point in his story, Fredrik fell silent. His eyes were bright with tears. The fire hissed and crackled quietly.

"She didn't want to," he said. "She said she was frightened."

"Of the pirates?" I asked.

Fredrik nodded. "A couple of years earlier they'd taken two children from Wolverine Isle, which isn't far away. But I said she was being stupid—I was only worried about the crabs."

He hid his face in his hands for a moment or two. Then he wiped a drip from the end of his nose and went on with his story.

He dropped Hanna on a very small skerry, putting the crabs in a rock crevice full of sea water. Fredrik told her to watch them carefully so that none escaped. He then rowed ashore and was given a thorough scolding and had his ears boxed. After that he hid and waited for Seaver to leave, but Seaver had decided to mend his nets. And mending nets takes time, particularly if you have as many as Seaver. So Fredrik waited and waited.

It was afternoon by the time Seaver finished and left. Fredrik hurried down to the rowboat, knowing that Hanna would be really scared by now. In fact, he was scared himself because he didn't want to be out at sea when darkness fell. He'd had nothing to eat for many hours and they almost certainly wouldn't be able to cook the crabs until the following day. But by now he was less concerned about them and only wanted to fetch his little sister.

Every muscle in my body went tense as he told the rest of his story. How he reached the skerry and found no sign of Hanna. How he went ashore and ran here and there over rocks and through bushes, slipping and sliding and shouting. How, when he'd run through the scattered trees and out the other side, he saw it. Far off by now, but gleaming so white there could be no mistake: the pirate ship.

The blood ran from his body, Fredrik said, and, instead of blood, his veins and organs were filled with icy terror. Terror made its home in him. His stomach became a nest of fear that was still there now, although he was a grown man.

I looked at him in amazement. So much in our stories matched. Almost everything, in fact!

"But there's one great difference between us," Fredrik said. "I was too cowardly to go and fetch her back. Like a wretch I stayed at home on Fell Holm and a couple of years later moved to Tillersay and took this job on the *Pole Star*. I've never been home since. Not once! I'm too ashamed."

He chewed long and hard on his dry bottom lip and fixed me with his kind, red-rimmed eyes. For a moment I thought he was going to cry again. Instead, he said in a very calm voice: "I'm going to help you bring your sister home. I've been thinking about it all day. I've been sailing the seas for twelve years, waiting for the day I can forget. But it's impossible to forget. I realize that Hanna must have died long ago—children don't last long in the mines. But if I…" He took a deep breath, so deep that the air rattled in his throat. "If I help you get Miki back, perhaps things will feel a little better. Just a little."

It's almost impossible to describe how I felt on hearing this. I began snorting and laughing like a mad thing—it must have sounded idiotic. He was going to help me! Fredrik, who had a gun and was so big and strong he could lift three sacks of grain with an outstretched arm! I couldn't possibly have a better help. Suddenly everything seemed easy, more like a good adventure than a dangerous undertaking. I wasn't alone after all. There were two of us now!

We sat talking by the fire for a long time. I told

him about the day on Iron Apple and Fredrik was also amazed by how similar our stories were. Then I drank some honey water after all and my stomach felt so warm and good that the moment I rested my head on a sack of grain I fell asleep. I wasn't aware of two strong arms picking me up and carrying me back to my hammock, where I lay until morning dreaming long, strange dreams about arriving at a village with paved streets, where a man with flowing white hair was holding a crab pot. And when I looked into the pot, there were no crabs, but a little girl in worn winter boots. However often I asked the man if his name was Whitehead, he just laughed and said he was someone else.

◆ ◆ ◇ ◆ ◆

8

A Gun in Bed

The following day Fredrik produced a sheet of paper from the depths of his sailor's kitbag. There was only one small oil lamp alight on the lower deck and there we sat while Fredrik unfolded the paper.

It was a map of our waters. I'd never seen one like it, only Dad's rough sketches of what things looked like. But this map had been drawn by someone who knew what they were doing. They'd drawn whales here and there and in one place two small sea parrots sat looking out over the sea. It was a very fine thing.

Fredrik pointed to Tillersay, the *Pole Star*'s home port. Then he traced our route with his finger. The first stop was Blue Bay—my village. Blue Bay lay on an island called Little Bluesay, but, of course, I already knew that. His finger moved on past Iron Apple and all the other islands that belonged to Blue

Bay, and out over the vast, cold Ice Sea. We'd soon be calling at the Wolf Islands to unload and load goods, after which we'd set a course for Outersay, the big island where Seglen was. I shuddered to think of that place, and I shuddered even more seeing the surrounding islands. They were tiny, like flies that Outersay had shaken off. And one of them was Whitehead's.

"How will we find the right place?" I asked.

Fredrik chewed his lip. "We'll have to see about that when we reach Seglen," he said. "Amongst pirates, the biggest windbags are those who like their beer, and the port there is full of dodgy taverns: the Seglen Arms, the Green Door, Two Little Pigs. We'll take lodgings somewhere and then—well, and then we'll ask around."

I looked at him sitting there with the lamplight dancing in his eyes. He was the best person I knew. Dad and Miki were good too, of course, but they were far away. As if in another, imaginary, world. In the real world, the world of the huge, cold, unstable sea, there was one small, bright spot and that was kind Fredrik with his warm, blue eyes. That made him the best thing I could think of.

"I see," I said hesitantly. "If we're going to stay at an inn…well, I don't have much money. In fact, I have none."

"Don't even think about it," Fredrik said. "As

you know, I've been cooking on the *Pole Star* for many years. I'm owed a fair amount."

His eyes returned to the map and wandered over all the small dots representing islands around Seglen, as if he was trying to work out which we should go to. Then, with no more ado, he folded the map.

"Best let Urstrom know about this at once," he said.

"D-do you think so?" I said. "Won't he be angry?"

Fredrik smiled. "That worm is nothing to be afraid of. Come on, let's go."

He climbed the ladder ahead of me and at the upper deck he strode towards the captain's cabin. He seemed taller, straighter and bolder, as if his decision had given him a boost. He knocked on the door, took a deep breath of fresh air and gazed expectantly across the rolling sea.

"Yes?" came a voice through the door.

Fredrik opened it and stepped in. I followed. There wasn't much room in the captain's cabin and Fredrik had to stoop not to bang his head on the ceiling. Four oil lamps fixed on the walls were all alight, and several large volumes stood on a shelf. The cabin was nicer than the crew's quarters, naturally enough, with a proper wooden bunk instead of a hammock. The feather mattress looked thick and comfortable, and there was no ordinary wool blanket but a lovely, glossy embroidered one. Urstrom's gun hung above his bunk.

He sat behind a small, low table with his nose in some papers—cargo lists, I think. He looked up briefly before continuing to stare at the documents.

"Well now," he said, "does the porridge cook itself these days?"

Fredrik didn't answer. He dug his hands into his pockets and looked at Urstrom.

At once, Urstrom stopped staring at his papers, put them aside and folded his hands on the tabletop. "So? What do you want?"

"I'd like to be paid my wages," Fredrik said.

"Your wages?" Urstrom was surprised.

"Yes. And while I'm at it, I should tell you I'll be signing off when we reach Seglen."

"Signing off? Why?"

Fredrik nodded at me. "I'm going to keep the girl company. Help her find Whitehead and get her sister back."

Urstrom blinked a couple of times and his brow furrowed slowly. "Have you completely lost your mind?"

"Not at all," Fredrik said. "This is the first sensible decision I've made in very many years."

"Sensible?" Urstrom snorted. "You're saying it's sensible to go after Whitehead?"

Fredrik was silent.

Urstrom snorted again and shook his head. "You're risking the lives of me and all my crew if you take it upon yourself to challenge that man—you do understand that?" he snarled.

"It's the only right thing to do." Fredrik's voice was determined. "You ought to agree with me instead of thinking of yourself. So now I'm asking for the money I'm due. All of it! The girl and I need to buy ammunition and various things when we arrive at the Wolf Islands."

Urstrom's eyes flashed like lightning. He stood so abruptly that his chair almost toppled.

"You'll sail with us all the way back to Tillersay, as agreed!" he roared, spit flying from his mouth. "And you can scrub these stupid ideas about Whitehead from your mind once and for all! Understand?"

Fredrik put his knuckles on the small table and calmly leaned close to Urstrom's face.

"My wages, Urstrom."

Urstrom was breathing so violently that his whole body shook. Seconds ticked by as I waited for his next outburst. I looked again at his gun, fixed directly above his fine bunk. It reminded me of the saying in Blue Bay: fear sleeps with a gun by its bed. There was little doubt that of all the men on the *Pole Star* the captain was the most fearful.

Urstrom realized he'd lost the battle. He walked to a cupboard by his bunk, fished a key from his pocket, opened the cupboard and took out a large box. He sat down at the table again and counted out the money owed to Fredrik. Fredrik looked at me from the corner of his eye and I'm pretty sure he grew a little taller as he took the handful of coins. There were rather a lot—a great pile of copper coins and quite a few silver—all of which Fredrik put in his purse.

Urstrom's face, meanwhile, was as black as thunder. "And who's going to cook our meals between Seglen and Tillersay?" he asked. "Have you bothered to consider that?"

Fredrik shook his head. "I've no doubt you'll find someone in Seglen. There's no shortage of seamen there."

Urstrom snorted. "I won't have seamen of that sort on board my ship."

"Whatever you say," Fredrik said. Then he nodded his thanks and the two of us left.

When we got back to our hammocks Fredrik put his purse in his kitbag.

"There we are!" he said. "Now we have enough money for bullets and lodgings. Both! What do you think?"

"We have!" I said. "So much money! Who'd have thought it possible?"

* * ◇ * *

The Wolf Islands

Three days later we reached the Wolf Islands. I was up on deck when we berthed early in the morning and I was excited. Ever since I was a very small child Dad had talked about the white wolves with teeth as long as knives. They were as lethal as they were beautiful, and thousands lived on the Wolf Islands. They could be seen out in the wilds and sometimes they even entered the villages. Then people were quick to close and lock their doors.

The port we'd entered wasn't very big—hardly bigger than the one at home. A couple of other cargo vessels were already there, but most of the boats moored along the quay were small fishing boats.

Dockers started unloading goods from the *Pole Star*: timber and grain from Tillersay and barrels of herring and herring oil from Blue Bay. The port office stored the cargo in warehouses until the buyers of the timber, the grain and the herring came to claim their goods. Urstrom stood in conversation with the fellow from the port office: I was pretty sure they were talking money.

Then I saw Fredrik, already going down the gangplank. We were going to buy more ammunition for his gun and a few other things, so I hurried to catch up. I wore my woollen sweater with the collar and a jacket as well.

Land felt good beneath my feet after more than a week on the *Pole Star*, though as I gazed around the bay everything still seemed to be swaying. The ground was gray with filthy snow. Steps led up to the port office door, beneath a hanging sign with a golden knot painted on it. Crates of lamp oil and barrels of brandy were stacked by the steps. The Wolf Islands needed all the light and heat they could get.

Fredrik pulled his cap down over his ears. "Time to go to the general store," he said, and that's what we did.

Even though it was early, people were up and about, washing in the snow and packing their sleds. The cottages were low, ramshackle structures—one, for instance, had an upturned boat for a roof. They were obviously short of building material here and the timber brought from Tillersay probably cost a fortune.

When I looked closely I saw that the people, too, were in a pretty poor state. Their faces were covered in scars—caused by claws and teeth.

"Look over there!" I said. "A wolf!"

A little farther up the village street a man was walking a wolf cub on a leash. The cub came to his knees and trotted along nicely at his side. The man—although his arm was bandaged—seemed pleased with his little companion. He stopped and stroked its head and the cub chewed his trouser leg even more ragged than before. It looked so funny and sweet that I laughed.

"Come on," Fredrik said. He wanted to avoid having to rush back to cook porridge. I would have liked to stay longer watching the wolf, but Fredrik said the place was full of wolf cubs and we'd see plenty more.

And we did! Not on the street, though. In the shop where we were going to buy our things I gave a small whoop of joy because there in the corner sat a little cub in an iron collar attached to the wall by a chain.

"May I pat it?" I asked, hurrying over.

The man behind the counter nodded, but he also said I'd have only myself to blame if I set out on my next voyage without hands. Then he greeted Fredrik and laid out the various bullets and cartridges we had to choose from.

I kept a safe distance from the wolf cub and crouched down.

"Hello you," I whispered.

The cub pulled and struggled to come to me. You could see he wanted to play so I slid a little closer. I stretched out my hand to see what the cub would do, so he could just reach my fingertips. If the worst came to the worst I could sail away without fingertips.

The cub started licking my fingers. It was so lovely and soft and warm that I burst out laughing.

"Look!" I said. "He's hungry."

Fredrik and the man were busy talking about ammunition but they looked over at me and smiled.

"Come on, I'll give you something to feed him," the man said.

I hurried over. The man, whose sideburns were so long they practically met under his chin, disappeared behind a curtain and came back with a piece of dried fish. "He likes this," he said. "You can have him for a good price if you want."

"Is he for sale?" The words burst out of me.

"He certainly is. And the sooner the better. He's eating every bit of fish in the house."

I went back and held out the fish. The cub gobbled it down in no time. Then I risked patting him on the head. Oh, how lovely and soft he was and his ears were like two little pleats.

"If only I had money!" I said. "He's so beautiful!"

Fredrik gave a little laugh, then he and the man went on talking business. A little later the man disappeared behind the curtain again and came back carrying two new woollen blankets, fur gloves, a tinder box and various other items. He wrapped everything in the blankets and tied it with string like a parcel. Fredrik took out his purse, paid and tucked the bundle under his arm.

"Ready then, Shrimp?" he said.

I held out my hand to the cub one last time. That little pink tongue was the sweetest thing in the world.

It had started snowing and I wiped the snowflakes from my eyelashes. The village street was even busier now and shopkeepers were opening their shutters. I daydreamed of a black-haired girl walking along the street with a wolf cub on a leash—and that girl was called Siri! Oh, how badly I wanted a little wolf! I was so happy that I laughed and hopped, skipped and jumped in the snow.

As we approached the wharf we heard raised voices. Soon we saw two men on a large sled struggling with a wolf cub. One of the men—

with boots that came to his knees—was trying to put a chain around the cub's neck, but the cub was fighting him off with its paws and showing its teeth. The man's face and hands were already bleeding.

"Get hold of it!" he snarled at the other man, who had a slouch hat and long thin beard.

"Okay, okay!" the man with the hat snapped back.

When he tried to approach the cub from behind, it spun around and lashed out with its paw. The man backed off in fear.

Fredrik and I went closer. Watching that little cub struggle and fight made me feel ill. It was out of its mind with fear. The fur on its neck and back was bristling like a scrubbing brush.

The man from the port office went over to help. He was big, with long gray hair and a fur cap. He began hitting the cub with a broom.

"Stop it!" I shouted, but none of them listened to me, of course.

"Don't watch." Fredrik pulled at my arm but I couldn't drag myself away from that awful sight.

The port official kept hitting and hitting the cub, which was jerking around to defend itself. Then the man in boots managed to attach the chain.

"I've got it!" he roared.

"Pull then!" the other man said.

The man in boots pulled and heaved to drag

the cub down from the sled and the cub pulled and heaved to stay where it was. The second man came over to help and the cub crashed to the ground, landing on its snout. They dragged it towards a cargo ship called *Homeless* moored in front of the *Pole Star*. The cub growled and snarled and resisted for all it was worth, and kept looking back at the sled and howling.

Going closer, I saw why the cub was howling. An enormous shaggy white beast lay on the sled— the cub's mother. Her tongue hung from her mouth and her chest wasn't moving. A clot of dried black blood on her neck showed where the shot had struck home.

Tears came to my eyes but, at the same time, I felt stupid. I don't know how I imagined the man on the street had acquired his cub or how the man in the shop had managed to lay hands on his. I suppose I thought they'd caught orphaned cubs that had strayed into the village.

"Wolf cubs are valuable booty." Fredrik patted me on the head as the port official took his broom back inside. "Lots of people come here hoping to make good money for a year or two. They buy a gun and go out into the wilderness. Then the cubs are shipped to well-to-do people wanting them to pull sleds."

"But what about their mothers?" I asked, drying

my cheeks on the back of my hand.

"It's hard to catch a white wolf cub unless you shoot the mother first," Fredrik said. "And they use the mothers for fur. Didn't you see the piles of skins in the shop?"

I shook my head.

"That one's so sad," I whispered. The men were dragging the cub up the gangway. It was still fighting with all its strength to avoid being taken on board. "Why must they take them when they're so small?"

Fredrik sighed and patted me on the head again.

"Once they get bigger they're impossible to catch," he answered. "They have to be harnessed to the sled early on, you see."

◆ ◆ ◇ ◆ ◆

An Errand with Urstrom

'll now tell you what happened the day we were due to leave the Wolf Islands and sail on to Seglen. We'd been in port for a couple of days and, according to Fredrik, the *Pole Star* usually stayed longer at the Wolf Islands, but with winter approaching the ship had to sail home to Tillersay as soon as possible. The temperature had become several degrees colder at night. It was rare for the Ice Sea to freeze over, but it could happen, and anyone at sea when it did could say goodbye to life: the immense force of masses of ice could crush a ship as if it were egg shell.

It was almost departure time. We'd cleared away the dinner things and Fredrik had gone for a nap. I'd stayed in the galley because it was raw outside and it was nice to sit by the fire and do nothing.

All of a sudden Urstrom turned up. He was chewing a plug of tobacco and he looked hard at me. "You're to come with me on an errand," he said.

"Me?"

He nodded. "Get a move on."

"W-what kind of errand?" I got to my feet.

"I'll tell you on the way," Urstrom answered. "Come along."

On the upper deck the wind tore at my hair. The tiny, spinning snowflakes were like grains of sand hitting my face. The sailors were at work all over the ships, and I assumed they were preparing the ship for departure just like us: it wasn't only Urstrom who hated the ice. Fredrik had said that *Windreef* was almost certainly going the whole way to Northwick; *Homeless*, the ship with the little wolf cub on board, was going to Saltholm; and a new ship had come into the bay—a beautiful big ship called *Wulf*.

The sea looked turbulent and impatient, as if the waves were longing for us, wondering when we'd come so that they could wrap their wet arms around us and send us to eternity. They also seemed to be asking, Do you dare?

"Can't I tell Fredrik first?" I asked. "He'll wonder where I've gone."

"Fredrik's asleep," Urstrom said. "And we have to hurry."

He stepped onto the gangway and I followed, but then I stopped.

"What if he wakes up? I think I should tell him,

so he doesn't run around looking for me."

Urstrom sighed and raised his voice. "Come on, let's go! I'm your captain, aren't I? And Fredrik's?"

"Yes, you are," I mumbled. Then I pulled my cap further over my ears and walked across the gangway.

Urstrom moved quickly. Once ashore he went straight to the port office door and knocked.

We were kept waiting for a while. I was nervous about speaking to Urstrom, but it felt strange to be standing there in silence.

"Have we come to fetch something?" I forced myself to ask.

"Nope." Urstrom spat, making a brown patch on the snow.

The door was opened at last by the office man. He was amazingly big. Fat, too. A bunch of keys hung at his waist.

He gave Urstrom a brief look. "Ah, I see, that business is it?"

He fetched his fur cap, with a shining badge on the front showing the same golden knot painted on the sign over the door. He stepped out into the whirling snow and across the big empty square. Urstrom and I followed. I didn't like this walk one little bit but, as Urstrom had already pointed out, he was the captain and I had no choice but to obey his orders. It was best to hurry along and get this over with.

The port official turned and said, "I have an old warehouse that should be suitable. There's nothing the matter with it, but it's a bit out of the way and no one can be bothered carrying things there. You wouldn't believe how lazy the dockers have become. Even though they're paid to carry things."

Urstrom grunted in agreement.

Soon we arrived at the old warehouse and the office man unlocked the door.

"In we go now," Urstrom said, nudging me in the back.

I swallowed hard and did as he said.

It was dark inside, which didn't stop me seeing that it was completely empty. I turned to Urstrom. "What's all this about?" I tried to sound firm, though I was actually scared. "What are we doing here?"

"We're dropping off some cargo that's been with us since Blue Bay," Urstrom said. "This is your final destination."

His words sent icy shivers through me. Perhaps I'd been scared because I suspected something like this. But I hadn't wanted to believe it. No, I simply couldn't believe he'd do it. He was going to leave me behind!

I rushed at Urstrom, to force my way past him, but of course the port official helped to block my path. They pushed me back so hard I landed on the cold floor.

"Just wait until Fredrik finds out!" I spluttered through tears.

Urstrom sucked in his cheeks. "The only thing Fredrik will find out is that you decided to run away." From his pocket he pulled something brown with a clasp on it. "With his savings!"

The brown thing was Fredrik's purse. Urstrom must have got his hands on it while Fredrik and I were busy in the galley. He opened the purse, poured the coins into his hand and pocketed them. Then he threw the purse on the floor beside me.

"That should be enough to drive silly ideas about Whitehead out of his red-haired skull," he said.

I cried. I cried so hard my chest hurt. Urstrom had worked it all out: if Fredrik believed I'd stolen his purse he wouldn't bother trying to find me. He'd simply take me for a thief, someone who could forget—for money—all we'd meant to do together. Maybe he would assume that the idea of a wolf cub had got so fixed in my head that I'd decided to buy one. It was nasty and humiliating.

"You can't do this!" I said.

"The *Pole Star* is my ship!" Urstrom answered. "I can put ashore anyone I want to."

I looked at the man from the port office. What about him? Surely he realized it was wrong, didn't he? And that Urstrom had no right to lock me up?

He must have known my thoughts because he

shrugged and said: "I simply store goods for Urstrom. I've done it many times before, no questions asked."

Urstrom hesitated, then sighed, almost as if his conscience was troubling him. But then he put his nose in the air and shoved his hands into his pockets.

"Now pay careful attention," he said. "Never ever show yourself near the *Pole Star* again. If I'd had my way back in Blue Bay I'd never have taken you on board. This ridiculous journey of yours can only end badly, but Fredrik's too stupid to understand that."

"He's not stupid, not at all!" I said.

"Anyway," Urstrom said, "he's good at making porridge. Chasing around for a new cook would delay our return home in the winter storms. I should put you both ashore since you insist on endangering our safety. As it is, I'm doing it this way."

With those words they shut the door on me. The lock squeaked as the port official turned the key. I attacked the door, pounding it for all I was worth.

"Let me out! I'll freeze to death in here!" I screamed.

"You won't be there for long!" Urstrom shouted back. "You'll be let out as soon as we've cleared the headland, so stop your whining."

"Let me out NOW!" I yelled. "What you're doing is wrong! It's just wrong!"

Silence was the answer. I pounded and kicked

at the door as hard as I could, and ran at it time after time, hurling my full weight against it. But it wouldn't open and in the end my shoulder—in fact my whole body—felt broken.

I sat on the floor with my arms around my knees. Some of the time I wept and every now and again I leapt to my feet and kicked the door again. After some time—it felt like an ice age—the vile man from the port office returned and unlocked the door.

"You can go now," he said with no sign of sympathy.

I ran past him, straight back to the wharf. I knew already, of course, but I had to see it with my own eyes.

The *Pole Star*'s mooring was empty and there was no sign of the boat out at sea. I sank down on an old crate and hid my face in my hands. So that was the situation. I was alone again.

◆ ◆ ◇ ◆ ◆

The Signal

A woman came past as I sat weeping by the water. She wore a fur hat and well-made fur trousers. Her face was weather-beaten. She parked her sled and looked at me. Probably children weren't a common sight on the Wolf Islands.

"Why are you sitting there?" she asked.

I saw no point in answering—no point in anything.

The woman stood there for a while before going into the port office.

When she came out she had a parcel under her arm. She must have asked the man in the office about me because she said, "The ship sailed without you, I hear."

I still didn't reply.

The woman hesitated, studying me carefully.

"Is it really very sensible to go after Whitehead when you're just a skinny wee thing?" she asked, and when I still said nothing she went on: "Shouldn't you be glad that someone put a stop to that idea?"

"I'm not in the least glad!" I snarled. "My ideas are my own business, aren't they?"

It was her turn to be silent. After a while she asked, "Are you hungry?"

I nodded.

"Come home with me then." She took off her glove and held out her hand: "Nanni."

"Siri," I answered and stood up. I suppose it was pretty crazy to go off with a complete stranger, but what else could I do? Without a fire to sleep beside I'd freeze to death. The port official, who was partly to blame for my misery, showed no concern.

We followed the village street northwards, past small, ugly cottages and shops. Nanni told me that the parcel had come from Goat Holm by ship. Her sister lived on Goat Holm and once a year sent over new socks. Socks wore out quickly when you never took them off.

"Why do you never take your socks off?" I asked.

We'd left the village now and the runners on Nanni's sled were cutting through new snow, though we could feel the wolf hunters' tracks beneath it. Nanni didn't answer my question, she just smiled.

Soon the village was merely columns of smoke far behind us. After an hour or so, two small, gray huts appeared in the deep snow. Nanni's huts.

She'd built them from driftwood she'd found along the shore. Many ships came to grief out on the Ice Sea and collecting ships' timbers was the easiest way if you needed planks. The slightly crooked huts had a sad look about them. Outside, Nanni had fixed a rope in a rather peculiar way: running from a hole in the wall of one hut to a pole stuck in the snow.

"Doesn't the washing freeze when you hang it out?" I asked.

She just smiled again and parked the sled. She lifted rags from the sled to reveal a gun. She picked it up, opened the door to one of the huts and I followed her in.

The first thing I noticed was a big white pelt on the floor, and another on the bunk. A third pelt was pinned on the wall with a second gun alongside it.

"Are you a wolf hunter?" I asked in surprise.

Nanni threw some wood onto the small hearth. Then she turned round with a gleam in her pale eyes. "Obviously," she said.

"But…" I didn't know what to say.

Nanni picked up a pan and went out, bringing it back filled with snow. She hung the pan on a hook and chain over the fire, then she opened a chest and took out two pieces of meat, which she put into the pan along with a pinch of salt. That seemed to be all that was needed for wolf soup.

I stood a few steps back, saying nothing. I didn't want to sit on the fur however soft it looked and I had no intention of eating the broth or the meat, if that's what she thought.

But my stomach was craving something. It was a long time since dinner.

"Aren't you going to have some?" Nanni asked as she served it.

I shook my head.

Nanni sat down and ate. The meat was so tough she had to chew and chew.

"I don't think people should shoot wolves," I said.

"You don't?" Nanni wasn't looking at me.

We were silent again, the only noise Nanni's chewing. There was crunching when she had gristle between her teeth, and the slurping of soup.

How my stomach ached! My head felt empty and giddy and my temples were pounding.

"I don't suppose you shoot mother wolves, do you?"

"What was that?" Nanni said.

"I don't suppose you shoot mother wolves?"

Nanni wiped out the bowl with her thumb, licked her thumb clean and put the bowl down.

"I shoot every wolf I see." She took a piece of uncooked meat from the chest and went outside. It was evening by now.

Suddenly I heard a clatter behind my back. I jumped. I looked around to see tin cans tied at the end of the rope coming in through a small hole in the wall. Obviously the washing line I'd seen earlier.

Nanni returned. She took one of her guns—a muzzle loader—and loaded it with a musket ball from a box on a shelf. Then she placed the gun close to the hole in the wall and lay down on the bunk.

"You have to keep quiet now," she said, as if I'd been talking non-stop since we met.

She fell asleep. It all felt so stupid: there was me standing up shivering while she, a complete stranger in fur trousers, lay sleeping.

Several hours went by, or so it seemed. I was so tired and hungry I could hardly think. The pan was beside the hearth and the food must have gone cold, but I could still smell it. I could almost taste it in my mouth and feel the soup running down my throat to fill the aching hole in my stomach.

If I took just one piece of meat, she surely wouldn't notice. One tiny piece. Just for a taste.

I tiptoed silently across the floor. It was dark and the oil lamp was almost flickering out. With the spoon I fished out a small piece of meat, put it in my mouth and chewed. It was dry and tough but it tasted good. I couldn't help taking another piece. And another, and another, then I put the pan to my lips to drink the well-thickened gravy—and at that moment there was a clatter over by the hole in the wall. It scared me so much I dropped the pan at the same moment that Nanni leapt up and rushed for her gun.

A shot rang out. I hugged my head and threw myself down, my heart hammering so hard I thought my ribs would burst. Nanni filled the oil lamp to give more light. She reloaded the gun and went out, gun in one hand, lantern in the other. She didn't even look at me.

She was soon back. She paused in the doorway. "I imagine you'll be pleased to hear that I missed." She cast a glance at the pan on the floor. "Or have you changed your mind about shooting wolves?"

I didn't say anything. I turned the pan the right way up and I don't think she saw me scrape gravy off the floor and eat it. But the wolf skin on the floor also had gravy on it and I couldn't do anything about that.

"Well, it's your problem." Nanni threw the skin up onto the bunk alongside hers. "I'm not the one who'll be sleeping in that mess."

She left the cabin with more meat and very soon the tin cans clattered again.

This contraption, which she called the Signal, was Nanni's own invention. The rope that went through the hole in the wall to the pole stuck in the snow wasn't a washing line. Nanni tied meat to the pole, and when a wolf attracted by the scent began eating the meat, it moved the rope, which made the cans rattle. Nanni had to be quick with her gun, but however quick, she might still miss, particularly at night with only faint light from the stars. Still, she had so much wolf meat out in her store that she could never eat it all herself. Nanni had come here from the island of Underholm a few years before and didn't know how long she'd stay. As she put it, very few people were born on the Wolf Islands, but quite a few died there. The life of a fortune hunter was a dangerous one.

When Nanni had re-baited the Signal she came back in and lay down. I'd already crawled under the wolf fur and even though it was wet and greasy it was still fine and warm. It smelled remarkably fresh, with a strong, musky animal smell, exactly as the wolf must have smelled as it loped across the wastes thinking there was nothing dangerous or wicked in the world. And perhaps there'd been a small cub with it, running to keep up.

I wondered what Dad would say about this. About me lying under a wolf skin in the hut of a woman who let meat get old because she had too much of it. Dad was always scrupulous about not taking more from nature than you absolutely needed. Anything else was greedy, he said.

In the end my eyes grew heavy.

Nanni and I were lying head to toe and the last thing I recall before falling asleep was being glad that today of all days in the year she was wearing new socks.

◆ ◆ ◇ ◆ ◆

12

I Fire a Gun

Taking your socks off at Nanni's was out of the question, as I found when I got up the next morning. The fire in the hearth had long gone out and the floor was so poorly built you could see the ground in places.

For some reason we didn't seem such strangers that day. I almost felt I lived there. And when Nanni cooked wolf meat for breakfast, although I didn't greet it with a cheer, I said yes and reached for my bowl without any trouble.

There was a full snowstorm outside, with flakes the size of mitts. Nanni's hut had no windows but you could see a little through her shooting hole. We opened the door as seldom as possible. It was a strange and huddled life, I thought. You sat like an eel in a hole waiting for prey to swim into the jaws of danger. And then—bang! Then you consumed the small parts you wanted and spat out the rest.

In fact, there were piles of skeletons around the hut where Nanni lay in ambush, but layers of snow covered the bones so there was no need to think of them unless you wanted to.

Almost as if she knew what I was thinking, Nanni said: "Is it really so bad—shooting wolves?"

She handed me a cup of hot water. I wrapped my fingers around it and the heat made them tingle. I put my lips to the rim, blew on it and drank noisily.

"Do you need to shoot so many?" I asked after a while.

She laughed. I don't think it was unkind, but I felt stupid all the same. Her teeth were short and there were gaps between them. "Shooting lots of them is the whole point," she said.

"But why? Surely you only need enough meat to fill your belly? And you could leave the cubs alone…"

"The cubs are what I want most," Nanni interrupted. "I lie here in the dark every night hoping that a mother and her cubs start eating the meat out there. If you only knew how much I get paid for a live wolf cub!"

She took a purse from her jacket pocket, unlaced it and showed me. Oh my heart! So many silver coins! Far more than Fredrik received when he drew his pay.

"All of this came from wolves," Nanni said. "Wolves I sold to the store down in the village. And the store sells them on to the skippers of ships. And the skippers take them far, far away. To the big islands where rich people want white rugs on their floors and a team of wolves to pull their sleds."

She laced up her purse and put it back in her pocket.

"Everyone does what they have to in order to survive," she said. "Wolves do, and so do I."

She sighed and peered out through the shooting slit. "Is there no end to it?" she muttered.

She meant the snow. It had been snowing for hours and the only thing visible was white spindrift. Nanni hadn't been out to check the Signal; she was waiting until the snow eased a little. But as time went on she grew impatient. The tin cans hung still and silent on the end of the rope and eventually she started pacing the floor, grunting restlessly. The meat must have fallen off the pole, she said. She seemed to suspect that it had fallen into the snow and a wolf had gobbled the lot and run off, hunger satisfied and pleased with itself.

All of a sudden she marched over and snatched up her gun. "I'm going out anyway," she said. She had to heave the door with her full weight because so much snow had fallen.

I closed it after her. I looked through the

shooting hole but saw no sign of her in all the whiteness.

How silent it was out here in the back of beyond. The fire made a slight crackling, but that was all. Outside the snowflakes landed silently on the soft roof and there was no wind roaring or tugging at the hut.

But it wasn't completely silent. I heard a low, dull sound like heavy furniture being dragged across a floor. It came from somewhere out in the snowstorm.

"Siri!"

It was Nanni shouting, half choked with fear. The voice cut off and then I heard something that turned my blood to ice: a yelping bark!

I ran to the door but turned back at once to fetch the gun from the wall. I grabbed the ammunition box and went outside.

I landed in snow well above my knees, tumbled over and dropped the gun. I groped about until I found it. I looked around: everything was white, white and dense and wet. All I could see was white.

"Where are you?" I yelled.

"Here!"

I trudged towards the sound but quickly lost all sense of direction.

"Where? Shout again!" I called.

"By the pole!" Nanni shouted. "Hurry!"

Of course, by the pole! Now I knew what to do. I rushed back to the hut and worked my way along the wall to the shooting slit. Tucking the ammunition box into my pocket, I held the rope and began running towards the pole. Nanni had told me the rope went about a dozen yards, and that takes a while in deep snow. My heart was pounding hard with fear. Fear of the wolf I knew was there, fear of it coming at me with gaping jaws, fear of my stomach being ripped open but, most of all, fear of being left on my own. If a wolf killed Nanni but not me, I'd be all alone, which is why I was going as quickly as I could, the rope burning one hand and the cold barrel of the gun burning the other.

Suddenly I could pick out the shape of a white back in the whiteness.

"I—I'm here!" I yelled. I think I was shouting at the wolf, however stupid that must sound. "I have a gun!"

"Shoot!" Nanni shouted.

The wolf turned and looked. Seeing me, it hesitated, scenting the air to see what kind of creature I was. It was big, but its body looked thin. It drew back its lips, showing its teeth. I jumped and felt for the tin box in my pocket. I found a musket ball and put it in the muzzle. Falling snowflakes were filling the box. Closing it, I was clumsy and balls fell out, leaving only two. The wolf was coming towards me. It was big and terrifying with fangs long enough to stab right through me. I took aim. Yes, I wanted to kill it! I hated the beast! When I saw how cold its eyes were, every muscle in my body screamed with horror and vomit rose in my throat. That wolf cared nothing for me, cared nothing that I'd wept about that little cub down at the wharf. Things were just as Nanni had said: each one cared only for their own survival.

I pulled the trigger, the shot fired, the gun recoiled and made my shoulder throb with pain.

I missed, but it was enough to startle the wolf, which arched its back, turned and ran a few steps before stopping to look again. The shot and the smell of powder had frightened it.

I reloaded the gun, pointed the barrel straight up in the air and fired again. The wolf ran a little farther away. Then it stopped and watched, almost as if it knew that my ammunition box was nearly empty. As if wondering how I'd use that last bullet.

As I reloaded, my arms were trembling so hard that the gun seemed to have a life of its own, twitching this way and that like a fish that's just been caught. I aimed at the wolf, then I aimed in the air, not knowing what I was going to do. The wolf watched me with its strange cold eyes. It waited. Nanni was yelling at me to shoot, but the falling snow muffled everything so much that she

sounded almost unreal. The only thing real was the wolf in front of me. Time came to a standstill, I think. It could have been years passing.

Then the wolf loped away into the milk-white world. I fired my last shot into the air and watched until it was out of sight.

＊ ＊ ◇ ＊ ＊

13

Some Are Cut Out
to Be Hunters

It was a while before Nanni made her way
cautiously back across the snow. Her eyes were
wet and her mouth still terrified.

"Is it dead?" she asked.

I shook my head. We followed the rope back to
the cabin and helped one another push the door
shut. Nanni checked the locks and bolts.

I was shaking so hard I could barely stand. While
Nanni put more wood on the fire I went over to
the bunk and sat down. With new life in the fire,
my hands, which were bright red with cold, ached
and stung as warmth returned to them. Nanni came
and sat beside me.

"It appeared without a sound," she said. "I was
just going to check the meat was still there and
brush the snow off it when all of a sudden, there
it was. As if by magic. I was going to shoot it, but I

dropped my gun and it disappeared in the snow."

She hid her face in her hands and sat in silence for quite some time. All I could hear was her heavy breathing. Then she raised her head and gave me a steady look.

"You were brave," she said. "Braver than many men who come here and think it'll be easy coming face to face with a white wolf."

It was then that the dam burst in me, releasing a flood of tears.

"I wasn't brave at all!" I said. "I was scared! I've never been so scared in my life."

Nanni stroked my back. "There, there," she said. "It's over now. You don't need to cry any more."

But I carried on crying and for a long time we just sat there, me sobbing and Nanni with her hand on my back. She tried to comfort me several times but it didn't work.

Eventually she said, "Will you stop crying if I tell you a nice story?"

"I don't know," I said, sniffing. "I might, I suppose."

Nanni thought for a while, then decided to tell me a story from the Wolf Islands. She had heard it herself just after she got there and it had cheered her up when everything was feeling strange and new. It went like this:

"Stupid and No-one bought a gun and wanted

to learn to shoot. No-one went first. He took the gun and fired a shot, but the bullet ricocheted, hit him in the forehead and he fell to the ground. Stupid ran to the village, where hunters were sitting in the tavern. 'No-one is dying!' he yelled. 'That's good,' the hunters said. 'Can't you hear what I'm saying!' Stupid yelled again. 'Yes, and it's a jolly good thing no one is dying,' the hunters said. 'For heaven's sake, can't you help me? No-one is dying!' the poor fellow shrieked desperately. The hunters all looked at him and said, 'Are you stupid, or something?' 'Yes!' said Stupid."

Nanni laughed when she came to the end. And I also felt laughter stirring deep in my body, the way water begins to stir in a pan over the fire. In fact, it was quite a silly story, but I laughed anyway because it was such a joy to feel the fear leave my body and to know I wasn't going to die today.

Nanni wiped tears from the corners of her eyes and looked at me again with that steady gaze.

"Say what you like," she said. "But I think you'll fit in here. And it's nice to have company in the hut."

She stood up and looked out through the shooting hole. It had finally stopped snowing and the last few scattered snowflakes were falling almost timidly, as if wondering where the rest of their flock had gone.

"I'm going to see if I can find the gun," she said.

"I dropped the musket balls too," I said.

Nanni said that didn't matter as she had boxes and boxes of them. She drew back the bolt and opened the door. The sky was still gray but visibility at ground level was better and it was safe to go out.

Once Nanni had shut the door behind her I sat there thinking about what she'd said. Would I be able to shoot? Be like her? A hunter?

I stood up and walked around, pretending it was my hut and my possessions. I stopped at the pelt pinned on the wall and stroked the dense white fur. What if I'd been the one who shot and skinned that wolf? And my purse had been full of silver coins? What if I returned to Blue Bay so wealthy that...?

No, I could never go home. But what about other places? Places where the streets were paved, where I could buy sweet things? What if Fredrik had been wrong when he said it was impossible to forget? What if snowberries and sisters and mines eventually faded from your memory if you really wanted them to?

The door opened again. Nanni had found her gun. She smiled at me and I realized I was still stroking that pelt. I pulled my hand away.

"A wolf skin on the wall." Nanni's cold eyes glittered. "That's something many people want."

I don't know what came over me then. I hadn't thought about it since leaving home, but my mouth opened and out came the words: "Guess what we have on the wall at home in Blue Bay?"

Nanni looked at me. There was no mistaking her curiosity.

"A mermaid's flipper." I felt my lungs fill with air and my chest puff up with pride.

Nanni smiled as if I was being stupid again.

"A little bit of one, I mean," I said.

"Who fooled you into believing that?" Nanni said. She sat down on the bunk and began inspecting the gun.

"No one fooled me," I said. "It's hanging there. I glued pebbles around it."

She nodded, still smiling.

"It was my dad who pulled her up in his net," I went on. "She was small."

Nanni laid the gun across her knee, looked at me and said, "Siri, there's no such thing as a mermaid."

I laughed because now at last it was Nanni being stupid, not me.

"Where did the piece of flipper come from if mermaids don't exist?" I said. "Ha ha! You didn't think of that, did you?"

"Your dad was just pulling your leg." Nanni sounded almost irritated. "Don't you get that?"

"He wasn't! I was there when he came ashore and told us. And it wasn't a joke."

Nanni smiled and rolled her eyes.

I put my hands on my hips and said, "I should be the best judge of whether my dad was joking."

"Well, in that case he must be a fool," she mumbled.

"What?" I said.

"Maybe he wasn't trying to play a trick, how should I know?" Nanni said. "But I know one thing: mermaids don't exist in the same way that fish or birds or wolves exist. So if your dad came ashore and really did say he'd seen one, then he must be a fool. You must realize that, so there's no need for us to fall out over it."

She carried on working on the gun and I watched how lovingly she dried off the barrel with her sleeve and how carefully she blew the melted snow out of the lock.

No, I certainly didn't intend to see it her way and take my dad for a fool! I was the fool. I'd been standing there dreaming of shooting. In just one day I'd changed into someone who wasn't the real me, into someone like Nanni, who looked after her gun as if it were her child.

Oh yes, I could see how impatient she was for the storm to end—it was nothing more or less than greed. Ugly, all-consuming greed.

"I have no intention of ever shooting with you," I said.

"All right then," she answered without looking up.

I waited, mulling it over before I said, "If you hunt wolves for money, you're no better than Whitehead. You're just the same."

Nanni stood up so violently that I jumped. Her face was taut with rage, her eyes wide open and blazing.

"You'll take that back!"

"No, I won't! I'll never take it back because it's true!"

"There's a huge difference between hunting wolves for money and hunting people for it!"

"And people are the ones who've decided that, aren't they?" I yelled, picking up my jacket, gloves and cap and rushing out.

◆ ◆ ◇ ◆ ◆

14

A Boat Called *Cuttlefish*

Siri!" Nanni called after me, but I didn't turn around. I didn't want to see her again! Not ever! She thought there was a difference between people and animals, but it didn't occur to her that a short while earlier two hunted animals had trembled at the possibility of death in the snowstorm. There hadn't been much difference between them then. And what about the little animal Whitehead had stolen from me so he could send her down a mine to make money for him? I was going to follow that little animal. I wasn't going to give up.

The tracks Nanni and I had made the day before were gone. But screwing up my eyes I could make out the thin coils of smoke rising from the village chimneys. It wouldn't be too hard to find my way. I put on my jacket, cap and gloves and set off on the long walk through the snow. I had seen vessels besides the *Pole Star* in the port and I might be able to sign on as a crew member. Even if they didn't go directly to Seglen they might take me part of the way. Halfway, even. Sometimes you had to make do.

Nanni shouted a few more times. She was probably trying to clear her conscience, and I didn't think much of her manky old conscience. She could put a leash on it and sell it at a village shop for all I cared.

In the end she stopped shouting and I was alone in the silence. Snow was getting into the legs of my boots and there was still a long way to go. I felt fear creeping up on me. Visibility was good now it had stopped snowing, but the great wild expanse of open country was white. And so were wolves.

I jumped. Someone was right behind me!

No, there was no one. I'd imagined it.

But over there? Behind that hummock? I stopped and stared. But no wolf came charging out, yelping and howling with frothing jaws. All was still.

I walked and walked and every step of the way I felt there was a monster at my heels. Eventually I was half running, stumbling and staggering, sodden with sweat and heart pounding. The columns from the village chimneys grew until I caught the good, familiar smell of smoke. At last I turned into the village street.

It was late afternoon by now. The merchants were closing their small shops and dusk was falling.

I walked down to the wharf. *Windreef* and *Homeless* had both sailed but *Wulf*, the splendid big ship that had recently arrived, was still there.

The fat man from the port office stood on his office steps, eyes following two scruffy-looking individuals wandering among the fishing boats. I disliked that man so much I didn't want to speak to him, but I had no choice. So, putting on a cheerful face, I walked straight over to the steps and gave a little cough. He carried on watching the scruffy pair.

"Good evening," I said.

He threw me a quick glance and gave a sort of growl.

"I wanted to ask you when the *Wulf* will be sailing? And if you know where it's going?" I said.

"Hey, you two!" the port official roared. The men on the quayside halted and looked at him. "Unless you own one of the boats the two of you can shove off!"

One of them—he was short and bald—held up his hands. "Can't we even admire the fishing boats these days?" he shouted in a shrill, unpleasant voice.

The port official snorted. "I'm supposed to believe that you two are fishermen, am I? I know riff-raff when I see it. Get away with you now! Scram!"

The bald man looked as if he was going to cause trouble, but the other one—with a beard and long hair—said something to his companion and they left.

The port official glared after them and only once they'd disappeared up the village street did he look down at me. "Well?"

"I was just asking when the *Wulf* will be sailing." I nodded towards the ship. "I want to talk to the captain about a job."

The port man sighed. "Didn't Urstrom tell you to forget those stupid ideas?"

"Yes, but there's nothing wrong with asking, is there?" I muttered.

"No ships will be leaving before next spring," he said. "So if you want to go you'll have to swim."

"What about the *Wulf* then?" I said.

"That's our ship and it'll be moored here for the winter. Now you know."

With that he turned on his heel and disappeared into the office. He wasn't the sort to be overly concerned about a child who'd missed her boat— not if he could help it.

I walked on. The shutters were down on almost every shop in the street. A man opened his window and emptied his chamber pot, another was trying to kick free his sled which had frozen to the ground. No one looked at me. No one bothered to ask what I was doing there or if I needed help. Nanni was the only one who'd asked, and I'd run away from her. A knot of anxiety was twisting tighter and tighter in my stomach. I had nowhere to go and night would soon cover the Wolf Islands with its black cloak. There were already stars in the sky. What could I do?

Suddenly I heard a mumble of voices, and I saw the two scruffy men from the port. They hadn't seen me but they were standing in an alleyway, where they'd put down their bags. I was going to hurry away because they made me uneasy, but I overheard them and that brought me to a standstill.

"I still don't know if it's a good idea, joining Whitehead," the bearded one said in a low voice.

"Got a better idea?" the bald one answered.

"Maybe not," Beardy said. "But working for someone like that could be stupid. I mean, if his crew's captured, what then? What do they do to pirates?"

I hid behind broken packing cases beside a cottage wall. No more than five yards away, I could see and hear them clearly.

"Which 'they' do you mean?" Baldy snorted. "Not a single person around the whole Ice Sea will risk going after pirates."

"There is that," Beardy said. He seemed to be thinking it over. Then he sighed: "Shouldn't we wait a bit anyway? I'll bet that port fellow's still on the lookout."

"We'll leave tonight," Baldy said firmly. "The sooner we get away the better."

"I don't know about that. The big ships have

stopped sailing and you still think we should set out in a little fishing boat!"

"You have to take some risks in this world if you don't want to end up a worthless pauper," Baldy said. "Anyone who joins Whitehead's crew gets incredibly rich. You know as well as I do that he lets his pirates keep all the valuables for themselves. He doesn't want any of it!"

Beardy snorted. "He wants something, all right."

"He does." Baldy was trying to sound nonchalant. "But when did you start worrying about a bunch of kids beings sent down a mine? I can't pretend I had a bundle of fun myself as a boy. If the winds are with us we could get to Seglen in two or three days."

"And if they're not…"

"Cut the cowardly drivel!" Baldy snarled. He took off his gloves and fished a medallion from his jacket lapel. I craned my neck to see. It was the image of an oarfish and it looked new. People said that wearing an oarfish would protect you from bad luck.

Baldy held the medallion tight in his fist. "Now we'll have the winds behind us," he said.

They shouldered their bags and left the alleyway. As they passed the pile of junk where I hid, I made myself small and hardly dared breathe. But the men didn't notice me as they set off briskly for the wharf.

The moon had come out so it was easy to keep them in sight. Running quickly from one shadow to the next, I followed them all the way to the shore.

The boat they intended to steal was gaff-rigged and quite big, as small boats go. Opposite the port office was a large warehouse, which I hid behind while the men made ready to depart. They threw their bags into the boat, and they were about to climb down themselves when there came a roar from the warehouse. Beardy had been right—the port official had been watching and was running over as fast as he could.

"Cast off!" Baldy yelled, snatching at the ropes.

But the next moment the man grabbed hold of his jacket and hurled him away from the boat.

"So that's what you're up to!" he roared. "I knew it, I just knew it! Sailing off with someone's boat! You wait until I fetch the owner—he'll have something to say about it. He'll have you thrown in the sea! That's what we do with thieving scum here!"

But Baldy rushed at the port official, threw his arms around his huge belly and pulled him to the ground.

"Find me something to tie him with!" he snarled. Beardy ran into the warehouse, quickly returning with ropes. Between them they got the man back on his feet and tied his hands behind him as he shouted and roared. Then they led him into the warehouse. It was his turn to be locked in a store. He was in for a cold night.

And it was my turn to move fast. I ran and jumped down into the boat, where I crawled under the afterthwart and eased the lid over me. There was plenty of room.

The two men returned from the warehouse, untied the mooring ropes and climbed down into the boat, which rocked as they pushed out from the quay. They hoisted the sails, then one of them sat on the thwart where I was hiding and took the tiller. As the sails filled, the boat picked up speed and began to heel over. I had to brace myself so as not to roll and crash into things. The offshore wind meant we'd make rapid progress.

"*Cuttlefish*," Beardy spat scornfully above me. "Have you ever heard a stupider name for a boat?"

"What's so stupid about it?" Baldy wondered.

Beardy couldn't come up with an answer at first but eventually concluded that stealing a boat called *Cuttlefish* could only mean bad luck. Fate was unlikely to have anything good in store for a boat named after a bottom-feeding loser!

We sailed out of the inlet and the sea grew rough. Beardy sighed and muttered. There was a good deal of truth in his mutterings: it was little short of madness to set out on a winter voyage in a boat like the *Cuttlefish*.

◆ ◆ ◇ ◆ ◆

15

Wood

I was woken by weak light filtering through a crack in the lid. The roar, the ceaseless roar that grew louder on the crests of the waves and duller in the valleys between, had lulled me to sleep, but now dawn was breaking. I was cold and stiff and my whole body ached, but I couldn't risk moving. The slightest tapping against the wood would make the men jump up and lift the lid on my hiding place. And what would they do when they saw me?

Beardy had evidently managed to sleep. Perhaps they'd taken turns at the rudder. Now he was yawning and grunting as some people do when they wake up. He asked Baldy what the wind had been doing and Baldy said it hadn't been bad at all. They'd been sailing large and holding a south-westerly course. It sounded as if they had a sea chart.

I lay where I was, pinned down, as if my body had been pressed into the curved gray wood and become one with the *Cuttlefish*. This must be what a boat felt, every thump and twist shooting pain through its body. What it most likely wanted to do was to stretch out, break free of its timber ribs and this ceaseless, angry rocking. How awful to be a boat, locked into a fixed shape.

"Shall I take over the tiller?" Beardy asked.

"Nope," Baldy answered.

No more was said. After a while, however, Beardy gave a little sigh and said that they were tempting fate by going to sea when all the larger ships were moored for the winter.

"You really do go on, don't you?" Baldy said. "Do you think fate was treating us well back on the Wolf Islands?"

Beardy didn't reply.

"Well, do you?" Baldy said. "Was fate treating us any better back there?"

"Maybe not, but at least we weren't doing completely crazy things."

"Weren't we? Wasn't it crazy to carry on as we did? Month after month getting nowhere?"

"Everyone has to learn the ropes when they start…"

"When they start? What are you talking about—all we did for a whole year was start and then start again."

They carried on arguing and I learned that the

year Baldy and Beardy spent on the Wolf Islands had been one long failure. They hadn't shot a single wolf. It was almost uncanny, and Baldy reckoned that if fate was so against him that it wouldn't even let him shoot one wolf, he'd get his own back on fate. He'd show fate who was the boss, which was why he'd acquired an oarfish medallion.

Beardy muttered that he didn't think you could do much about fate, because fate was stronger that people, wolves and oarfish combined.

Baldy responded with a snort, after which they were so annoyed with each other that neither spoke for several hours. But if they were silent, the wind and waves made up for it. The wind grew ever stronger, the waves grew angrier, and more and more spray splashed over the sides. I felt dizzy as the boat surged up onto the crests then down into the troughs again. The men said nothing, just sailed stubbornly on as if the whole business had turned into a competition, with the loser the first to concede that it was a touch breezy!

Finally, at long last, Beardy thought it was time to reef the mainsail.

"No," was all Baldy said. He had no intention of reefing anything.

Beardy kept nagging, saying they ought to reef the sail even if only a little bit. It was stupid to push an unfamiliar boat so hard.

Baldy wouldn't budge. He wanted them to make haste. He'd allowed fickle fate to govern his life for too long. Speed didn't frighten him.

At that point I could tell that Beardy was beginning to untie the mainsail rope because Baldy started yelling at him to leave it alone. And so a new quarrel started, with Beardy screaming that Baldy would be the death of them both, and Baldy shouting that if Beardy had his way he'd lower both sails and let fate decide where it took them. Meanwhile the wind increased and, lying there in the darkness, I was terrified by all the noise—the men's bellows and the roar of wind and waves. The sea was hammering at the hull with its hundreds of fists, demanding to be let in.

In the midst of all the roaring and pounding there was a crack and a splash. The *Cuttlefish*, which had been leaning one way for a long time, suddenly heeled over hard the other way, causing me to roll over and bang my head. The men swore and Baldy shouted for Beardy to untie the rope. The sail was flapping madly in the wind. The gaff had snapped and the sail had fallen into the sea. Beardy must have leapt to the rail to salvage it while Baldy carried on yelling and water splashed in over the sides.

"We're getting waterlogged!" Baldy shouted. "Fix up a drift anchor!"

A drift anchor is something thrown into the water to stabilize the movement of a boat—the best kind is a bucket on the end of a long rope. Once Beardy had rescued the mainsail, he began looking for a bucket. I bit my lip hoping against hope he'd find one stored under another thwart in the bows of the boat. After a little while, however, I heard him tell Baldy to stand up.

Light suddenly flooded in, hurting my eyes. I closed them tight. Someone pulled me up by my arm, as easily as if I were made of paper. My body, which had been lying curled and motionless, felt broken in ten places. I screamed and the man screamed back, asking what the devil I thought I was up to, swearing and threatening to throw me overboard. But a new shower of ice-cold water told them they had to attend to the boat, or it would nose-dive under the waves.

They couldn't find a bucket so Beardy emptied one of the sacks they'd brought on board, tied it to a rope, and threw the sack overboard.

The speed of the *Cuttlefish* was immediately checked, as if a strong rider were pulling on the reins and calming it down. The wind still howled and whipped the boat, the waves were still wild, but we were no longer completely at their mercy. We were soaked and the air in my lungs was like ice. My body was still stiff and the light still hurt my eyes. And what was going to happen to me now?

Baldy kept a firm grip on the tiller and I was down on the bottom boards, but he watched me the whole time with a piercing, ugly look. The boat pushed on across the leaden, foaming sea. Beardy had packed away the salvaged sail and was bailing out the water swilling at his feet. He looked at me now and then, but not with the fixed stare I was getting from Baldy.

"You're that kid who was talking to the port official last night," he said.

I shivered and tried not to look into his evil eyes.

"When did you hide under the thwart?" Baldy asked.

"When...when you were tying him up," I said in a quiet voice.

Baldy thought for a while. "Do you have any idea at all where we're going?" he asked.

I nodded. "To Seglen. I heard you in the alleyway."

His eyes narrowed. "And why do you want to go there? What's a snotty little kid like you going to Seglen for?"

I swallowed hard. "Whitehead took my sister and I'm going to take her back."

The men looked at one another. They said nothing for a while and then they started laughing. Not the jolly kind of laughter that comes from hearing something funny, but the breathless, snorting laughter people make when they find something incomprehensible.

The storm passed as quickly as it had come and soon we were bowling along over a long, gray swell. Baldy hauled in the drift anchor and we sailed on using only the small, triangular foresail. We'd been blown about and they had no idea where we were now. Islands and skerries came into view, sometimes a series of them, one after another like pearls on a string. But they were all uninhabited, home to nothing but snow and ice.

Baldy, who'd been thinking things over, became a bit more cheerful about my presence on board. The way he saw it, a new child for the mines was practically the best present they could take to Whitehead. It would ensure them a warm welcome on the *Snow Raven*.

"That's assuming we get there before our fresh water runs out," Beardy muttered, staring at the map.

Large ice floes and icebergs drifted around us, and now and again one would collide so violently with our hull I was sure we'd sink. But the *Cuttlefish* sailed on, damaged and cautious, across the waters.

All of a sudden Beardy jumped. "I saw something!"

"What?" Baldy asked.

Beardy continued gazing into the distance. "It's gone now," he said.

"What was it?" Baldy asked.

"A seal, maybe." Beardy was still staring. Then he rose to his feet: "There it is again!"

Baldy and I craned our necks and as we came closer all three of us saw it. Baldy swore under his breath, sounding almost frightened. What we saw rolling in the waves was alive, something that seemed to be desperately waving its arms, something with pink skin, something crying. If I didn't know better I would have thought we were looking at a naked child.

♦ ♦ ◇ ♦ ♦

16

The Child in the Water

We turned to starboard and Beardy dropped the sail. The *Cuttlefish* slowed down. Baldy leaned his elbow on the rail and peered down at the naked thing rolling in the water. Now and again we saw two flippers moving, very much like a seal's.

"What on earth is it?" Beardy asked.

Baldy shook his head and continued to stare as if in a dream. "No idea," he muttered.

We glimpsed a small, round head in the foaming water and heard sobs again. Two small, fat arms desperately beat the surface.

"A mermaid," I whispered.

"What did you say?" Baldy asked.

"It must be, mustn't it?" I said, staring at the little creature in the water. "A mermaid's child, a merchild?"

Baldy and Beardy laughed as if relieved to have the seriousness of the situation wiped away by the foolishness of a child. But I could tell they weren't convinced that what I'd said was stupid. Whatever it was, with a head, arms and flippers, if it wasn't a merchild what was it?

Baldy made his mind up in seconds.

"Get the bag net," he said.

"Are you sure?" Beardy answered. "It might break it."

"Of course it won't."

"But what if it does? The bag net's worth having…"

"We have to lift that thing out of the water. It could be worth a fortune."

Beardy lifted tangled ropes out of the way and managed to find the net.

"We'll have to get closer," he said.

Baldy looked at me. "Can you row?"

I nodded—I didn't dare do anything else. I untied the oars, put them in the rowlocks and then, following Baldy's commands, rowed over to the child.

As we approached, the child took fright and dived, leaving on the surface a white flower of foam.

"Damn!" Baldy hissed. He stood up, grabbed the boathook and looked at me. "Hold the boat steady!" he roared. He went down on his knees in the prow, leaned over the rail and stared into the water. He told us that there were doctors in the great cities who'd pay a fortune for new species of fish, which they preserved in spirits and dissected. If they were willing to pay that much for fish, how much more would they pay for something like this, something...

What was it we'd seen? Beardy, who seemed a bit timid, fidgeted and said that *if* there were such things as mermaids they must surely be creatures from hell? That's what he'd heard, anyway. And they could weigh many hundreds of pounds and kill a man with a single blow if they felt like it. What if there were a whole herd of them, directly under our boat...?

Baldy kept on peering down and paid no attention to him. Now and then his hand felt for the oarfish round his neck. He'd touch it gently, as though asking it for help. He gave a sudden jump.

"There it is!" He jabbed the boathook down as far as he could, sharp end first, hoping it would catch in the creature's flesh.

"Stop that!" I said.

Baldy's first attempt had missed and he pushed the boathook down again, taking aim and trying to send it straight. It was tricky, of course, because the wooden shaft wanted to float.

I rowed, pulling on the oars for all I was worth to move away from the creature. At the same time I stamped on the bottom boards to frighten it into diving deeper and hiding in the shadow of the slushy ice.

"What are you doing?" Baldy screamed. "Keep still and keep quiet!"

But I carried on stamping and rowing hard. Baldy wouldn't be able to find the spot once we'd moved away. He lost his temper. He hurled the boathook into the bottom of the boat, rushed over and hauled me up by my jacket. He held me out over the side.

"You've made me lose a prize catch!" he screamed, and I thought I saw tears in his eyes. "The only decent catch I've had in my sights for a year!"

"It…it was so small!" My feet flailed frantically to get a grip on the gunwales, but the wet wood was slippery.

Baldy glanced at the sea, then fixed me with his ugly, spiky look.

"The more I think about it the more I reckon you won't be the sort of kid Whitehead wants," he said. "The last thing he'll want is a troublemaker."

And with that he let go of my jacket. I hung in the air for a surprisingly long time—or perhaps I only imagined whole seconds passing. I do know that I flailed my arms, trying to grab hold of anything I could, and I found the leather thong with the oarfish. Baldy was caught by surprise and I dragged him with me. For one moment I thought we were going overboard together.

But Beardy came to the rescue. He caught

Baldy around the waist and held him tight until the leather snapped and I fell. The oarfish followed me into the deep.

I've fallen into the water before. Several times, in fact, and the feeling is always the same. If I had to describe it I'd say that you suddenly know who you are. The thing is, most of the time you don't think about that. Everything you do is pure routine: scrubbing, gutting fish, rinsing the washing, sleeping and getting up—you do it all without a thought of who is actually doing those things. But when you fall in the water, you suddenly realize, "I am Siri! And I'm the one who has fallen into the water."

The worst thing is that your clothes get so heavy. Wool, for instance, becomes as heavy as lead in water, and now it felt as if a strong hand had grabbed me and was pulling me down.

I reached the bottom and that's when I became frightened: if I'd gone down so far, this was the end. I'd never reach the surface again unless I had something to climb.

But was this really the bottom?

I looked around at all the blueness and in one direction it was dark but in the other, light. I realized I'd landed on the underwater ledge of an iceberg.

I let go of the leather thong so I could grip and climb the uneven surface of the ice. The oarfish drifted on down and disappeared in the gloom.

The air in my lungs was quickly running out. Dad used to say that drowning people die because they eventually go mad from lack of air. Something goes wrong in their heads and they breathe in even though they're still in the depths. That's when water rushes into their lungs and they die.

But it was lighter above me. Small ice floes drifted on the surface like a flock of glaucous gulls. I forced myself up the last bit before I could black out, and at the surface I took an enormous breath, sucking in air until my throat ached. I made my way from floe to floe towards a nearby skerry where at last I felt solid ground beneath my feet. I waded ashore and collapsed on my knees. I was so cold I thought my arms and legs were about to fall off.

◆ ◆ ◇ ◆ ◆

The Inhabitants of Snowrose

The first thing I did once I'd got my breath back was to stand up and run. You have to do it to keep your body temperature up. After running back and forth across the small white beach I noticed tracks. Not ordinary footprints, but something else. Possibly the tracks of small, flat-bottomed boats being pulled up the beach.

I looked around. Maybe the skerry wasn't uninhabited after all. There might be people on the other side of those cliffs. There might even be a village.

I had no idea how big the skerry was, but I was sure I could walk all the way around it before darkness fell. Well, I had no choice.

My clothes froze to ice and armoured me against the cold. That's strange, isn't it? They formed a shell. The heat of my body dried out the woollen pants and woollen shirt I was wearing next to my skin.

Pack ice in lumps the size of houses had piled up against the cliffs. I climbed up and down, up and down, sweating in spite of the cold. But there was no shortage of snow, so I didn't have to go thirsty.

There's life here, I thought. I'll find life. I have to.

Darkness began to fall over the skerry, at first so imperceptibly I thought I could blink it away, but then it closed in and the roof of the sky came lower. My legs wanted to rest but I forced them to go on. I strained my eyes for more of those tracks, for a place where human beings dragged their boats ashore, where there were houses and food and fire.

At last I found some and my heart missed a beat. I ran the last bit, afraid I'd imagined them. But there they were: more tracks left by boats.

"Hello!" I shouted. "Is there anyone there?"

I called again and again, shouting until I was hoarse. But no answer came.

That's when I saw footprints in the snow. But they weren't the prints of people who rowed flat-bottomed boats, they were my own.

I sank to the ground. I'd walked around the whole skerry. It had taken the strength out of me, though it had taken less time than I expected. And nowhere had I found life.

Perhaps this skerry was a hunting ground for people who lived far away on another island. People might come here only once or twice a year, the way

Miki and I rowed out to Iron Apple. They might even have a name for the place. Snowrose?

It made no difference. The stars were in the sky and the night chill, fast and piercing, had arrived. Walking round the skerry I'd been tempted to take off my coat, but now my whole body prickled with goose-flesh. I ran and jumped, rushing between the walls of pack ice and beating my arms. I'd have to keep it up all night to stay warm, then perhaps, just perhaps, the sun might peep through. There might be a couple of hours when the sun was willing to shine on Snowrose and I'd be able to sleep in its warmth. But now, under the stars, I was running to stay alive, and my running grew slower and slower—it was no good pretending otherwise. My legs wouldn't obey, my feet skidded on those strange boat marks and I fell over. I stood up and fell again. Stood up and fell and stood up again.

Then, after landing on my belly in the snow yet again, I didn't bother to get up. I didn't have the energy. I actually didn't *want* to! I didn't care if the cold overcame me, I only wanted to rest, to shut my eyes with my forehead resting on a cold pillow. It felt so good. If freezing to death felt this good, maybe it didn't matter one way or the other. I wasn't thinking of Miki any longer, or of Dad or Fredrik. I had only one thought, which was to rest for a while, and then decide.

I heard weeping. Or was it me weeping? Perhaps. Was I already dead and weeping over the empty shell of my body? I sat up and listened. No, I wasn't dead, and someone else was crying. I stood up.

At first I couldn't tell where it came from, then I suddenly heard splashing as if someone was kicking the sea, and the crying became despairing grunts and sobs.

I hurried down to the water and in the moonlight could see a small body. I knew at once whose it was.

The merchild was face down, struggling to push itself forward with its lower body, where it had two flippers instead of legs. It was naked and helpless at the water's edge.

I crept closer and crouched down beside it. The merchild fell silent, watching me expectantly. Was it shy? Then it began struggling. The rocks were slippery and the child was soon grunting again. It sounded angry and looked at me as if it thought I should be helping.

I wrapped my arms around the small body and carried it up from the water's edge. I took off my frozen gloves to feel how cold the child was and, remarkably, it wasn't cold at all. It was warm and even seemed to be sweating.

The merchild pulled itself to sitting. Its eyes,

deep-set in a pink face, shone blue in the moonlight. Its nose was small and short and it had a couple of new baby teeth. Its skin was thick and rough and down near the hairy flippers was something floppy and much smaller than my little finger. It was obviously a boy.

The merchild raised his arm and pointed. He stretched his head back and made a long, hissing noise. I looked over to the cliffs but I couldn't see what he was trying to show me.

He repeated this several times before dropping back onto his stomach and wriggling in that direction. He pushed himself along with his hands and glided so smoothly across the hard snow that I almost had to run to keep up.

There was an opening in the cliffs that I hadn't noticed before. The child slid through and I hurried along behind.

It was pitch-black inside and I clambered over things that crunched under my feet. I had no idea where the child had gone.

"Come back!" I shouted. "It might be dangerous!"

I could hear no sound of the child. I put my hand on the cave wall and felt my way farther into the darkness. The crunching under my feet grew louder. What was I walking on? It wasn't twigs and it wasn't ice. Could it be bones?

Then I heard the child call out: "Na-naa!"

I put on a spurt, sensing light ahead. The moonlight must be finding its way through an opening in the roof. And there was the child. It was warm in the cave, almost as warm as springtime at home. But the air was tainted with a rotten smell and I crouched for a closer look at what was under my feet. Mussel shells! There were heaps of them all round me and everything became clear—mermaids eat mussels. The child had been living in this cave with his mother—others too, perhaps. Maybe a whole herd? And they must have gone to sea and lost contact with one another in the storm. The child had probably spent hours trying to find his way home.

He was shouting now and it sounded as if he wanted me to come. When I reached him he was lying down and I realized he was in a nest, a big nest made of twigs and dry seaweed. He was making little humming noises. Once I'd taken off my icy clothes and lain down in the nest, I cuddled his small warm body close to me. He took hold of a lock of my hair and began to suck on it.

The tracks on the shore weren't made by flat-bottomed boats, I thought before falling asleep. They were tracks of the inhabitants of Snowrose.

◆ ◆ ◇ ◆ ◆

Looking for a Boat

The merchild woke me by pulling my hair and sucking and chewing on it. He sounded unhappy and after a while began climbing onto me. Whining and snuffling, he scratched and pulled at me. He was heavy and ungainly and still so tired he could barely hold his head up. Time after time his little forehead banged into me, and time after time he uttered that sorrowful *Na-naa*. I assumed that was what he called his mother.

"Are you hungry?" I yawned and sat up.

The child whined and writhed.

"I don't have any food for you," I said. "Nor for me, for that matter."

The child whined even more. He seemed to understand exactly what I said but had no way of answering. His little mouth turned down at the corners and tears of despair came to his eyes.

"Shh now, shh…" I said, putting on my damp

clothes. "Come on, let's go and see what I can find."

I wrapped my arms around his chubby stomach and carefully carried him through the dark cave, clambering over all the smelly shells.

The light hit us like fists as we left the cave. The sea was gray and choppy, with small waves stirred by the wind. The temperature had dropped during the night and my breath came out as dense clouds of steam. I put the child down and he used his hands to push himself along and slide to the shore. I looked around. What was there to eat on Snowrose? There were no hens to provide eggs, no bushes to produce berries. I had no fishing gear and no nets to catch sea parrots. The answer was obvious: on Snowrose you had to eat as mermaids do. The merchild was already in the shallows busily gathering mussels.

I joined him. The seabed was covered in shining, blue-black mussels, there for the taking. By the time I'd pulled up six or seven my hands were aching with cold. I broke open the shells, pulled out the cold, slippery flesh, stuffed it quickly into my mouth and forced it down. It wasn't so bad, perhaps: many times at home we'd had to eat herring that had gone bad, and that was worse. Clearly, though, it would have been nice to have something else to fill my stomach. Life on Snowrose seemed likely to be gloomy and monotonous, with only a stinking cave to live in and nothing but mussels to eat.

The child was really tucking in, crunching the shells open without cutting himself and slurping down the contents. Every so often he looked at me with his small blue eyes. He was happier now and seemed to think that we were having a wonderful time together.

By the time I'd eaten three handfuls of mussels I'd had enough. I wiped my mouth on the sleeve of my jacket and turned my gaze to the sea. If only there was a boat, if only someone came sailing along to tend their nets or drop creels. If only a passing sailor saw me standing on the shore, marooned and miserable.

I wandered aimlessly around Snowrose for several hours, always keeping an eye out to sea. The child wouldn't leave me in peace—he was under my feet the whole time. He pulled and chewed at the legs of my boots. And time after time he held his arms out and asked to be picked up.

"Na-naa!" was all he said.

"That's what you want, is it?" I said eventually, when my legs were starting to feel tired. "You want to sit on my lap for a while?"

The sun had broken through the woolly gray blanket covering the sky and was giving some real warmth. I picked up the child and went over by the mouth of the cave. There was a rock that looked as if it would make a good seat, but just then I tripped over something in the snow. I fell and dropped the child, setting off floods of tears that took much sympathy and patting to quieten. I kicked snow aside to see what had tripped me and discovered the shattered timbers of a boat that must have lain there for many years. After looking all day for a boat it felt eerie to find the carcass of one. It clearly wasn't going to be much use to me.

But…perhaps?

I put down the child and this time ignored his whines and howls. A tiny spark of hope had been struck in my heart. I kicked aside more snow and dug with my hands. I found fragments of beams and planking, dowels and nails and even a broken rib, but I was looking for something else.

After digging for some time my gloves were so heavy and wet they almost slid off my hands. But at last I found what I was seeking, buried with the rest of the rigging a few feet from the hull. The mainsail.

Pulling it from the snow was laborious, verging on hopeless. I had to remove my gloves to get a good grip, while the child persisted in crawling over the sail and ropes, so I had to push him away.

Once I'd salvaged the sail, I inspected it. It was a spritsail, four-sided, thick and in good condition, without a single tear. Two of the corners had begun to rot and gone slightly black, but that made no difference. I also dug out the mast that had carried the sail and as much of the ropework as I could find.

"Now then," I said, giving the child a smile. "We're going to the top of Snowrose."

The child laughed, no doubt thinking it sounded like a great adventure. I took firm hold of the stiff, rolled-up sailcloth, bent my knees, hoisted it onto my shoulder and set off.

Oh, how I toiled and struggled that day. First of all I dragged everything—sail, mast and ropes—up to the highest point of the skerry through snow that kept giving way beneath my feet so that I sank to my waist. Then I began fixing the sail to the mast so that the heavy cloth would stay attached. What made it so awkward was that the sail now had to hang with its short side to the mast instead of the long side as it had been designed. I swore such strings of oaths that I think the sun hid its face behind a cloud for a while. But then it was time for the hardest job of all: making the whole thing stand upright.

I built a cairn of rocks that I dug out of the snow. The bigger the stones, the better, and how my back ached afterwards! The child was well-behaved and even tried to help, crawling around with stones scarcely bigger than potatoes, which he placed on the cairn and then a moment later thought it was great fun to take them away to put elsewhere. He was a sweet little fellow.

The sea turned violet in the twilight. The choppy waves had calmed down and the surface was smooth as a mirror. The ice floes barely moved. Soaked with sweat and with every muscle shaking, I eased the foot of the mast down into the cairn. I'd left a hole of exactly the right size and it took the last of my strength to raise the mast upright. Then I stepped back to look at my work.

Despondency and gloom came over me. Was this really what I'd hoped for? I'd slaved all day with only a few mussels in my belly and this was all I'd achieved. What good could come from this pole and its sad piece of sailcloth?

But just then, a gust of wind came sweeping across the skerry and took hold of the sail. My heart began to beat faster. Now it looked better, now it looked just as I'd thought it would. The sailcloth fluttered and flapped while I gazed out over the great silent sea. The surface rippled and the ice floes began to bob a little. There was no boat in sight, not as far as the eye could see, but perhaps, just perhaps, one day someone would come sailing by and see my flag.

◆ ◆ ◇ ◆ ◆

The Game

The temperature on Snowrose dropped quickly. The slush ice along the water's edge grew thicker with every passing day and the sea creaked and cracked. But the cold didn't penetrate our cave, where eternal spring ruled, dark and raw. Not a single ship sailed past the skerry and the only thing to do was to wait.

The day I'm going to tell you about now was my sixth on the skerry. We'd had breakfast and I went as usual to gaze out to sea for signs of life. Enormous icebergs drifted slowly and silently along the horizon. As usual the merchild was with me, getting under my feet, and also as usual biting at my trousers and the legs of my boots.

"Stop that now." I pushed him away quite roughly. "Can't you see you're ruining my boots?"

He fell over but rolled back at once to sitting and sank his teeth into my leg so that I yelled out.

"I'll soon have nothing left but rags," I said. "You'll have to find something else to play with."

But understandably the child didn't want to play on his own and when he started chewing at me yet again I couldn't help laughing even though I was annoyed. Defending myself against this plump little creature was hopeless.

I bent for a stone and held it in front of his pointed nose. "See this?" I said. "Can you fetch it for Siri? Off you go!"

I threw the stone and it landed with a tiny splash on the water's edge.

The merchild gave a shout and wriggled after it. He found the stone straight away and brought it back.

"That was clever," I said. "Can you do it again?" The stone landed in the water this time and he rushed after it just as happily. He brought it back to me at once with an eager look.

I tickled him under the chin and smiled. "Is that good fun?" I asked.

The merchild whined and wriggled, wanting me to throw it again, which I did. So we had found a game to play on Snowrose!

We played and played it! I threw and the child fetched, hour after hour. He never got tired, and I found it fun too. I decided to throw it a little farther out each time so his swimming would improve.

I remembered seeing him from the *Cuttlefish*, when he had just rolled around pathetically. It was good for him to try swimming, and the game helped him do so without thinking about it.

"You're getting fast in the water now, aren't you?" I said, weighing the stone in my hand.

The child laughed, ready to chase it.

It was time to make the game a bit harder. I hurled the stone with all my strength. I regretted it the moment the stone hit the water: it had landed too far out.

"Wait!" I told him, but he was already on his way. He made two or three rapid strokes, then dived.

I paced at the water's edge. Splashes from the waves soaked my trousers but I didn't care. I only wanted him back on shore.

When he surfaced he took a mouthful of sea water, coughed and snorted and rubbed his nose.

"Come here!" I shouted.

He didn't answer.

"I don't want you going so far out!" I said. "Come back now—I don't care about the stone."

But when he'd cleared his throat, he flicked his fat little flippers and dived again.

Time passed. I stared at the spot where he'd disappeared, as the surface bubbles slowly dispersed. I had no idea how long a merchild could last without air. If it was the same as for humans, it was time he came up. But what if he was too small to know that? What if he drowned?

I grew more and more anxious; I could feel the air in my own lungs running out. I was ready to go in myself, however stupid that would have been. But at last, bubbles appeared a little way out and up he came. He was shouting with joy and his flippers thrashed the water to foam as he made for the shore.

As soon as he came ashore I ran over and threw my arms around him as if I'd never let go. "You gave me a fright," I whispered.

After a while he slipped from my embrace, wriggled a short distance away and sat up. For the first time, I noticed what he was holding, and it wasn't a stone. It was a small, shiny object on a thong—the oarfish.

The child fiddled with it and tried to sink his teeth into it.

"I'll show you how to wear it." I sat down beside him and took the oarfish. I tied a new knot in the thong and hung it around his neck. I laughed because it looked both funny and elegant. A mermaid wearing human decoration.

But the child clearly didn't like the thong. He tore it free and threw the oarfish down.

"Don't you want it?" I asked, and tried it around my own neck.

The child shoved a piece of ice in his mouth

and chewed it to splinters with his sharp baby teeth. He'd lost all interest in the medallion he'd swallowed so much water to fetch.

I drew myself up to my full height, feeling quite grand. I had a lucky charm all of my own now. There couldn't be many children who owned such a thing. Some people back in Blue Bay had bought oarfish charms, but they were better off than us.

I took the merchild's hand. "Shall we play now?" I asked. "I'll find another stone if you like."

But he was tired after all the diving and so I carried him back to the nest and lay down beside him. I stroked his back and kissed his forehead, and it made him so happy that he cuddled up to me and said *Na-naa* as if I was his mother. We lay like that for a long time before we fell asleep. My nose was pressed into his thin, fair hair and I thought how good he smelled. Like land and sea at the same time.

That night I dreamed I was standing on the skerry, watching a ship approach across the water, strangely slowly. Its sails were filled although there was no wind. When it stopped I saw that the sails weren't made of cloth, but of snow and ice. The hull too was formed of frozen water. On board, a man with long white hair was tightly gripping the arm of a chubby, naked girl only about a year old. I told the man I had an oarfish with which I'd buy the girl from him. He nodded, picked her up and threw her in a wide arc over the side of the ship, but she landed in the water and sank. The man laughed and asked if I didn't know that oarfish brought bad luck.

◆ ◆ ◇ ◆ ◆

Leaving

The little merchild reminded me of Miki. When she was small she was chubby and soft and lovely just like him. Our mother was dead so she couldn't feed Miki herself, of course, so Dad fed her cream and Miki drank and drank. I remember how you could hear the milk gurgle in her tummy.

Thinking of Miki was painful. My poor little sister, who'd be crawling around in Whitehead's mine carrying so many diamonds her back was likely to break. Or she might have lung disease from the damp. She might already be lying in a pit, hacking and coughing so badly that blood poured from her mouth. She might even have died. The darkness might have driven her mad and crushed all the spirit out of her—or even life itself. Was she dead?

It was painful to think about Miki, but it was also painful thinking of the merchild, because I couldn't stay on Snowrose forever. For Miki's sake the day would come when I had to leave him.

"It's not going to be easy to go," I said one afternoon as we sat soaking up the last of the sun's heat. "I'm going to miss you a lot."

The merchild stared at me. There was a new look in his eyes, a look that seemed to reveal anger and surprise at the same time.

"But surely, you know, don't you?" I said, stroking his hair, which the salt water made so stiff. "I can't stay here with you for ever. You know I'll have to move on, don't you?"

He jerked away from my touch and snarled.

"You...you know I must leave. I have to save my little sister from the pirates. You understand that, don't you? I know you'll manage very well. The rocks here are covered with mussels, aren't they, and you've become such a good swimmer. I taught you that. Don't be angry." I swallowed hard to stop the tears coming.

But the merchild was more than angry, he was furious. He started thrashing around, whacking the snow and sending it spinning all round. When I tried to hold him he pulled free. I felt both desperate and stupid—I'd been so sure he understood all this.

"You helped me make the flag, after all!" I said.

When I saw that he didn't understand I pointed towards the high point of the skerry where the flagpole stood. You couldn't see it from where we were on the shore, but he knew it was there.

"The flag's there to signal anyone passing in a boat," I said. "So they'll know I'm here, so they'll come and save me."

The child shook his head. His mouth suddenly twisted and he began to cry.

"I didn't mean save," I said. "I meant fetch. Oh, you dear thing, come here and let me hold you."

He threw himself away from me with a furious look, his face red and wet with weeping. Then he turned and wriggled off.

I sat waiting for what must have been an hour. The sun no longer gave any warmth and I was shivering harder all the time. I walked up and down the shore in front of the cave opening, looking left and right, but there was no sign of the child.

I decided to go and look for him.

"Hello!" I shouted as I clambered up and down over the pack ice. "Hello! Where have you got to?"

Startled by my yelling, a bird—a king eider with beautiful bright cheeks—flew up from the sea and disappeared in the sky.

"Little fellow!" I shouted. "Come on now. Let's find something to eat. It'll probably be spring before anyone sees the flag. We don't have to think about it yet."

Silence was the only reply.

I turned to search in the other direction and there he was! Right behind me. He was out of breath and had snow in his hair, but he was no longer angry. He looked at me with his beautiful little eyes and smiled.

"Where were you?" I said. "I've been looking for you."

"Na-naa!" he answered, holding out his arms.

I picked him up and kissed his forehead.

"I'm not Na-naa," I whispered. "Now let's have something to eat."

I held him tight as I carried him back to our part of the shore. We ate mussels until we were full. From the far distance came the moaning, gabbling call of the king eider. Dusk fell, shimmering pink and violet and bitingly, mercilessly cold. Dusk was like this on Snowrose—magnificent but terrible, beautiful but dangerous.

Whenever it happens, I thought, whenever I eventually leave, I'll always remember this dusk with the merchild.

Four days later I was the first to wake in our nest. I lay watching the child in the scant gray light that filtered through the roof of the cave. I watched the rise and fall of his stomach, his small open mouth moving as he dreamed, his eyes fluttering nervously behind his eyelids. He was so lovely.

I decided to surprise him with breakfast. I

slipped out through the long, foul-smelling entrance and hurried down to the shore. A strong wind was blowing and the slush ice was as thick as porridge. But there was no shortage of mussels, and now that I was used to gathering them I soon had a sizable pile.

I rested, sucking my fingers and looking out to sea. I screwed up my eyes against the wind and traced the line of the horizon… And all of a sudden a surge of amazement ran through my body. There was a boat! A boat under sail!

"Here!" I screamed, leaping to my full height, jumping and waving. "Here! Over here! Look this way!"

Whoever was in the boat didn't turn around. No doubt he was old and half-deaf. But why hadn't he seen my flag? Since he had the wind behind him he must have sailed very close to my skerry.

I screamed and yelled and the merchild came hurrying from the cave, understandably frightened out of his life. When he saw the distant boat he realized why I'd been making so much noise.

My throat was sore from shouting, but the boat was growing smaller and smaller and was soon impossible to pick out among the waves.

Angry and upset, I ran to check the flag. Perhaps it had fallen down? I was followed by the whimpering child.

When I reached the top of the skerry I stopped

and stared like an idiot. I walked around the cairn. It still looked good, though it had collapsed slightly on one side. But where was the flag?

Then, ten feet or so from the cairn, I noticed a long, narrow pile of snow that hadn't been there before. I went over and kicked some aside, revealing a piece of the mast. I took a firm hold of the end and heaved the whole thing clear. The flag hadn't fallen; it had been torn down and buried by someone with no intention of being left alone on Snowrose if he could possibly prevent it.

A muffled sound made me turn. The child had caught up and sat watching me warily. He held out his arms and in a quiet voice said, "Na-naa?"

I dropped the flag, walked over and pushed him as hard as I could. He fell with his face in the snow but quickly sat up again and looked at me fearfully. Tears burst from his small blue eyes and his bottom lip trembled but I was still shaking with rage.

"Can't you see what you've done?" I shouted. "Can't you? Can't you? I never want to see you again!"

He sobbed so loudly and deeply it seemed he might shake himself to pieces. Then, quite suddenly, I threw myself down and embraced him.

"I'm sorry," I whispered. "Dear merchild, I'm sorry."

I sat holding his trembling body and hating

myself for pushing him over and saying those things. The words rang in my ears. I stood up quickly and rushed over to the flag. I began tearing at it, using my nails and teeth, and when it was free I dragged it to the cliff and hurled it over. Then I fetched the mast and sent it after the sail. I sat down in front of the child, took him by the shoulders and looked him in the eye.

"Listen," I said. "I'll never leave you. I promise to take care of you, as if you were mine."

◆ ◆ ◇ ◆ ◆

A Visit from the Sea

After I'd pushed the child over, my conscience nagged me from morning till night. Now I couldn't leave him. How could I when I'd promised not to?

But how could I save Miki without leaving the child? I couldn't possibly take him with me. For instance, what if Baldy had been right about doctors who preserved mermaids in spirit and dissected them with knives? It was too dangerous to take the merchild to Seglen.

I was stuck. Caught between two small lives, both of whom needed me. There was no answer.

That's what I thought, anyway. But there was a solution, so obvious and at the same time so disappointing. It came from the sea one night when the moon shone like a silver coin in the sky and the stars twinkled in their thousands. Icebergs creaked in the distance and the whole world seemed uneasy.

I was curled up in the nest of sea grass and twigs. The temperature had dropped at least ten degrees in the last few days and we went outside less and less often. In the safety and warmth of the cave I slept well.

Suddenly, however, I was woken by a far-off scream and at first I thought I'd been dreaming. But when I reached out and felt all round I realized the child wasn't there. I sat up and listened towards the cave mouth—and heard him scream again. What was he doing out there in the middle of the night?

I rose to go and see what was happening, but something made me freeze on the spot. The child wasn't the only one shouting out on the shore, there was someone else. Someone had come! Someone had landed on Snowrose and found the child.

I rushed towards the cave mouth but stumbled and fell. As I lay with my nose in the stinking empty mussel shells I heard that other voice again and it sent cold shivers up and down my spine. It was a man's voice, angry and dark. The child screamed and screamed and the man's voice bawled in response. I was so frightened I thought I was going to faint.

This person—what if he knew the doctors in the towns? What if he took the child to sell? I couldn't let it happen.

I stood up and ran again on legs so soft they'd scarcely carry me.

At the mouth of the cave I stopped. It took quite a few seconds—remarkable seconds—before I understood what I was seeing out there on the shore by the light of the moon and stars. There was no boat pulled up at the water's edge, nor was there a man.

The child was screaming at something quite different—an enormous creature, fleshy and shapeless, with breasts as big as sacks. She had long, dishevelled hair, a pale face with a pronounced jaw and small nose. Her flippers were pounding the ground, sending snow and ice in all directions.

The child was throwing himself at her again and again, butting her, biting her and hammering her enormous belly. He tried to climb up onto her lap, and she picked him up in her huge arms, from which fat and loose skin hung. The child felt her cheeks, felt her nose, bit her time after time wherever he could reach. He kept screaming and now it was clear that those weren't cries of despair coming from that fat little throat. The merchild was happy. And when that huge creature roared back at him I could tell she wasn't angry at all. That was the sound his mother made.

I stood and watched them laughing and touching one another. The warmth of the mother's body had melted a hollow in the ice even though it was so cold that the ice creaked and cracked.

"Na-naa!" the child said over and over until I was sick of hearing it. I covered my ears. I hated her. I hated that she'd come and that he was sucking and chewing her hair not mine. Why had she stayed away so long? Didn't she know he would have died of loneliness if I hadn't come? Didn't she know that *he and I* slept in the nest now?

I strode firmly over and kicked a stone loose from the frozen ground.

"Do you want to play?" I asked the child. "Look what I've got for you!"

I threw the stone out into the water but he didn't rush after it. He just stared at me through half-closed eyes and rested his head on his mother's breast.

His mother, however, put him behind her and started up a terrifying roar. She threw her head back and forth so violently that her collar of fat swung this way and that. She was ugly and horrible and must have weighed many hundredweight. She rolled onto her stomach and came closer, spitting with rage.

"I'm his friend!" I said. "Leave me alone!"

She slid even closer, beating the air as if trying to knock me over. At last I understood that I'd frightened her and that it was impossible to talk to her. I backed away, ready to turn and run when I slipped and she was over me like a shot. Her mouth gave off a foul stink of mussels and filthy teeth. She pulled at my jacket, prodded and hit me as if to see how much resistance I was capable of.

Then she heard a splash behind her and turned. The child had decided to dive for the stone. His mother followed him into the water, unwilling to lose him again. It took her two seconds to catch up. Taking firm hold of his little arm, she swam to shore. There she sat cuddling him on her knee, stroking his wet head and sniffing at it. She'd decided I wasn't worth bothering about and it seemed the merchild had done the same.

As long as I didn't make too much fuss, perhaps they'd let me go on living in the cave. I could find somewhere to sleep so they could be alone together.

But what if his mother considered the cave to be theirs alone and didn't want me there? If they drove me out, I'd freeze to death. Did the child understand that?

Before long I realized that I wouldn't have to fight for my place in the cave. Once they'd spent some time cuddling and laughing and poking one another, the mermaid turned onto her stomach and put the child up on her back. Yelling with excitement he caught hold of her hair. For a brief moment he turned and looked at me. I'd never seen him look so happy in all the time he'd been mine. His mother put her palms to the icy ground and pushed off into the water. One beat of her flippers and they were gone.

I stood waiting for a while but I knew they wouldn't be coming back. They'd decided long before this to leave. It was just that they'd been delayed.

◆ ◆ ◇ ◆ ◆

22

Snow

I didn't want to go back into the cave. I didn't want to move, or do anything. The merchild had only been gone a short time but I was missing him so much it hurt. The air was bitingly cold. I'd never experienced cold like it in my life—the muscles in my face refused to move and my eyes were motionless in their sockets. But I didn't intend to go inside, didn't want to see the nest where we'd lain together and which we'd never share again.

The icebergs out at sea were moving slower and slower as the temperature continued to fall. The sea crackled and cracked like gunfire. Even the stars in the sky seemed to shrink with the cold. When dusk fell I walked to the water's edge to dip my finger in, but the sea had frozen over and been transformed into a pavement. I stepped straight onto the ice and walked away.

Walking on water was a strange sensation. For

a while I was nervous that the sea might only be frozen around Snowrose, that I'd encounter open water farther out, but I walked on and nowhere did I come to an edge. The ice in front of me went on forever. Perhaps, just perhaps, I might come to an island with people, and I might even reach it today. I noted the skerries I passed as landmarks so that I wouldn't start walking round in circles.

And now it was cold, so cold. I looked up at the sky in case birds came crashing down with frozen wings, but all I could see was an empty, pale-gray ceiling.

I looked down into the hard, gleaming depths. Where the water began, far beneath my feet, bubbles crept slowly along like leeches of air. How were the merchild and his ugly mother managing for air? What if they'd been down on the bottom collecting mussels when the sea froze above them? What if they were still down there?

I ran a little, I don't know why. Maybe to run away from those thoughts. But his mother must know where they could surface, where there was open water. In fact, that must be why they left Snowrose. They knew it would freeze over. They probably had other islands to live on in winter.

I'd been walking for a couple of hours when the gray ceiling overhead began to release small, soft flakes. It was fun at first. The flakes lay on

the ice and made it easy for me to slide, and I had snowflakes everywhere: in my hair, on my eyelashes and nose. I stuck out my tongue and tasted them. But then the wind picked up and the flakes whipped my face. I pulled my cap over my ears and struggled on. I knew that when it snowed like this it wasn't as cold as before, but the wind had decided to blow straight into my face. The falling snow grew thicker with every step and soon the skerries I'd been using as landmarks disappeared into the surrounding whiteness. All I could do now was walk on in the hope that I was heading for some form of shelter. I had to reach an island with rocks to hide among, where I could sit out the storm.

I walked and walked but I reached nowhere. Was I simply walking on the spot? Was the wind holding me back that much? Would I walk on the same spot until I wore a hole in the ice?

Frightened by my fantasies I began running again. I could no longer blink the wet flakes from my eyelashes and the snow blinded me. I ran on in darkness, ran and ran, praying that my feet would strike stones.

I stopped, wiped my face with my sleeve and peered around. What was the outline looming ahead of me? Cliffs?

I hardly dared believe it but I ran anyway, my hair damp with sweat. The image of the cliffs flashed before my eyes but each time it vanished just as quickly. Was I going mad?

No, there they were. Real cliffs! Black gashes emerging from the whiteness, and closer than I'd thought. I laughed as I ran the last bit, laughed at this wonderful discovery that was going to save my life.

I shaded my eyes with my hand and studied the rock wall, seeking any sort of hollow, perhaps even a small cave. There might be a cave here like the one I'd shared with the merchild.

Climbing was difficult. The texture of the snow varied, and time after time the crust gave way and my legs sank deep. I couldn't find a cave and in the end I had to be satisfied with a protruding rock. I dug away as much snow as I could, pressed myself in beneath the rocky roof, and waited.

Heavy snow kept falling. From time to time I kicked away drifts that built up round me. They formed small avalanches that wended their various ways to the shore. When at last it stopped snowing I felt like a hibernating animal poking its head out and sniffing the air after months in silent darkness.

Visibility was good and I could pick out the far-off shapes of other islands. The white blanket over the ice looked soft and beautiful. I had just started to climb down when a sound echoed through the air. No. Surely it couldn't have been…?

I looked all round, trying to work out where the

sound had come from. From over the crest? I began climbing up, growing more eager as I went. When I reached the top and saw what lay down in the bay my muscles seemed to turn to water and flow out of my body.

A ship. An evil white ship with three masts and a bird's head at its prow. *Snow Raven*.

It was real! Whitehead's *Raven* lay down there, frozen in, buried in snow, brooding in the ice and barely alive, or so it seemed. But there was a hatchway open on deck and the pirate standing at the rail having a pee wore nothing but long johns and a knitted jumper. And then he farted again.

Craning my neck I saw that the island was bigger than I'd thought when I was huddled and waiting for the storm to finish. Somewhere over in the middle a pillar of smoke rose into the sky. Whitehead's mine! That's where Miki was!

I stood rooted to the spot, unable to believe my eyes. My mouth was so dry my tongue stuck to the roof when I tried to swallow. The pirate shivered slightly and yawned a couple of times. When he'd finished peeing he climbed back through the hatch. He hadn't seen me.

I turned and rushed back down the cliff. It was weeks since I'd left Blue Bay determined to find Whitehead's island. I'd journeyed by ship and small boat and on foot and now that I'd finally reached my goal I was so frightened that my heart beat like a mad thing. I was scared of Whitehead, of course—terrified of a man who wore his hair up in a bun and who treated children as if they were animals. I wanted to get away and hide, to find some protection.

Then the snow gave way under me, my foot caught in stones beneath it and I fell. I tumbled down the steep slope, rolling and sliding on and on. I went head over heels so many times it seemed my head and feet had changed places, and at the bottom my head struck something hard and everything went black.

I don't know how long I lay there or if I dreamed of hands taking hold of my jacket. I don't know if I dreamed of being lifted from the ground, or hearing someone say incomprehensible things in my ear. But when I found myself flying effortlessly above the ice at the speed of a razorbill, I knew it must be a dream, that it couldn't be anything else.

♦ ♦ ◇ ♦ ♦

23

The Boy on the Stool

I woke in a bed, with a dry feather mattress under me and a warm blanket over me. I breathed in the smells of wool and dirt. My head hurt—I must have struck it really hard. The room was in half darkness, but I could see ceiling beams and a small attic window. There were voices and noises outside. The sounds of a village. A boy sat on a stool looking at me. He had black hair, blue eyes and a handsome face, and a cut on his cheek.

"Where am I?" I asked.

"Seglen," the boy said.

Seglen? I swallowed. The village where pirates and riff-raff gathered like flies on a plate of herring bones. The village you went to if you wanted to find Whitehead.

But I'd already found him. I'd already been ashore on his island and seen the *Snow Raven* below my feet. And I'd turned and run away. I'd run away and I had fallen because I was a coward.

My eyes filled with tears at the thought, but I wiped them away quickly. I had no desire to lie here crying in front of a boy I didn't even know.

"How did I get here?" I asked.

"You were left at the door."

"Who by?"

"Nobody knows, except whoever left you." The boy raised his voice: "She's woken up!"

Shortly someone came up the stairs, a wiry woman with big hands, sunken cheeks and gray eyes. She placed a mug on the table by the bed and a plate on my stomach with bread and dripping. The dripping smelled rotten.

"Are you from here?" she asked.

I shook my head and took a bite. It didn't taste bad after all.

"How did you get to Seglen?" she asked.

"I don't know. Someone carried me in from the ice," I answered. It really was amazing. Creepy, in fact. Some stranger had carried me all the way to this cottage. But *why*? And *who*?

"Here in Seglen we don't let children go out on the water on their own," the woman said. "Do you know why?"

I nodded.

"Pirates." The woman answered her own question. "There are swarms of them around here.

Some of them are happy just stealing skins and ironware. But there's one captain who's out for something else."

"Yes," I whispered. After a pause I asked, "His island...is it far from here?"

The woman laughed, but it was a cold, frightened laugh.

"Not many know where that island is," she said. "A fisherman's widow and her son least of all. And we want nothing to do with it anyway." She looked down at her worn hands then back at me. "You've been in bed here for three days. You were so pale and in such an awful state I didn't think you'd pull through. Eat and drink now, and get better." She stood up and looked at the boy. "I'm going out with some things."

She disappeared down the stairs and I heard the outside door open and close behind her.

I sat up slowly and with difficulty, finished eating the bread and drank the water in the mug. The boy watched me the whole time, as if I was some kind of mystery he was trying to work out with his eyes.

"What did you do?" he said.

"How do you mean?" I answered with the last bite of bread still in my mouth.

"Out on the ice," he said.

While my tongue worked at grains of rye stuck between my teeth I wondered what to say. Should I tell him? That Whitehead had taken my sister and I was out on the Ice Sea to get her back?

No. He'd just run to his mother and she'd say it was far too dangerous. She'd stop me going on.

"I can't tell you," I said.

The boy's eyes narrowed as if the mystery had suddenly deepened and made him even more eager to solve it.

I looked around, though moving my eyes was painful. On the far wall hung all kinds of bits and pieces: boots, coffee pots, a couple of coats, a harness, a bread spade, a spale basket, a ladle, a parrot's cage, a dead eider. On the floor stood a stool, its seat polished with wear.

I suddenly remembered my oarfish. Did I still have it? I reached inside my shirt and found the thong—yes, the medallion was still there. And it was amazingly warm from lying against my chest under the woollen blanket.

The boy looked and I couldn't tell what he thought. Perhaps that I was showing off. I tucked it away.

A strange silence fell. Neither of us could think of anything to say. When he looked out of the filthy little window I took the chance to study his face. His eyes were like two ice-cold seas and the slash on his cheek was red, fresh, deep and absolutely even.

I wondered if it was a pirate who'd cut him. And if this was a village where a pirate might leap out and slash you with his knife the moment you stepped out of the door. Was the boy covered in scars beneath his clothes?

I couldn't contain my curiosity, so I cleared my throat and said: "How did you get that?"

He turned from the window almost as if he'd been waiting to be asked.

"Get what?" he said calmly.

"Your cut. Where did...I mean, did someone hurt you?"

The boy touched his cheek thoughtfully and then he smiled. "I can't tell you. But if you tell me what you were doing out on the ice, I'll tell you where I got this."

"Not a chance!" I laughed.

"We can promise each other it won't go any further," the boy said. "How about that?"

"It doesn't matter to me how you got that scratch," I said.

"Really?" the boy said. "I was close to death because of it, if you must know."

"Death?" I said suspiciously.

He fixed me with his eyes. "If you tell me, I'll tell you. But we'll have to be quick. Ma'll be back soon. Can you stand up?"

"Of course I can." I threw aside the blanket and

got up like a shot just to show him, but my legs gave way and if the boy hadn't caught me I'd have crashed to the floor.

"Take it slowly," he said. "It might be better if we wait a while."

"Don't be stupid," I said, blinking away my dizziness. "Well?"

"We're agreed then, are we?" the boy said.

"Sure." My curiosity swept away caution. "As long as you don't tell your mother a thing."

"My mother will be the last person to find out where I got this," he said. "I told her I did it myself with one of my father's old fishing spears." He gave a laugh. "I told her I tripped when I was pretending to be a fisherman and the spear stuck in my face. You should have heard her go on about it. She said I'd come within a hair's breadth of losing an eye. If she only knew."

He smiled again and there was a glint in his eyes. Then he became serious and said, sounding almost grown up, "I'll show you something but you'll have to come out to the shed. Do you want some help down the stairs?"

"No thank you," I muttered, walking over and taking firm hold of the banister.

◆ ◆ ◇ ◆ ◆

The Blanket

My spinning head made everything sway so I went slowly down the stairs. We put on our jackets and boots. Several torn and ragged items hung by the door and the boy told me his mother earned money by taking in things to mend. A burnt cooking pot, a decaying decoy bird, a gun with a bent barrel, a shoe with a hole in the sole—she could mend it, patch it, glue it, whatever it was. Also girls with cracked skulls, it seemed, and I assume that's why I was dropped off at her door. The boy told me his mother could bend a poker with her bare hands, which is why she was called Iron-Anna. His name was Einar. His father had drowned some years before.

The shed was behind the cottage where Einar and Iron-Anna lived. A kick sled leaned against the outside wall. Einar opened the door and we stepped in. It contained a lot of fishing gear which hadn't been used for a long time. The nets were covered in dust.

"Ma never comes out here," Einar said. "It reminds her too much of Dad."

He crouched down by a bundled-up blanket, carefully opened it and lifted out something the size of a turnip. It was an egg.

"Is there a chick in it?" I asked, for I knew that bogle birds hatched their chicks in winter.

Einar nodded. He put his ear to the egg.

"It will hatch soon. I can hear it moving." He touched the cut on his cheek. "I've wanted an egg like this for ages and I swear the mother bird tried to kill me when I took it."

I touched the shell. It was marked with black spots. I'd handled these eggs many times, but never one with a chick inside.

"When the chick hatches out it'll be mine," Einar said. "All my own. What do you think about that?"

I smiled. I had to admit it wasn't a bad idea. Imagine having a bogle bird all of your own. A little tooth-beaked creature to look after and make a fuss of, to give a name and somewhere to sleep—a heap of straw in a sugar box, perhaps? I had to admit I'd have liked one of my own.

Einar carefully wrapped the egg back in the woollen blanket, stood up and looked at me.

"Your turn now," he said. "What were you doing out on the ice?"

I hesitated, but we'd agreed to tell and I had no good reason now to hold back.

"Looking for Whitehead," I said.

He frowned. "What!"

"Whitehead," I said again. "The pirate captain who doesn't stop at stealing furs and iron. You know, the one who steals children."

"Why the heck are you looking for him?"

"His crew took my sister several weeks ago," I replied. "I'm on my way to get her back. And I actually found his island, but then I fell down a snow slope and then…well, I don't remember any more until I woke up at your place."

Einar's eyes were big and shiny, with more than a hint of fear. "Had you really found his island?" he whispered.

"It's an island which has a big bay with only a narrow entrance," I said. "The bay is surrounded by high cliffs and when the *Raven*'s at anchor in the bay it can't be seen from the sea. And smoke was rising from somewhere in the middle of the island."

"The mine." Einar swallowed hard. He thought for a while and then he asked, "Do your parents know what you're doing?"

"My mother's dead," I answered. "And Dad couldn't stop me."

A sigh escaped me as I said that. Dear Dad, how would he be managing at home? With the herring running out, the berry jar empty, the fireplace cold in the morning, and all alone. That would be the worst thing. The two people who brought light to his darkness were no longer with him.

"I have to find my way back to that island," I said. "Obviously whoever found me could tell us where it is. If only I knew who it was."

Just then we heard a tentative little crunching, like very thin ice being broken by the toe of a boot. The crunching was accompanied by bad-tempered peeping.

"It's hatching!" Einar said.

He dropped to his knees and unfolded the blanket. The thick, spotty shell was already showing several cracks. Einar carefully picked off a piece of shell to help the chick. An almost transparent, toothed beak poked through the shell and squawked and squawked. I'd never heard anything like it. Then the whole egg fell apart and the chick stood beating its wings and wobbling on unsteady legs. When it grew its adult plumage it would be white with black patches, but now it was brown. It was small and beautifully downy, and its eyes were golden. Every so often it toppled over but got straight back to its feet and squawked as if it was absolutely furious with everything.

When Einar put out a hand it pecked him.

"Ouch!" Einar said. "I didn't think it would be so wild."

"Ha ha!" I said. "A chip off the old block! If you don't know anything about bogle birds you're going to have trouble with that little thing."

He looked at me. Not so much annoyed as with a touch of admiration.

"Do you know about bogle birds?" he asked.

"A bit," I said.

Einar's eyes gleamed. "Show me then," he said.

I hadn't actually had anything to do with bogle chicks, but I was familiar with the adults. I knew, for instance, that the most important thing, if you wanted to avoid those sharp teeth and spiky claws, was not to show fear.

I knelt alongside the screaming fledgling and trapped its wings against its body. It twisted round to bite but couldn't reach my hand. Once it realized I wasn't afraid of its small attacks, it calmed down.

"Does your mother have any fish?" I asked.

Einar, who'd been watching wide-eyed, nodded and hurried from the shed. He was soon back with a salted herring.

"Fresh fish would be better," I said.

"But salt herring tastes so good." Einar tore off small pieces of gray fish. He passed them to me to feed the chick, which gulped down piece after piece and shrieked when I was too slow.

"This is really going well!" Einar said excitedly.

"It is, isn't it?" I laughed.

Once the herring was finished I put the chick down and stood up. But as soon as I straightened my legs everything went black and I suddenly found myself held up again by Einar's arms. He looked at me and said: "If you want to know what I think, you should thank your lucky stars you escaped alive from that island. The chances of doing it a second time are nil."

♦ ♦ ◇ ♦ ♦

Blood in the Snow

In the following days I helped Einar with his chick as much as I could. As soon as Iron-Anna had gone out to deliver things she had mended, we'd creep down to the shed with herring in our pockets. Einar said that his mother mustn't find out he had a chick. He wouldn't tell me why. Whenever I asked, he simply said: "You and I have promised, haven't we?"

The chick was almost a week old by now. Its beak had gone from transparent to pitch-black and its teeth were as sharp as nails.

"If you don't lick that thing into shape, it'll bite your nose off," I said to Einar.

"It seems to like you better than me," he sighed, jumping back as the chick tried to peck him.

"You have to be much firmer. And stop throwing the fish on the floor. You have to feed it by hand or it'll never take to you."

Einar retrieved a piece of herring he'd thrown down. He held it out to the chick and put on a stern face.

"Like this?" he said. "Come and eat from Einar's hand or there's no dinner for you."

I laughed. "It doesn't understand talk," I said.

But the chick almost seemed to understand. It bent its neck and made a noise like a cat sneezing. Then it scuttled over to the herring and gobbled it down like a shot.

"It worked!" But in his joy Einar forgot about his hand. The chick lunged and stabbed for more fish. Einar yelped and leapt to his feet.

"Ow, ow, ow!" he wailed, clutching his hand.

"Let me see."

He showed me the wound on the back of his hand. The sight of bright blood pouring out turned my stomach. The floor was already splashed with it.

"That will need to be bandaged," I said.

We left the chick pecking at the splashes on the floor. I locked up carefully and we went over to the cottage.

Iron-Anna was still out. I found a rag hanging by the wash basin and wet it.

"Sit down," I said.

Einar obeyed. There was still some life in the fire and its kindly flickering light reflected off the ceiling. The curtains moved against the window. Iron-Anna's kitchen, with the dim light and the smell of gutted herring, felt ordinary and homely. I washed the wound as Einar followed my movements. Then he looked me in the eye and said:

"Don't you think we're alike?"

"How do you mean?" I said.

"Well, we have the same hair and eyes and we're both from fishing families. Your mother is dead and so is my father. And I've got a medallion too. Look!"

With his good hand he fished a small charm from around his neck. A fish hook. I'd noticed it before but hadn't looked closely. Einar told me his mother had given it to him right after his father drowned.

He turned the charm over and over in his hand, then he looked at me again and laughed.

"It's as if we're brother and sister or something."

"Perhaps," I said with a smile. "Although your eyes are much bluer than mine."

"I don't think so," Einar muttered, almost as if I'd said something unpleasant.

Once the wound was dry I fetched another rag to bandage his hand. Then I washed out the bloody rag and emptied the pinkish water into the sludge in the slop pail.

"Right, shall we go?" I asked.

Einar, who'd been sitting there silent and a bit dejected, nodded and stood up.

"I'll bring some more fish." He lifted the cloth from the pot where Iron-Anna kept the herring. He picked out a magnificent female, her belly plump with roe.

"Don't you think your mother will notice?" I asked.

"No," Einar said, throwing open the door.

We both jumped back when we saw Iron-Anna. She was looking at the blood on the steps and following its trail with her eyes. It led across the snow to the closed door of the shed. Then she saw Einar's bandaged hand. She put her hands on her hips and her face hardened in anger.

"Have you been playing with that fish spear again?" she asked.

Einar was so surprised he didn't say a word.

"I told you not to mess about with those old tools." Iron-Anna gestured at the mark on his cheek. "No sooner has it healed up than you go back for more. Don't you know that cuts can go septic?"

"Of course I do," Einar muttered.

"And what makes it worse is that you took Siri with you," she went on. "Don't you think she's been ill quite long enough? I've a good mind to go and clear everything out of the shed."

"No, don't do that!" Einar howled.

"I'll have to unless you start doing as I tell you!" Iron-Anna said.

Einar squeezed her arm. "Please don't," he said.

Iron-Anna stood looking at him for a moment, her face tense and angry. Then all at once her face softened and she stroked his hair.

"My little boy," she said, almost in a whisper. "Are you going to be like your dad when you grow up? Is that why you run off every spare moment to play at being a fisherman?"

Einar said nothing, just stared at the ground and gave a little nod.

"Are the two of you coming in now?" Iron-Anna asked. "It'll soon be time for dinner."

We were following Einar's mother through the door when she noticed the herring in his hand. "What on earth are you doing with that?" she asked.

Einar was lost for words again, but I was quick with an answer.

"It was my idea. I thought it would be more realistic if we used a fish. It was stupid of me."

Iron-Anna smiled. She took the herring and when we'd hung up our outdoor clothes she said, "I want the two of you to promise me you won't play with those sharp things again. Never. If you do, I'll have to get rid of them."

"We promise!" Einar and I said together.

◆ ◆ ◇ ◆ ◆

26

No Finer Fisherman

So the days passed in Seglen. My awful dizziness slowly improved. Einar noticed that I hardly needed his support to stand up or go down the stairs. He knew, too, that the healthier I grew, the closer my departure, and I think that made him sad.

One evening all three of us were at the table eating fish soup. Iron-Anna was a kind woman. She fed me and gave me a bed without once asking where I came from or what I'd been doing out on the ice.

Now she seemed to know I was thinking about those very things. She said, "You can stay as long as you want to."

I looked down at my bowl where small bits of fish floated amongst barley grains. I liked Iron-Anna's fish soup. She spiced it with lovage and other things.

"I'm quite steady on my feet now," I said. "It won't be long before I can move on."

Iron-Anna put her hand over mine and looked me in the eye for a long time. She seemed sad.

"Wherever it is you're going and whatever it is you're doing," she said, "I hope it's worth it." Her eyes narrowed. "In Seglen we don't allow children to go out on the sea alone," she said.

"I know," I said in a low voice.

"And if you'd been my child I'd have chained you by the door," Iron-Anna went on. "But you're not. All the same...I have a feeling it's best I don't know."

I nodded again. Yes, it was probably for the best. For her peace of mind, if nothing else. I'd heard her say a dozen times that children should stay away from the sea. She'd be reluctant to let me leave if she knew.

"You'll soon be rid of me," I said. "I promise."

Iron-Anna didn't answer and went to fetch herself another helping. Then she looked at Einar, who'd stopped eating and was just staring at the table.

"What are you looking so miserable about?" she asked.

"I'm not!" he snapped and went back to spooning up his soup.

The following day Iron-Anna went out to deliver a pair of trousers she had mended for an old man. I was sitting by the window looking out at the cobbled street she'd disappeared along. I had stomach pains just thinking about the big village out there, the village I'd told Miki about so often and which occupied so many of my thoughts. I ran my fingers along the window frame—there was mildew on it. Everything here felt and smelled exactly as it did at home. In this cottage you'd hardly know you were in Seglen. But soon, I thought, soon I'll make my way along those cobbled... Pain shot through my stomach again.

I suddenly noticed Einar behind me, watching my finger as I ran it over the soft mildew.

He looked at me and said, "You think we're poor, don't you?"

There was something about him I didn't recognize, something hard in the way he asked the question. I took my finger away. "No." I didn't know whether I was lying or not. Maybe Einar and Iron-Anna were poor, but that meant I was poor too, didn't it? It meant practically everyone was poor.

"Is that why you don't want to stay?" Einar asked.

"How do you mean?"

"You don't think this is a nice place to live."

"Rubbish," I said. "You know very well why I can't stay."

Einar nodded. "You'd rather go off and get yourself killed."

"No! Because I have to rescue my sister. Why do you say things like that? I don't want to argue with you before I leave."

"You won't leave!" He sounded angry, but then he smiled and took me by the shoulder. "When you hear what I've worked out, you won't leave," he said. "Just wait."

He ran up the steps and hurried back with a piece of paper.

"Look at this," he said.

He unfolded the paper. A couple of years earlier his mother had mended a decoy bird and taken out the paper used for stuffing. I could see it had been crumpled.

It looked like a page from a book about birds. I recognized the one in the picture because it was an adult bogle bird. And there was a heap of information that Einar went on to tell me: how much it weighs, how they build their nests, how deep they can dive. He'd underlined one sentence in particular: *There is no finer fisherman in the Ice Sea than the bogle bird.* Of course it meant that the bogle bird was the most skilful of all animals when it came to fishing.

I looked at him. "What are you trying to tell me?"

"This is my plan." Einar gave me another smile. "I've kept it secret because I wanted it to be only mine. But I've decided to tell you. I promise you'll think twice about leaving when you've heard it."

And Einar told me the plan he'd come up with.

When his chick grew to an adult he would tie a rope around its leg and a second rope around its neck. He'd pull the second rope so tight the bird could only just breathe. Then the work could start. From his dad's old jetty, Einar would send the bird down into the water for fish, but when it tried to swallow its catch, the rope around its neck would prevent it. So as not to choke to death the bird would need Einar to remove the fish. Once he'd caught plenty of fish he'd take off the neck rope and let it have one or two herring as a reward. But he had to make sure the bird never ate too much because then it would stop fishing. This plan, Einar thought, would make him the richest person in Seglen, perhaps even the richest person in the western Ice Sea.

"And you," he said, "can help. We'll do it together."

I looked at his pale face and his blue eyes and suddenly he didn't seem so handsome. I shook my head.

"No."

"Say yes!" Einar said. "With your help I'm absolutely sure it will work. Can't you see how wealthy we could be? Mother could stop slaving for all these people who want their trousers patched for next to nothing. And we could ask your dad to come and live here!"

"And my sister?" I said. "What about her?"

Einar sighed as if it suddenly occurred to him that I was being difficult.

"People in this village are very wary of Whitehead—they certainly don't go looking for him. Anyone taken by Whitehead…"

"…no longer exists," I said. "Thanks. That's what they told me where I come from too."

"So why should *you* be the one to go after him?"

"Because…because the whole thing is so wrong," I said.

"What whole thing?"

"Making others work like slaves so you can get rich."

The moment I said those words Einar's face went hard. Hard and distant.

"If that's what you think of me," he said, "it's just as well you're leaving."

"I don't have to leave right away though," I said.

"Yes, you do!" Einar snarled and shoved me. "Now! Immediately!"

"What are you doing?" I said.

But Einar shoved me again and there were tears in his eyes. "Get out! That's what I'm saying—you're not my friend. There's no place for you here."

I was so sad and upset that I could only do as he

said. I got dressed, ran outside and set off down the village street. Then I heard Einar running after me.

"Siri! Wait!" he yelled. "Listen, wait!"

He ran to catch up and grabbed my jacket. "I'm sorry!" he said. "I shouldn't have done that."

"It makes no difference." I pulled myself free. "I'm going anyway. I've waited too long already."

"Siri!" He took hold of me again.

"What now?"

"I just want to say..."

Einar's eyes were wet and full of sorrow. The cold made his breath white and glistening. I could have sworn he was struggling with something in his heart, but then he swallowed and looked at the ground. When he looked me in the eye again he said, "...that you should sit down. If you feel giddy, I mean."

I nodded. "I'm grateful to you. And to your mother. Say goodbye to her for me, will you?"

♦ ♦ ◊ ♦ ♦

27

The Shops in Seglen

My heart ached as I left Einar. He wasn't the same boy he'd been during those days in the shed when the two of us had worked at taming his chick. Now that I knew his motives, he seemed a very different person. But for all that, I was still sad we had parted in anger.

I wasn't used to walking on cobbled streets and my feet skidded about. What was I going to do now? I had no idea where to go or who I could turn to for advice. I didn't even know which direction my nose was pointing. Everything was new and unfamiliar.

At least the cottages looked the way cottages usually do. Huddled and gray with blackened window frames. They had little curtains at the windows and behind the curtains were little, gray, old women with hairs on their chins. Pigs snuffled around the backs of the cottages, licking at the frozen, gray puddles of slush. The sky was gray and even the children I met had gray eyes.

The closer I came to the water, however, the less gray everything was. The shops had opened their shutters and almost every one sold ammunition for guns. One shop had rows of silver foxes hanging upside down, their stomachs slit open and cleaned out. The owner was selling fox-fur hats. The shop next door had combs and boxes and dice carved from whalebone. And a walking stick made from the tusk of a narwhal. Another shop sold octopuses, five or six squashed together in a wooden tub. They were still alive, winding and crawling over each other to find room.

Then came copper and silver pots, shoes made of salmon skin, and sealskin boots, jewels made of teeth and jewels made of gold; you could even buy snowy owl eggs as ornaments. In fact, everything you could possibly desire was available in Seglen.

A man in white wolf skins came along the street. My eyes locked onto the two pistols in his belt. I held my breath in sheer terror as he passed. He didn't even notice me.

A little later I passed a woman who stank so strongly of dead birds I had to hold my nose. Looking closely at her coat I saw it was made of the skins of great auks and decorated all over with their curved black beaks. Great auks were easy prey because their wings were too small for flying. The worst sort of people didn't even bother to kill the birds before skinning them, and I'd heard of people who cooked them alive for a quick meal. They just tossed the lovely bird in the pot and lit the fire.

Next, I came across a woman wearing a jacket on which were two lines of knives hanging on straps. She had a hat on her head and warts around her eyes.

Could you tell if someone were a pirate? Did a pirate look meaner than other people? Or was it the other way round? Maybe the most cunning pirates were those who could trick people into believing they were nice. What if they had handsome faces and fine clothes and neatly combed hair? Then, just when you thought you'd found a friend, they stole your valuables and ran away.

I spent a long time roaming around these fascinating cobbled streets looking at people. What was the best way to go about things? Should I just take someone by the arm in a nice, friendly way and say, "You don't happen to be a pirate, do you? If so, would you be kind enough to take me to Whitehead's island, preferably at once?"

As I walked along, I came to an open shop that was more or less empty. The man who sat in the doorway seemed to have nothing but a couple of worn-out harpoons for sale and some unattractive jellied flounder heads in a tub. But right alongside the tub lay a couple of small purses made of a pale leather that looked both familiar and unusual. I felt one of them and it was soft. The man licked his lips and gave me a sly look. His expression said that I was holding something very special.

"Interested?" he asked.

"I'm just, er… What is it? The skin, I mean," I muttered.

He leaned closer, revealing his foul brown teeth in a smile.

"Something very rare," he said. "I don't think you'll have handled that kind of skin before, nor have most people. They're not free, if that's what you think."

All at once a great wave of vomit heaved in my stomach. On the ends of the thongs used to tie the purse were what I'd taken for pieces of snail shell.

They were fingernails.

I knew immediately what the purse was made of, threw it down and rushed away from that vile old man. All I could hear in my head was a small voice crying, Na-naa!

I told myself over and over that it wasn't him. It wasn't my little one who'd been made into a purse, it was someone else—it had to be!

I thought I was going to collapse. I found some old packing crates and sat there for a while with my head spinning. And I wept about everything, about the boxes and the hat and the dice, about people who made purses out of mermaids, about everyone who took more than they needed.

When I eventually stopped crying I dried my cheeks on my sleeve and looked around. I was down by the water. By the fishermen's huts, the nets hung up for mending had frozen into slim, graceful skeletons. Nearby, a group of gray men and women stood talking. I recognized them as fisherfolk. It couldn't be easy for them with these conditions, when it was impossible to make a living.

There was something extraordinary about this great frozen sea. The ships lay still in their moorings, neither rocking nor creaking, as if locked in a vice. One single-masted vessel had a beautiful wooden figurehead on its prow, depicting a woman in a dress smoking a meerschaum pipe. Splashes of water had frozen on her cheeks like tears.

A row of storehouses stood next to the wharves, as did a port office and the pilot's small booth with a lantern at the door.

My gaze suddenly fixed on a particular man, and that particular man, I thought, is probably a pirate! I don't know why I thought it, except that everything about him was ugly and unpleasant. His sharp and threatening eyes. His pursed and malevolent mouth. His quick and crooked walk, which stopped for no one and nothing. Everything about him said, "Don't come near!"

The man steered his way across the windswept square to an unpainted door a stone's throw from the pilot's scrubbed steps. He opened the door and stepped through, but before it closed behind him I heard people swearing and the rattle and clank of tin plates.

I stood and walked slowly over to the door. What was it Fredrik had said? *The biggest windbags among the pirates are the ones who are fond of their beer, and the harbour there is full of dodgy taverns.*

Over the door hung a rusty sign. I'm a poor reader at the best of times, but I puzzled my way through the indistinct, ornate lettering: *The Seglen Arms*.

I stood staring at the door for a long time. I was scared and would rather have run away, but I couldn't allow myself to be afraid. This was probably the very place for me to discover where to go from here.

I took a deep breath and went in.

♦ ♦ ◇ ♦ ♦

28

The Seglen Arms

blinked as my eyes adjusted to the gloom inside. The oil lamps along the walls gave little light. And there was a sour smell. The floor was wet and filthy like a pigsty from all the snow that had been carried in, and the walls dripped with damp. A man in a grubby apron was drying a mug behind the enormous bar, and I assumed that the barrels stacked behind him were full of beer. Over the very large fireplace hung a variety of pots on various lengths of chain. Bunches of dried cod heads and split ling dangled from the ceiling.

The men and women crowded around the tables were indescribably filthy. Their clothes were patched and so were their faces. Almost every seat was occupied: I suppose that pirates, like fishermen, can do nothing when the sea's frozen over. I saw no sign of pretty clothes or well-combed hair—these were people who didn't bother to put on airs. Some looked up when I entered, sizing me up.

I immediately regretted my decision. This was not somewhere I wanted to be and these were not people I wanted to talk to. I turned to leave but bumped into a man who had suddenly appeared behind me. He was so foul I could hardly bring myself to look at him. His face was a mass of boils and he wore a horrible hairy coat so infested with lice I could see them crawling. His hands were short of several fingers, his eyes ran and he looked ill.

He suddenly gave me a toothless smile. "What are you doing here?"

I swallowed hard. "Searching," I said.

"Searching? For what?"

I wasn't sure I should tell him straight out. And yet what if this ruffian knew that I had a genuine and dangerous reason for being in the Seglen Arms? I might even win his admiration. Best to appear brave.

"I'm looking for someone who can tell me where to find Whitehead." I looked straight into his runny eyes.

The man stared back for some time with a look that was hard to interpret. Then he nodded slowly. "That's how it is, is it?" he said. "Amazing the things a fellow hears before his time to be popped in a sack and chucked in the briny!"

"Is there anyone here who knows the Ice Sea

really well?" I asked. "Anyone who knows where his island is?"

The man's eyes narrowed. "Well now." He licked his lips thoughtfully. "If you can pay your way…"

"I don't have any money," I mumbled.

"Perhaps you have something else?"

"How do you mean?"

He eyed the thong around my neck. "Can I see that?"

I wanted to refuse but didn't dare. I pulled out the oarfish from inside my shirt. The man's eyes gleamed. He reached out, but I stepped back—I wasn't about to let that repulsive, mutilated fist touch me.

"Listen here, you!" the man roared. "I only want to feel it. Keep still!"

Two other men were suddenly on their feet. One had a long, dirty moustache and a fur cap with ear-flaps, the other had one eye sewn up so it looked more like a furrow than an eye. The tip of his nose was blunt, as if someone had cut off a piece.

"What's she got there?" asked the moustache.

"Keep out of it!" the boils snarled. "Get back to your seat!"

"Why should you get all the valuable stuff?" One-eye said. He leaned over me and a strong, foul stench came from his mouth. He caught hold of the thong. "Give me that!" he snapped.

"Let go! I came here for information." I jerked away the thong.

"Information?" said One-eye. "What kind of information?"

"She says she's looking for Whitehead," said Boils.

"Is she? As if you'd know anyway," One-Eye said.

"Nor you, you creep!" replied Boils.

Now it was Moustache's turn to poke his nose in. "I'll tell you where Whitehead's island is. Out in the ocean! So there! Give me that medallion now!"

"No!" I shouted, knocking his hand aside.

He lost his temper and grabbed me by the jacket. I looked over at the barman for help but he didn't seem bothered by what went on.

"Are you looking for a fight, you midget?" Moustache snarled. "Fine by me!"

"Put me down!" I said. "Don't hit me!"

"I'll hit anyone I damn well like!" he said. "The last I heard, Whitehead was looking for children, not the other way round. What do you want him for?"

"Nothing." I felt the tears coming. "I'm actually looking for my dad. Can't you take a joke?"

"Your dad?" One-Eye said with a snort. "He's supposed to be in here, is he?"

I dried my eyes.

"That's exactly where!" I spat out. "And you'd better watch out or I'll tell him you tried to rob me. He carries a knife!"

The men laughed.

"Well, I never," said Boils. Of course, they all carried knives. "Just point out your dad and we'll leave you alone."

They pushed me farther into the room, between tables full of horribly smelly people, each uglier than the last. They all looked at me, but none gave a fig that I was being violently thumped in the back, and none came to my rescue.

What could I do? If I tried to run for it I'd never make the door, and there was no dad into whose arms I could throw myself. I didn't know a soul in the place.

But I did! I couldn't believe my eyes. The alcoholic fumes from all the drinks must be making me see things. But there, alone at a table at the far end of the room, there really was someone I knew! He was asleep, one arm thrown across the table and his face resting on it. A line of dribble escaped from the corner of his mouth.

I walked over with quick steps, caught his outstretched arm and shook it. "Wake up!" I said. "Don't just lie there asleep—I've been looking for you."

The man sat up like a shot, spluttering from the sudden awaking. He stared at me and no doubt could hardly believe his eyes.

"Well?" I looked at the three men who'd been

elbowing me along. "Here he is. Now leave me alone!"

Boils, One-Eye and Moustache were quick to obey. Not so much because the man at the table might have a knife in his belt, but because he was wearing a smart captain's coat and had thick gold rings in his ears. They didn't need to be awfully smart to know that my dad wasn't just any old ruffian.

• • ◇ • •

29

Disaster

Urstrom looked much the worse for wear. His captain's coat was dirty and he had gray bags under his eyes. He looked at the three men who had just left us.

"Who were they?" he asked.

"Nobodies!" I said.

He straightened himself up and took a sip from his mug. We said nothing for quite some time and then he said: "So you're here."

"I am," I said.

He nodded. "How did you get here?"

Well, of course he was wondering about that—and he could carry on wondering for all I cared. I was happy to have saved myself by coming to his table, but seeing him again made me furious. This was the wretch who'd tricked me and then sailed away from the Wolf Islands leaving me to the snow and cold.

When Urstrom saw he wasn't going to get an answer he stared down at the table. After a while he looked up.

"The man you see before you is a captain without a ship. No doubt you think that's what he deserves?"

"How do you mean?" I said.

Urstrom smiled, but it was a bitter, insincere smile. And he told me that the *Pole Star* was no more; the ship had been crushed by the ice.

I shuddered. To think that such a big and beautiful ship had been reduced to splinters.

"How did it happen?" I asked.

Urstrom took a swig and dried his mouth on his sleeve. There was an air of gloom about him, a feeling of defeat and disaster. The ship and its captain had both been crushed.

"We were becalmed," he said. "The wind died and as we lay there the cold crept up on us and froze us in. At first I thought that if we waited out the freeze-up we'd be free. But the cold didn't let up." He took another swig. "We lay there for many days with the ship creaking and groaning, and suddenly one night it was all too much. The hull gave way and the ship was reduced to matchwood." He swallowed and continued in a trembling voice. "The whole crew went down to Davy Jones's Locker, and I was the only one who escaped with his life."

All at once I found it hard to breathe. A lump grew and ached in my throat. The whole crew? Every single crewman, and the cook! My wonderful friend with the warm smile and the big heart. It was so terrible I didn't want to believe it. Fredrik was dead.

Urstrom went on with his story and the lump stayed in my throat. He told me how he had raced across the ice in the black of night, frozen to the marrow and with little hope of surviving. How he had glimpsed the lights of Seglen in the distance and had managed at last to get safely ashore. He laughed when he said that if the *Pole Star* had sailed a knot faster—one miserable knot faster—between the Wolf Islands and Seglen they might have arrived before the freeze trapped them.

I had an unpleasant sensation in my stomach. It seemed I had Urstrom to thank for my survival, for the fact that I wasn't dead at the bottom of the sea with the rest of the crew, my cheeks white and my hair swaying around my head like thousands of fine tentacles.

I looked at him sitting there bent and despondent. It was irrelevant now, and perhaps I should let sleeping dogs lie, but I needed to ask and hear him tell me.

"Why did you leave me behind?" I said.

Urstrom raised his eyes. For a moment he said

nothing, almost as if wondering whether to be angry. But weariness came over him again and he shrugged. Then he said:

"I was afraid. Afraid of Whitehead's anger if he heard that you and Fredrik had come to Seglen in my ship. I didn't want to risk the lives of my crew." He shook his head. "But now they're all dead anyway—the whole damn lot! And I don't have a penny to my name. Everything I owned went down with the ship. Fredrik's money too, if you must know."

"You still have your rings though," I said. "They must be valuable."

Urstrom fingered one of his thick gold rings.

"I've promised them to the tavern keeper in exchange for food and lodging."

He gave a deep sigh and at that moment I actually felt sorry for him. Strange, after all he'd done to me.

"Telling Fredrik that I was the one who'd taken his money—that was really low," I said.

Urstrom snorted. "He didn't buy it for one moment," he said. "Once we'd left the Wolf Islands he just lay sulking in his cabin. If I went anywhere near him he yelled a string of oaths, and shouted that he smelt the stink of a liar. The sooner he could leave the ship, the better, he said."

I was so happy to hear that Fredrik hadn't been

taken in by Urstrom's lie. Nevertheless, he was dead. Big and kind as he was, he'd been swallowed by the sea. I would never get over that.

"Did you see..." I said, and the lump formed in my throat again. "Did you see when he drowned? Did he suffer much?"

"I never said that Fredrik drowned," he said.

I blinked the tears from my eyes.

"You said the whole crew..."

Urstrom interrupted: "Fredrik was no longer one of the crew when the *Pole Star* went down. He'd signed off several days before."

"Signed off? How do you mean?"

"When we discovered we were frozen in, he went straight to his cabin, collected his things and left. Climbed over the rail. I tried to tell him it was madness, that there was no way of knowing if the ice would bear his weight all the way to land. But you know Fredrik. He's stubborn. The sooner he could leave the ship, the better was what he'd said, and he meant it."

"So what happened to him after that?" I asked. "Did he reach land?"

"I've no idea," Urstrom said carelessly. He took another small swig and wiped the foam from his lips. "What I do know, though, is that there's supposed to be a red-haired madman camping just outside the village. He spends his days shooting sea parrots as they fly over. People here talk about him but no one knows his name or where he comes from, and no one's keen on going too close. He's a very good shot apparently."

I jumped up so quickly I almost tipped over the chair. My heart pounded frantically at my ribs.

"Where?" I said. "Where's he camping?"

"Follow the bay eastwards until the houses thin out," Urstrom said. "You'll see a fire up on the hill."

◆ ◆ ◇ ◆ ◆

30

The Man on the Hill

I felt as if I had wings on my feet as I ran in the direction Urstrom had told me. Could Fredrik really be here in Seglen? Was I actually going to see him again?

But what if it wasn't him? What if it was some other red-haired man good at shooting sea parrots? And what if he shot me as I approached?

I hurried on, and there were fewer cottages as I reached the edge of Seglen. I could see a hill, but was it the right hill? Urstrom had mentioned a campfire, hadn't he?

Good! There was smoke, a long, thin bootlace of smoke. With my heart still pounding I slowed down. Best to play this cautiously, anyway.

I followed tracks in the snow. Footprints made by boots that were big—big enough to be…Careful. I didn't want to be overconfident. Not yet. That would be stupid, and disappointment would be unbearable.

Shouldn't I be hearing the sound of shots? Hadn't Urstrom said that the man on the hill spent all day shooting? Perhaps he'd broken camp and moved on. Perhaps the fire was about to die out. Perhaps I was too late.

Perhaps and perhaps not. Enough worrying, I said to myself, just go there and see.

And that's what I did. Every little bit of me held its breath. As if nothing existed in the world besides me and the footprints in the snow and the person who might be waiting where the footprints ended.

I came to the crown of the hill. I saw the fire.
I saw a hut built of driftwood. And a small coffee pot
on the ground, and a gun. And dead birds hanging
from a pole in the snow. And I saw the man—a man
with red hair and broad shoulders. He was sitting
staring into the dying fire, his legs drawn up and his
arms around his knees. He looked lonely.

"Fredrik," I said in a small voice. Much too small
and he didn't hear. I cleared my throat to say it again
and that made him raise his head.

At first he didn't look in the least surprised.

Perhaps he thought I was a figment of his imagination. But then it slowly dawned on him that I wasn't a fantasy, that I was real. His forehead furrowed and he stood up. I went right up to him and to make it a little easier for him I said: "It's me!"

He shook his head. "Is it really you?" he whispered. "Is it really you, Shrimp?"

He lifted me up and held me out in front of him and suddenly I started laughing. I just couldn't stop myself.

And Fredrik exclaimed, "Yes, oh yes, it is you!"

He started laughing too. And the more I laughed the more he laughed. We hugged each other, still laughing, because it was so good and strange and wonderful that the two of us were suddenly there together. If people happened to be passing at that moment or spying from a distance they would have decided there was more than one crazy person there on the hill.

In no time at all Fredrik had poked life back into the fire. We sat on his skin rug; it was old and worn, but nice anyway. He fetched one of the new blankets he'd bought on the Wolf Islands and put it over my legs.

"Are you hungry?" he asked.

I certainly was. I already knew, of course, that Fredrik could cook sea parrots, and how good they tasted. As for him, he was tiring of sea parrot, he said, because he had hardly eaten anything else since leaving the *Pole Star*.

"Will you tell me everything that's happened to you since we saw each other last?" I said.

Yes, he would do that by all means, he said, but first he wanted to hear what had happened to me. We argued for a while about who should go first. Jokingly, of course. Eventually I gave in and while Fredrik plucked and cleaned two big sea parrots I told him my tale from beginning to end. About Urstrom and the port official who'd locked me in the warehouse, about Nanni and her Signal, about the men who'd stolen the boat and set off across the sea, about the little merchild with whom I'd lived in the cave, about the snowstorm and the *Raven*, about Einar and his mother, and finally about Urstrom again and how I'd met him in the Seglen Arms.

"Did you know that the *Pole Star* has gone to the bottom?" I said.

Fredrik stopped plucking for a moment. He nodded. "Yes, I did. I sell a few of my birds to a poulterer in the village. So I can buy coffee and a few other things. He's an acquaintance of the landlord of the Seglen Arms and I heard it through him."

He gave a deep sigh and went back to plucking the birds.

"They weren't all decent fellows exactly, the

crew who worked the *Pole Star*," he said. "But none of them deserved to die. And the only one who survived sits drinking all day and feeling sorry for himself."

We said nothing for a while. Fredrik stuffed the parrots with raisins he'd taken with him when he left the ship, then he roasted the birds on a stick. Fat dripped from the meat and hissed as it fell into the dancing flames. When they were ready he took the roast birds off the stick and gave one to me. It burnt my fingers, but I was soon chewing my first mouthful of tender meat.

The food seemed to put life back into Fredrik even though he'd said he was tired of parrot. Once he'd eaten half his bird it was his turn to tell his story. He started at the beginning, when he'd woken from his midday nap that day and realized I wasn't on board.

I had to interrupt him already. I said, "How did you know it wasn't me who'd taken your money?"

Fredrik fixed me with his shining blue eyes. "You, Shrimp? If you were the sort of person who thinks of no one but themselves you'd never have set out on the Ice Sea in the first place. Would you now?"

"Perhaps not," I said, ecstatically happy that Fredrik had recognized the truth.

Fredrik took a few more bites before going on.

Urstrom, of course, wasn't going to admit that he'd hidden Fredrik's money, hoping that Fredrik would soon forget about our plan. But he didn't. As soon as the ice froze around the *Pole Star*, Fredrik set off for Seglen. He had no idea what had become of me, or if I was still alive. And that was why he'd decided to go and find Whitehead himself and try to rescue Miki. After all, that's what he'd said he was going to do. He couldn't take lodgings in an inn; Urstrom's theft of his money had seen to that.

"But..." he said, smiling at me, "...I'll be darned if I don't think things are better like this."

"They are," I said. "I wouldn't stay at the Seglen Arms, not for all the fish in the sea. Can you believe that three ruffians there said they could tell me where to find Whitehead, but it turned out none of them had a clue."

"Captain Whitehead..." Fredrik nodded. "His reputation is such that he seems to live on every single island around here. Whoever you ask gives a different answer."

He dried his hands on his trousers, brought over his sailor's kitbag and took out a map. He placed his finger on one island after another and said, "One man I met in the docks assured me I'd find Whitehead here, a couple of nautical miles south of Outersay. Someone else said he's on Eelsay, out there to the east. The fellow I sell sea parrots to says he's somewhere north of Fat Holm, though that doesn't sound likely because the skerries up that way are hardly bigger than my pocket."

He sighed and folded the map. We went back to eating our birds and talking about how to go about ferreting out where Whitehead's island actually was. How stupid and annoying that I'd already been there but still had no idea where it was.

By the time we'd finished eating I felt pleasantly satisfied. In fact, my stomach felt more than a little bloated. "That was the best food I've tasted since...since the last time you cooked sea parrot for me," I said.

"It should have egg in it really," Fredrik said. "But I don't have any. I don't think it's as good without egg."

"Once I've had a rest I'll go and see if I can find a bogle bird's nest with eggs in it," I said. "If you prefer it with egg, then egg you shall have!"

"There are no bogle birds here." Fredrik started to clean out the coffee pot with a brush he'd made from twigs.

"What did you say?"

"I said there are no bogle birds on Outersay," Fredrik said.

"Why do you think that?"

"I know it for a fact. The poulterer told me that the last bogle bird on the island was shot more than fifty years ago. So if you're going to find eggs you'll have to go a long way. Out to the small skerries in the open sea."

He measured coffee grounds into the pot and filled it with snow, mumbling to himself: "This time of year, of course, the eggs will have chicks in them."

I shot to my feet.

"What's up?" Fredrik asked.

"I've just worked something out," I said. "Can I have your map, please?"

"What do you want it for?" he asked as he passed it to me.

"I know who can point out Whitehead's island," I said. "I'll be back soon."

* * ◇ * *

Who Found Me on the Ice?

When I got back to the gray cottage I waited a while across the street. No sign of Iron-Anna's bent figure. Perhaps she was still out. I went up the steps and knocked on the door. It seemed strange to be doing so because I'd almost come to think of that door as my own.

No one answered.

I went back down the steps and over to the shed. The kick sled was still leaning against the wall. You can travel a long way quickly across the ice on a kick sled, I thought. You can fly along, like a razorbill.

I put my ear to the shed door. I could hear Einar whistling and talking in a coaxing voice, and I heard the angry, hissing answers.

I opened the door. Einar, who was kneeling on the floor, spun around to look up, his face terrified.

"I thought it was my mother," he said, standing.

"Sorry, I didn't mean to frighten you." I stepped inside and closed the door behind me. "What are you doing?"

Einar sighed and shook his head. "It doesn't want to come out." He nodded towards a pile of rubbish: a bailing bucket, tangled nets and a broken basket. "It's been behaving this way all day. I told you it likes you better than me."

We stood staring at the floor and saying nothing for a while, although we stole an occasional glance at one another.

"Why have you come back?" Einar asked.

"Because it was you."

"How do you mean?"

"It was you who found me out on the ice."

Einar made a dismissive noise. "It wasn't me," he said.

"Now I know why it was so important to keep the chick secret from your mother. She'd have been really angry if she'd known. Maybe even made you get rid of it."

He sighed, unable to think what to say.

"Because if there's one thing Iron-Anna would never let you do, it's go out on the frozen sea. That's right, isn't it? And I've just found out something about bogle birds that I didn't know: there aren't any here on Outersay."

"All right," Einar said reluctantly. "It was me."

He opened the door to check that Iron-Anna hadn't come back yet. Then he sat on the floor and looked at me. "You talk a lot, you do," he said. "You stay in our cottage and eat our soup. And tell me I'm wrong to teach my bird to work for us. Tell me I should catch my own herring. Do you know what famine means?"

"Of course I do," I said.

He said nothing for a moment. He looked at the pile of rubbish where his chick was hiding. "Bogle birds can always find fish. They don't have famine years."

"Maybe not."

He pulled out the medallion he wore around his neck, the one Iron-Anna had given him when his dad died. "She told me to wear this so I'd never forget that my dad died because of a herring."

"A herring?"

"Yes, a herring," Einar said.

He fingered the charm, the small fish hook that looked like a real fish hook, touching the point with his index finger.

"I was four at the time. The fishing off Outersay was bad—bad for all the families. Dad was afraid. If you have only fishing and the fishing fails, you're going to be afraid, aren't you? Time after time the only thing he caught was kelp, but one day when I went with him to check the nets, there was a herring. One miserable little herring. Dad was pleased and said it was for me, just for me. But the herring gave a sudden flip and escaped. Dad reached to catch it but fell overboard. And I was too small to help him." He swallowed hard. "And my ma seems to think I need help to remember that!"

I didn't know what to say, so I said nothing. It must have been dreadful for him to watch his dad die. I could remember my own mother's death, but that was different because she was ill. She slipped away, so to speak, but Einar's dad must have been shouting and fighting for his life as he went under. Imagine that.

Einar shook his head. "I don't intend ever being so hungry that I risk my life for a herring," he said. He looked again at the heap of rubbish, from which a bad-tempered churring came. "As soon as I came across that page I knew what I was going to do. Get hold of a bogle bird to keep famine at bay. Always!"

"But you didn't have a boat," I said.

"No, we haven't had one since Dad died," Einar answered. "And you already know there aren't any bogle birds on Outersay. A couple of times I came close to borrowing someone else's boat on the quiet, but I wasn't brave enough. But the morning I woke to find the sea completely frozen over…it was like being given a sign."

"So you went out on the kick sled?"

He nodded. "Ma was in a hurry. She had to go and help a family whose landing stage had been damaged by the ice. She said she'd be away all day. The moment she left I set off. I found it out by Grubb Skerries. The nest, I mean." He smiled at the memory and put his fingers to his cheek, where there was only a white scar left now. "What a struggle I had with the mother bird! She followed me for ages when I set off for home, screaming like a mad thing. But I was happy and it was the first time I'd felt really happy since Dad died. Then the snowstorm came."

How could I forget the snowstorm? That was why I'd headed for the shelter of the cliffs.

"By the time it stopped snowing I was lost," Einar continued. "I looked around for hours and the fresh snow made it all the harder. And suddenly, there you were. At first I thought you were dead but…" He looked at me with those eyes of his, the colour of the sea. "But you were alive. I put you on the kick sled and tied you on with my belt. I didn't get back here until the afternoon. Ma was still down at the bay and when she came home I told her I'd found you on the doorstep."

Neither of us said anything. The only sound was the sinister, ill-tempered churring of Einar's chick.

"Why couldn't you have told me all this earlier?"

I asked. "You knew I needed to know."

He gave a snort, not so much sneering as weary. "You were planning to take on Whitehead. One child against the coldest, most evil man on the Ice Sea. Do you get it? I didn't want to be guilty of your death."

I smiled. It was kind of him to think like that. I might have done the same if someone else had been going after Whitehead. But there was something I hadn't told Einar yet, something so wonderful and good that it made my heart sing.

"I'm not on my own any more," I said. "I have a friend—called Fredrik. We lost each other for a while but I've found him again and we're going to Whitehead's island together."

I unfolded Fredrik's map on the floor of the shed.

"Do you think you can point it out to me? The place where you found me?"

Einar got to his knees and studied all the islands.

"Here's Seglen," he said. "This is the way I went when I set out. Over here to the Grubb Skerries. But I went all over the place during the storm because on my way home I passed both Wet Holm and Cat Skerry." He touched an island to the north of Wet Holm. "This must be the one. There's a large bay with a narrow entrance. I'm sure you could anchor a ship in there without it being visible from the sea."

He thought things over for a while and then he said, "Do you have any weapons?"

"I don't. But Fredrik has a gun."

Einar said that was all very well, but it was only fair that I should have something too. He looked around the shed, which contained a rusty old fishing spear and various hooks, as well as a bag net and some ordinary nets. Then he took a stone down from a shelf, about the size of a cod's head, with sharp edges.

"This is what my dad used to kill fish," he said. "They died immediately."

I laughed. "And I'm supposed to kill the coldest and most evil man on the Ice Sea with a stone? Is that what you think?"

Einar smiled and shrugged. "What works on a catfish will work on a seadog!"

"Yes, you're quite right," I said, putting the stone in my pocket.

I left him and as I closed the shed door behind me I heard him clucking to the chick, coaxing it out of its hiding place. I was glad that the last thing we'd done before parting was to share a joke.

♦ ♦ ◇ ♦ ♦

The Corpse of *Cuttlefish*

The following day was bright and clear. Fredrik and I left our camp on the hill while Seglen was still asleep.

My Fredrik! I could hardly believe he was walking at my side as we made for Whitehead's island. He had a gun and he was so big and strong he could lift three sacks of grain on an outstretched arm. And the two of us were doing it together!

Hungry flocks of sea parrots flew overhead, calling for fish. But there were no fish to be had now that ice had locked the sea. Fredrik had shot a supply of them back in Seglen; he said it was best not to draw attention to ourselves out on the ice.

In the early afternoon we stopped and ate bread and butter before continuing our journey. The sun soon began to sink and the ice changed from white to blue or violet or a mixture of the two. The sky turned pink and yellow and shades in between.

Fewer flocks of sea parrots passed above us, and cold pinched the tip of my nose.

Fredrik stopped, put down his kitbag and took out the map. Einar on his kick sled would have covered the stretch between Seglen and Whitehead's island much faster. Dense white clouds formed around Fredrik's mouth when he spoke.

"Getting there in pitch darkness is no good. We can't risk getting lost. We'll spend the night out on the ice." He folded the map. "We need to find a good spot," he said.

We searched around and found nothing but tiny islets and small reefs—nowhere sheltered from the wind and the cold.

After walking a while into the fiery sunset Fredrik put his hand up to shade his eyes and said he could see a boat.

I felt a stab at my heart; for a second or two I thought he was talking about the pirates' ship and imagined the ship had grown so ravenous it had broken out of the bay and was smashing through the ice in search of new children to devour.

But I quickly understood he meant a fishing boat, not a ship, and as we approached, I could see which fishing boat it was. I pulled at Fredrik's sleeve to draw him away.

"That's the boat I was in," I said. "*Cuttlefish*. Let's get out of here."

But Fredrik was in no hurry. He spied out the direction of the boat and the ice all round.

"No need to be frightened," he said. "The boat's deserted. Can't you see, the hull is shattered?"

Reluctantly I looked again. He was right: *Cuttlefish* was a wreck, a broken, pitiful corpse in the winter ice, its gaff pointing crookedly at the sky.

Fredrik headed over, saying it was at least worth investigating. I followed hesitantly. The mere memory of Baldy and Beardy made my skin crawl.

No, it wasn't pleasant to see the *Cuttlefish* again, to see its curved gray timbers and the thwart I'd spent so long under, my body aching. It wasn't nice to see the oars I'd been forced to row with or the boathook with which Baldy had tried to drag the little merchild out of the water.

Fredrik poked at a couple of items they'd left lying on the bottom boards. It looked as if they'd deserted the boat in a hurry.

"Difficult to say if they saved themselves out on the ice or if they drowned," he muttered.

I shuddered. It was horrible to think of them lying at the bottom of the sea, swaying this way and that, with staring eyes. Right beneath our feet even! But it was also horrible to think they might have survived and be on board the *Raven* this very moment, drinking beer with Whitehead. The pirates might even be tossing them in the air to celebrate their joining the vile gang to help out with their looting.

Fredrik put down his kitbag and began digging out the salvaged sail from the prow.

"We'll sleep here tonight," he said.

I wasn't too happy about spending the night in the *Cuttlefish*, but I could see it was the best solution. We needed shelter, and once Fredrik had dug away the snow and stretched the sail as a roof over the boat, I crawled inside and it actually felt quite cosy.

We spread Fredrik's big fur rug over the shattered bottom boards, then with his knife he sliced slivers of wood off the broken timbers. Then he arranged a smoke hole in the sailcloth and made a bundle of the slivers, and we soon had a small fire burning in a tin bowl inside our shelter.

We lay there eating parrot in the firelight. We ate the last piece of bread and talked about tomorrow. It was so unreal it seemed like a fairy tale: just one man and a little shrimp were going to challenge Whitehead, the coldest and most evil man in all the Ice Sea.

I burst out crying. It went on and on; I didn't even try to hold back the tears.

"Don't be afraid," Fredrik said.

"But I am afraid," I answered. "What if she's dead? What if we're too late? The mine breaks children faster than anyone thinks."

"She's not dead," Fredrik said. "We'll get there in time. You must believe that. I do."

I dried my tears and sniffed a couple of times. Suddenly I felt very stupid. I remembered that Fredrik, too, had lost a little sister, abducted by Whitehead. There was still hope for Miki, but Hanna, the little girl taken away twelve years before, must have died long ago. And yet, even though there was no chance of saving his sister, Fredrik was coming with me. That was Fredrik!

I knew at once that I wanted to give him a present. I took the oarfish from around my neck. "Here," I said. "This is for you."

Fredrik shook his head. "A real oarfish," he said. "I could never take that from you."

"But you must. I want you to have it," I said. "It brings luck, you know that, don't you?"

I hung it around his neck. Fredrik looked almost embarrassed, but he touched the oarfish anyway and thanked me.

"Luck," he said. "I've no doubt we'll need it tomorrow."

"Not me," I said. "Because I have you."

Then I crept close to him and pulled the covers over me. The fire was crackling in a homely way and my body was worn out after our long march. I was asleep before I knew it.

That night I dreamt I met a man with long white

hair and a rope around his neck. When I looked down his throat I saw a little girl stuck in it. I caught hold of her feet to pull her out, but however hard I pulled she slipped farther down. And all the time the man was screaming at me to pull harder because otherwise he was going to choke. But I couldn't pull her up and suddenly she was gone. That's when I woke with a jerk and sat up.

The fire in the bowl had almost gone out and everything was dark and as cold as ice. I pushed more wood into the bowl and waited for the fire to catch, then I cuddled in close to Fredrik again. I could allow myself a little more sleep. Tomorrow hadn't come yet. It was still hovering at a safe distance from our little shelter and it would be a few more hours before it found us.

◆ ◆ ◇ ◆ ◆

33

Target Shooting

Once morning came we quickly broke camp. We emptied the ashes from the bowl, rolled up our fur covers and packed what little we had. Then we left the *Cuttlefish*, which would remain stuck in the ice until spring eventually freed it to sink to the bottom.

We didn't have far to go. After a couple of hours we could make out an island in the distance. Even when it was little more than a dot I knew it was the right island. It had a kind of reek about it, of something ugly and dangerous, something utterly evil. As we approached and the dot grew bigger, the worse the reek became.

As we stood at the foot of the high cliffs, the only thing between us and the evil that lay beyond, my heart raced like a horse at full gallop and fear rang in my ears. I couldn't shake off the feeling that the pirates knew we were there and were watching us, listening to us, picking up our scent.

Fredrik opened the map and studied it for a long time. Then he said, "We need a good view of the island. We'll have to climb up high."

He put the map back in his kitbag and threw the bag over his shoulder. He took the lead and I hurried along behind him.

It was a steep climb. I knew it would be, of course, because I'd done it before. Time after time we had to take detours because of a lack of good footholds or because the snow was too deep. Once, Fredrik sank to his waist and it took him some time to pull himself out.

We reached the top at last and rested to catch our breath. Fredrik looked at me. My eyes hung on his kind blue gaze the way a young animal clings to its mother's fur. He wiped water and crystals of ice from his face. "We can't tell how this will turn out," he said. "Have you made up your mind? Are you sure you want to go on?"

I swallowed hard and nodded. "Yes," I said. "I'm sure."

At that moment a shot echoed back from the clouds. Fredrik and I ducked. It came from the other side of the cliffs. We looked at one another nervously. Were they shooting at us? But then came the cheerful voices of men laughing and shouting, followed by another shot.

"What do you think they're shooting at?" I whispered.

"No idea," Fredrik whispered back.

We heard more shots, followed by cheering. Fredrik whispered, "Let's take a look."

We crawled up the last bit and poked our noses over the edge. The first thing we saw was the *Snow Raven*. Its hull hadn't been crushed by the ice, probably because of its sheltered position. The danger comes from currents in the deep that make the ice move, but in a bay like this the water remains quite still.

I pointed out to Fredrik the thin column of smoke rising from the middle of the island. By straining your eyes you could just pick out a strange, tall tower and a cluster of smaller houses.

Some of the pirates were out on the ice. We counted a dozen of them shooting at a target. They had made a small mound of snow—representing a human figure, of course—a short distance away and were taking turns trying to shoot it. When anyone managed to hit it the snowman was blown to pieces, then they'd all cheer and help build a new one. Almost all were good shots, but two men still had a lot to learn: Baldy and Beardy, the two wretches I'd sailed with in the *Cuttlefish*. They'd obviously managed to find their way here and were members of the crew. It was little wonder they'd failed to shoot a wolf on the Wolf Islands; their shots always hit the snow yards away from the snowman. That was why their companions were laughing so much.

When Baldy and Beardy finished, it was someone else's turn to shoot and he had no trouble hitting the snowman's head. They carried on like that, each man taking a turn at shooting and rebuilding the target until it was Beardy's turn again.

He stamped his feet a few times, twisted his neck this way and that and swung his arm, as if loosening himself up. The rest of the pirates were so sure he was going to miss that they were already laughing.

As Beardy was raising the gun, one of the others took it into his head to creep up and throw a snowball that hit him in the back. Beardy lost his temper and spun round, forgetting to take his finger off the trigger. The gun went off and, scared out of their wits, they all turned to see where the shot had gone. It had hit the *Raven*!

But that wasn't all! Someone stood on the deck, someone who hadn't been there a moment before. A big, powerful man dressed in furs. He wore a cap fastened with a chinstrap, and the terrified pirates tore off their own caps and bowed. The man on the deck could only be Whitehead himself!

Whitehead took off a glove and felt the bullet hole in the ship's rail. Beardy was so frightened he dropped his gun, which fell at his feet. He'd come within a couple of inches of shooting the pirate captain. What would happen to him now?

Whitehead put his glove back on as if nothing had happened. He gave his men a brief nod. Presumably he'd ordered them to carry on, because the men began at once to reload their weapons. Now it was Baldy's turn. He was such a bad shot that no one saw where his bullet went, but no one was laughing now. They all took furtive looks in Whitehead's direction and waited for his reaction. Whitehead stood there motionless and silent. Then it was the turn of one of the pirate sharpshooters.

"We've seen enough," Fredrik said, ducking down.

But I stayed where I was, eyes fixed on the man on the deck. I could have lain there until the snow melted under me. That was the man I'd heard so many stories about, the man who'd been in my mind every night and every day since I left home. There he stood, watching and enjoying target shooting. Anyone can watch and enjoy target shooting, of course, but the fact that he could do so right before my eyes was so fascinating I couldn't take my eyes off him.

"Shrimp!"

I was startled out of my daydream and turned sharply to crawl back down. But that made something happen that should never have happened.

A great lump of snow came loose under me as I turned, and it went rolling down the slope towards the bay. It came to rest for a few seconds as if intending to stop, but the snow beneath it urged it on, and on it went, stirring up more snow. More and more broke free and slid and rolled and rushed downwards. It grew into an avalanche with spindrift filling the air around it. Fredrik desperately pulled me to safety. We looked at one another, knowing it would be only seconds before the pirates noticed.

We were right. They began shouting and a shot was fired, presumably at our ridge. Someone yelled, "Up there! Up there!" which meant that the lot of them would soon be with us.

Fredrik surveyed the great, empty expanse of sea ice on our side of the island. However fast we ran we would never manage to get out of sight, so he made a swift decision.

"Better they catch one than both of us." He stood up and put his hands in the air.

"No!" I whispered, but it was too late.

"Don't shoot!" he shouted to the pirates, walking towards them to save me from being discovered. They screamed at him, screamed for him to keep his hands up, screamed that now he was for it, that now they were going to shoot him, that he'd die for daring to think he could be on the island without their permission.

I felt as hard and cold as ice as I listened to them yell. I heard how they pushed and shoved him down the slope, how they ordered him to get a move on, but at least there were no shots.

Then the voices grew fainter and I risked a quick look over the ridge—just in time to see two pirates forcing Fredrik down the ladder to the lower deck of the *Raven*. The rest of the gang followed and behind them, in no hurry at all, walked Whitehead. The hatch closed and everything went quiet.

◆ ◆ ◇ ◆ ◆

34

Bragder

Down on the ice far below me a little arctic fox scuttled along, stopped to sniff at something, then moved on. That was the only living thing I saw. The rest of the world was holding its breath. The wind tugged gently at my hair as I lay huddled up, cold and with a pounding heart. Fredrik had been taken prisoner, dragged down into the belly of the *Raven*, and now I had to rescue him too. I absolutely had to rescue him! There was no way I could go on living if Fredrik died.

But how was I to do it? The *Raven* was full of pirates. I'd seen twelve of them target shooting on the ice, but there must be many more. It would take more than a dozen men to sail the *Raven*. And then there was Whitehead himself. They were all in there and I was out here and however hard I tried I couldn't think of any way to sneak on board.

Then something remarkable happened. I'd only

been lying there for an hour or so when the hatch in the deck suddenly opened and out stepped a pirate. Then another, both with guns over their shoulders and wearing good warm coats.

They were followed by a third and a fourth and more, one pirate after another emerging from the *Raven*'s innards. The deck was soon full of armed men and a few women. They inspected each other's guns and all seemed to be in high spirits. Even Baldy and Beardy were there.

Last of all, up came Whitehead! It was him all right, I could tell even though the pirates clustered around him so I couldn't see his face. I recognized the fur cap with the chinstrap. The pirates thumped him on the back and someone even fired a salute into the air. They clearly liked their captain very much.

One of them called out and gestured to a couple of distant skerries. They all climbed down the rope ladders that had been thrown over the ship's rail and off they went, eyes fixed on the far skerries.

I could scarcely believe my luck. The pirates were going off hunting. No doubt they'd left Fredrik chained in the hold, confident he couldn't escape while they were off shooting birds.

But had all of them gone? There was no way to be sure of that, and so I waited for a good while before scrambling down to the bay.

On reaching the ice I ran to the ship and put my ear to the hull. The white-painted timber was coated with glittering frost.

Silent. Dead silent.

I moved along a little and listened again.

Not a sound could be heard from the belly of the *Raven*, not even the slightest rumbling. I raised my head to look; the pirates were too far away to be visible.

I scurried around the front of the ship and crept under the two taut anchor chains frozen into the ice. The evil eyes of the raven figurehead glared at me, the bird's beak gaping and hungry. When I reached the rope ladders I quickly climbed up to the deck.

There I was on the pirate ship. I thought of all the children who'd been brought aboard, terrified and trembling. I took off a glove and felt the ship's timbers, felt the frozen curves. Very carefully I touched the ship's bell and I looked warily aft towards the captain's cabin. That's where he lived, where he ate and slept—and that's where he planned his raids. That cabin was the very heart of the *Raven* and that was Whitehead's home.

But I mustn't get lost in my thoughts. There was no time to daydream. The quicker I rescued Fredrik the better.

Using both hands I took hold of the great

iron ring on the hatch. It took every ounce of my strength to open it. Then I poked my head in.

Empty and dark, but I inhaled the smell of pirates, a smell of sweat and smoke, dirt and beer. I climbed down. There was a brick-lined fireplace towards the bows, more or less like the *Pole Star*'s, but more old-fashioned. An oil lamp hung on a nail, its flame turned low. I took it down and turned up the flame. Everywhere I looked was a mess of hammocks and kitbags, clothes and valuables. I realized that many were stolen goods because several of the seamen's chests were painted with the names of other vessels: not *Snow Raven* but *Sea Cat*, *Wave Clipper* and *Farewell*. I saw silver chains and pewter mugs and objects carved from meerschaum, gold trinkets and precious fur coats with buttons of horn and bone. The cannon lashed to the gun ports looked like ugly iron vases. The main mast came down through the decks all the way to the keelson and on it was a hook from which sea parrots hung. The birds smelled dreadful; they'd gone so rotten their heads were on the point of falling off.

There was one more hatch, the hatch down to the cargo hold. It wasn't as tight as the first but was still so heavy I had to put down the lamp to open it.

I climbed down the ladder and looked around. Baggage and firewood were stored in different bulkhead compartments. In one was a heap of pulley blocks, in another were sacks, probably of grain or peas. Being aboard a ship as motionless as a house was a strange sensation. The ship's timbers, which usually creaked and complained in the waves, were as silent as death. Not a sound could be heard.

Wait! There was something! The sound of breathing? Of someone breathing hard through their nose. Someone straining as though in pain. It was coming from the stern.

I hurried past the stores, and beyond a compartment stacked with beer barrels I found Fredrik.

He had an iron collar around his neck. A chain ran from it and was attached to the ship's timbers. His hands were tied behind his back and a rag was gagging his mouth, which explained the strained noises. I rushed over, and when the lamp lit his sweating face I saw the fear and desperation in his eyes.

"I'll get you free," I said.

Fredrik made snorting noises and jerked his head, trying to say things impossible to understand. I untied the gag. They'd pushed another rag into his mouth and once he'd spat it out he said tearfully:

"You should never have come here."

I looked at him, bewildered. Wasn't he glad that I'd come, that I was setting him free?

At that moment I heard footsteps behind me and I turned around slowly. Emerging like a monster from the darkness was the captain. It was him, even though I was sure I'd seen him leaving the ship. He had a fleshy face with a large nose and cheeks and chin covered in stubble. He held a gun. But his hair was dark and cropped short.

"Wh-whitehead?" I said.

The man gave a black, repulsive smile.

"No! It's a long time since Whitehead set foot on the *Snow Raven*. I'm Bragder. The mate."

He dragged over a beer barrel and sat on it after putting down his gun. The barrel blocked my exit.

He sat like that for some time, looking at me in an almost kindly way. As if someone he was fond of was paying him a visit. I was frightened, so frightened that my blood ran cold, but I was also confused. What had he just said?

"Doesn't Whitehead sail in this ship?" I asked.

"No," the mate said. "He doesn't. He has other things to look after."

"Wh-what kind of things?"

The mate smiled again and instead of answering my question he said, "I'm the acting captain. I'm the one who sails the *Snow Raven*. And I'm the one who traps children who come here thinking they can change the fate of their little sisters."

I looked quickly at Fredrik but he shook his head. "I haven't told them anything," he said.

Bragder fished a pipe out of his pocket and filled

it with tobacco. He pointed at the lamp I'd put down beside me. "Do you mind?" he said.

"M–mind what?" I said.

He smiled again, pulled the lamp over and used a spill to light his pipe. He sucked at the stem of the pipe and the smell of the smoke was sweet.

"Your friend tried to convince us that he'd found us by pure chance," he said. "And we swallowed it."

He puffed at his pipe and then, without warning, burst into raucous laughter that made me shudder.

Bragder and his crew had indeed swallowed Fredrik's story that he was just a lone hunter who'd come to the island for prey. But then they noticed the oarfish around his neck and one of the pirates claimed that it was his. He'd bought it on the Wolf Islands not long before and he recognized the plaited thong he'd made for it.

That was when Baldy and Beardy told them all about me, the girl who was planning to free her sister, the girl they thought they had killed at sea. How I'd survived was, of course, a mystery to them, but Bragder had said that, mystery or not, the important thing was to draw me out of hiding, assuming I was in the vicinity. Captain Whitehead was a very busy man and wouldn't want his work disrupted by attempts to free anyone.

It was Bragder who'd come up with a plan of action. He swapped clothes with one of the pirates, then ordered them all to go out hunting. When they went up on deck they had to behave as if they were happy and excited. Meanwhile, Bragder remained on board, waiting for me to approach.

He took a couple more puffs on his pipe and smiled. I was a welcome visitor, he said. There was always room for another child in Whitehead's mine.

♦ ♦ ◇ ♦ ♦

The Mine

Fredrik yelled and tugged at his chain like a tethered dog when Bragder tied a rope around my neck and led me towards the ladder. We climbed up, me first and Bragder following, then we walked through the filthy, stinking sleeping quarters. We climbed up the next ladder and when we stood by the ship's rail I looked all round, taking in the sea and the cliffs and the blanket of snow over everything.

Bragder seemed to know what I was thinking because he smiled and nodded to it all. "You can say goodbye to all that," he said.

We climbed down the rope ladders and I heard shots from the distant skerries where the pirates had gone. I also heard Fredrik shouting from the depths of the hold.

We began walking across the ice. There was no chance of running away since Bragder had a tight hold of the rope around my neck and a gun in his other hand. He poked me in the back with the barrel just to remind me.

When we reached the island I found myself trudging through snow that grew deeper. And after we had walked a bit I noticed something strange about the snow. Slowly, gradually, it was changing.

At first it was just a pale, pale gray, like the most washed-out stones in the sea.

Then it was a little darker, more or less like dried fish.

Then it was darker again, the same deep gray as our weather-beaten house back in Blue Bay.

Then it was even darker, like the skin of the gurry shark.

Then it was almost black, like the steels we use to sharpen our knives.

And finally it was as black as night.

Whichever way I turned it was the same. My eyes, used to whiteness, ached and stung from all this blackness.

I was afraid of that snow. Could it be real? Had the snow changed from white to black because Whitehead had emptied his evil soul on the ground around his diamond mine? I was so afraid that I didn't dare ask, I just kept on trudging through the blackness. And every so often Bragder nudged me in the back with his horrible, hard gun barrel.

Eventually we arrived at a cluster of cottages, the ones I'd seen from the top of the cliff. One looked to be a fine, well-built place with windows lit up and smoke coming from the chimney. There was a similar cottage alongside it, but smaller. Then there was one that didn't look nice at all; it reminded me more of a port warehouse without windows. The fourth building was the strangest of all, because it wasn't really a house, but a very high tower. A little like a wooden lighthouse but with no light at the top. There were huge piles outside the tower: not of snow, but of something black. Two pirates were on guard at the door, each sitting on a stool. They stood and raised their caps when they saw Bragder.

"Bringing something new, are you?" one of them said. He had a moustache and an earring in each ear and wore an ankle-length fur coat with a broad belt. He meant me, of course, as if I were merely a thing, a new bit of booty.

Bragder mumbled in reply and the other pirate, a bald man with a hunchback, long chin and sparse teeth, opened the creaky door. I heard the sound of picks working. It came from far away and was strangely muffled. It made my skin creep.

"How did you get hold of that one, Bragder?" the man with the hunchback asked, glaring at me. "You haven't found a way of sailing on ice, have you?"

"This one came of her own accord," Bragder answered, which made the man glare even harder.

Then Bragder poked me in the back with his gun barrel. "Come on then," he said. "On we go."

I didn't move. My legs and arms and whole body were trembling. The doorway in front of me was a threshold that divided my old world from the new. A new world I didn't want to enter. I suddenly knew I'd fight for all I was worth to avoid entering the mine. Those dark, narrow passageways! I'd been born with the terror of them in my blood.

"No," I said, shaking my head.

Both the guards laughed. I think they were laughing at Bragder and the idea that someone who barely came to his waist was resisting him.

Bragder sighed. "There's no point, you know," he said.

"I'm not going in." I turned and looked him in the eye. "I'm never going in. Let me go!"

I pulled at the rope around my neck. I pulled and tore at it as hard as I could, hissing time after time, "Let me go! Let me go! Let me go!"

The two guards were enjoying the scene.

But there were signs of anger in Bragder's face and the muscles in his jaw stood out. He wound a turn of the rope around his fist and jerked so hard and savagely that I fell to the ground.

I was dragged over the threshold and into the

great, mysterious tower. I screamed and tried to get up on my knees but couldn't. Bragder didn't even turn around, he just carried on walking. There was no floor, only trampled earth that tore holes in my clothes and my skin. The rope tightened around my neck and threatened to strangle me. Being dragged along like a sack hurt worse and worse.

Eventually Bragder stopped. "Get up!" he said.

I rose to my feet slowly, biting back tears. A number of lamps lit the tower and I saw a large hole in the black earth. It was from there that the sound of picks was coming. Over the hole a construction of beams reached right up to the roof of the tall tower. Attached to the beams was a block and tackle through which ran a thick rope with what looked like a wooden cage hanging from it. It was the lift down to the mine.

A huge pirate sat by the lift, half asleep. His bushy beard was filthy and he had long hair in a headband, though the crown of his head was bald. His face was wrinkled and weather-beaten, as if at least half his life had been spent at sea.

Two more pirates stood by the wall. One was a stumpy man in sealskins whereas the other had a distinctive feature I'd never seen before. On his cheek was a picture of a knife pointing at a heart from which three drops of blood were falling. Both these pirates were armed with guns.

Someone else sat at a table further back in the gloom. It was an ugly woman with white hair and eyes like milky water. On her table were a plate and a pewter mug and she chewed on a bird bone clasped in her bare hands. She wore trousers and a fur jacket and she too was armed, with a gun hanging on the back of her chair.

I found it strange that everything here was so miserable and black. I'd heard stories of piles of precious stones, some the size of eggs. I'd heard of a guard who'd had all her teeth replaced with diamonds. But looking at the woman eating, I saw that her teeth were the same neglected yellow as any other old woman's.

"Isn't this a diamond mine?" I asked, looking at Bragder.

Bragder smiled and said no, there were no diamonds in this mine and there never had been. This was a coal mine.

He looked over at the woman. "Good day, little Dove," he said.

The woman called Dove looked at him briefly and went on gnawing at the bone.

"Where do you want this one put?" Bragder nodded in my direction.

Dove spat a piece of gristle onto the floor, wiped her mouth with the back of her hand and stood up. She took the rope from Bragder and led me over to a wall where there were long rows of hooks, on some of which hung baskets. Dove tied my rope to a hook and went back to continue her meal.

"Right, I'm going, little Dove," Bragder said. "I'm off to have a word with the captain."

"Wait!" I said. "What'll happen to my friend?"

Bragder stopped and looked at me. "That's what I'm going to talk to Whitehead about. A man who falls into our hands is usually given a choice."

"Ch–choice?"

"The *Snow Raven* has plenty of room for another pirate and we need as many as we can get. Ships are getting better equipped all the time to resist our attacks. He'll be given three days to accept the offer. Most men don't need more than one day, but something tells me your friend's the stubborn sort."

"He doesn't like pirates," I said.

Bragder gave another of his raucous laughs. "No one likes pirates. Hell's bells, even I don't like them!"

"But…why become one in that case?"

Bragder pointed a finger at his head. "Because the choice is between a pirate and a bullet, of course."

◆ ◆ ◇ ◆ ◆

36

The Children

Tied to the wall I waited, listening to the muffled ring of picks down in the underworld. I shut my eyes and tried to imagine which of those picks was Miki's. Was it the one with regular strokes, like a clock? Or the slower one that seemed to pause for thought between each stroke? Or the one where each blow of the pick bounced so that it sounded like a double strike?

The pirates sitting by the wall seemed bored. They yawned and exchanged occasional remarks. Apparently guarding children at the mine was beneath them and they longed to be back with their companions on the *Snow Raven*. What they wanted more than anything was to be at sea, but they'd have to wait, of course, until the ice broke up.

Dove concentrated on her bone. When she finished chewing it, she ran her tongue over her front teeth to clean them, then she looked at me.

"What's your name?" she said.

"Siri," I answered in a quiet voice.

Dove nodded and studied me from my boots up.

"Are you healthy?"

"Yes."

"Strong?"

"I think so."

Dove nodded ominously towards the hole down to the mine.

"The stronger you are the more chance you'll survive," she said. "The weak, little ones don't last long."

I swallowed and felt faint. I saw nothing but darkness, a darkness imprinted with images of small children with pale cheeks and broken backs.

"My sister…" I said. "A small girl called Miki…is she here?"

Dove just looked at me with those milky eyes. Then she gave a short nod and said, "She is here."

I breathed a deep sigh of relief. "How…how does it all work?"

She leaned back in her chair and pulled her mug towards her. Then she told me about the work in Whitehead's mine.

In the morning you shouldered a basket and took a lantern and a pick. You were lowered down into the mine in the lift and when you reached the bottom you started crawling. There were many,

many galleries down there, a whole network of tunnels and rooms. Then you set to work with your pick and you went on working until work was the only thing you knew, until your aching arms swung the pick of their own accord, until you were on the verge of madness. When, at last, your basket was full of coal, you put it on your back and crawled back to the lift, because only when your basket was full were you allowed to come up.

I shuddered and looked at the mineshaft, the black throat that swallowed children in the morning and coughed them up when they'd finished their task. I looked at Dove.

"How long does it take to fill a basket?"

She took a mouthful from her mug. "That's what you'll find out tomorrow," she said.

Neither of us said any more. We sat in silence listening to the ceaseless sound of the subterranean picks and the drivel being talked by miserable pirate guards. The man sitting half asleep by the shaft had woken up and was cleaning his nails with a rusty knife.

Several hours later a ship's bell rang. It made me jump. I saw that the bell was attached to the beams that supported the lift and that a rope ran from the bell down the lift shaft. The pirates stood up and the one with the tattooed cheek yawned and said it was that time again. The biggest pirate, the one by the shaft, lowered the cage and my stomach turned over at the length of time it took to reach the bottom. While this was going on the other two checked their guns and made sure they were loaded.

The strong, bearded man began hauling the cage up. He didn't have to pull very hard, although of course it took even longer than lowering it.

And then, all of a sudden, it was up, with a boy on board. He was black all over and thin. He looked like an insect. His feet were black, his trousers were black, his shirt was black and so were his hands, neck, face and hair. His basket was full to the brim and black, the pick he held in one hand was black and the lantern in his other hand was so black you could hardly see the flame behind the glass. The only things not black were the boy's green eyes.

He stepped from the lift, blew out the flame and placed the lantern and pick on a shelf. He emptied the coal from his basket to make a small heap on the floor and then he hung his basket on one of the hooks where I was sitting. He looked at me without a word and walked over to the door where he sank at once to the ground. The armed pirates were already standing there, legs astride and looking grim, as if to show him he damn well better not try to escape. The boy didn't even look at them. He sat with his arms around his knees, forehead resting on his entwined fingers, perhaps already asleep.

A little while later the bell rang again and up came another boy, slightly younger than the first. Following the same pattern he put down his lantern, pick, coal and basket and went over to wait by the door guarded by the men with guns.

I was growing impatient. I wanted to see Miki come up with the lift. I wanted to talk to her and know if her back was holding up. The next time the bearded pirate hauled the wooden cage up from the depths it still wasn't Miki, but a tall, gangly girl of about twelve. Instead of shoes she had rags on her feet and her jacket was a peculiar striped thing that looked like a half-plucked bird.

Child after child came up from the underworld, all of them black and looking dreadful, and all with eyes that gleamed bright in their ghostly faces. They all emptied their baskets in the same place and the heap of coal soon reached Dove's shoulder. She stood overseeing everything, checking that the baskets were properly full, that everyone put their tools back in the right place and then took their place by the door, where the line of exhausted little bodies grew longer and longer.

By now the only sound from below was of a single slow pick.

Dove counted the children at the door—nineteen in all. She untied the rope around my neck, and called, "Right!"

The children immediately rose to their feet. Anyone who'd fallen asleep was roused by a kick from one of the armed pirates. The line formed up quickly and Dove went to open the door.

"Wait!" I shouted to her.

All the children turned and nineteen pairs of eyes looked at me in astonishment mixed with fear. It clearly wasn't a daily occurrence for a prisoner to order a guard.

Dove, however, didn't seem angry. She lifted her eyebrows a little and said, "Well?"

I pointed at the shaft. "There's still someone down there, isn't there?"

Dove nodded. "She can come up when she's filled her basket. After that she has to sort this coal."

Dove indicated the enormous pile. "That's the way we do things here. Last one up does the sorting. As I said before, being small and weak is not an advantage in the mine."

She opened the door and stepped aside for the line to pass through. Then she looked at me with a strange, almost sympathetic look and said: "And hardly anywhere else, either."

♦ ♦ ◇ ♦ ♦

Little Sister

It was night outside and the sky was as black as the snow. The stars that looked down on our silent procession were a beautiful scattering of thousands of small lights. It was so cold that steam rose above the small, tousled heads. I was last in the line of children and behind me came the two pirates with loaded guns.

I peered over at the big cottage, the one that looked so fine and well built. In one of the lighted windows I saw the outline of a man. Just briefly. A moment later he was gone.

"You!" one of the men behind me said. "Keep your nose pointing to the front. You wouldn't want us thinking you were about to make a run for it."

I didn't risk answering. I stared ahead and tried not to think about those loaded guns, and how it might feel to get a bullet in the back and fall face first into the snow with my life pumping out through my clothes as I lay in a warm pool of my own blood.

The line came to a halt outside the building that resembled a port warehouse. One of the men behind me yelled: "Sheepskull!"

There was a short delay, then the door was opened by a pirate with a great gray mane of hair and one eye with such a fixed and horrible stare it couldn't possibly have been real. Probably a glass eye. He stepped aside to let the line inside.

We entered a large room in the middle of which was a hearth and a chimney breast, with a cauldron hanging over the fire. There was a large bed with curtains against one wall and along the other three walls stood rows of small beds, each more wretched than the last. A couple had mattresses, but others had only a blanket or two or a fur rug. There were chamber pots underneath and to each bed was attached a chain with an iron shackle. Everything was black with coal dust.

The children were quick to get onto their beds. I saw that everyone had an allotted place. The man with the tattooed face kept guard at the door and the man in sealskin clothes picked out my bed. Three or four were empty and he chose one in the corner, between a girl who looked about ten years old, like me, and the boy with the green eyes who'd been first to come up from the mine.

I crawled up on to the stinking rags and

imagined the lice moving over a little, annoyed at having to share the space with me.

The man they called Sheepskull tied a filthy apron around his belly, put on a pair of thick leather gloves and took down the cauldron hanging over the fire. Already the children were sitting waiting with bowls in their hands. I dug amongst the filthy blankets on my bed, found the bowl that was now mine and copied the others, waiting my turn.

A gray sludge of peas landed in the bowl. No one possessed a spoon so we had to shovel the food into our mouths with our hands. I shuddered when I saw a small dead mealworm amongst the peas and flicked it out with my finger. The girl alongside looked at the maggot on the floor and then at me. She must have thought I was being picky and, if I thought about it, maggots are food too, as Fredrik had said to me.

The children quickly emptied their bowls and were then allowed a swig of water. Several of them were gazing hungrily at a full bowl waiting on a bed four along from me. Miki's bed. She'd be allowed to eat when she finally finished her day's labour. The peas would be cold by then.

There was very little noise now. The two men with guns lounged around over by the door, muttering things I couldn't hear and laughing. Sheepskull sat by the fire eating pea soup. The man with the tattooed face said he wouldn't eat that mush even if Sheepskull paid him.

I smiled cautiously at the girl in the next bed. She didn't smile back, but looked at me as if I were some alien creature. A fish with two heads, or something. I realized what was alien about me: I was a child from the old world, who looked as they'd all looked before coal dust painted them black.

I turned to the boy on the other side. "Why does the coal need to be sorted?" I asked.

At first he said nothing, but after a while he cleared his throat. "Are you the little one's sister?" He flicked his eyes at Miki's bed.

I nodded.

"You look like each other," he said. "It'll be a long time before she gets here. She has to sort the coal every night. Because she's no good at the pick work."

"That's hardly surprising," I said. "She's a lot smaller than the rest of you. Wouldn't it be fairer if you took turns doing the sorting?"

The boy smiled, and several other children did the same.

"You there!" Sheepskull roared.

The girl beside Miki's bed had dared to steal a handful of her soup. She cringed and curled up on her mattress to avoid Sheepskull's grim gaze.

But even though she tried to hide it I could see from the triumph in her face how much one small portion of peas meant.

The boy with the green eyes was right when he said it would be a long time. Most of the children had fallen asleep by the time the door opened and Miki stepped in, accompanied by Dove.

But seeing her again gave me no joy. It made me so sad and angry that a huge lump grew in my throat and I gritted my teeth against the tears. My Miki—the smallest, the blackest, the most ragged of all, even though she was the newest! And none of the children who'd been abducted and brought here to crawl through darkness and dig coal showed such terror in their eyes as she did. My little sister was beside herself with terror.

"Miki," I said.

Her eyes searched the gloomy room. When she saw me she blinked several times, finding it hard to believe her eyes. Then her face lit up with a big smile and it was so wonderful to see her little teeth with the gap. She ran over and threw her arms around my neck.

"Is it you, Siri?" she whispered.

"Yes," I whispered back. "Forgive me. Forgive me for sending you off to find berries."

Miki let go of me and sat back on her knees. "Siri, my boots have got too small. I need new ones."

I shook my head. She hadn't changed at all, apart from her feet growing bigger. How could she talk of such a silly, unimportant thing now?

"I can't get you new boots," I said. "You'll have to make do with those."

"Some of the children only have rags on their feet," Miki said, feeling her boots. They were the ones I'd had when I was seven.

That was all the time we had to talk because Dove chased Miki to her own bed, where she devoured her peas and was given a swig of water by the pirate called Sheepskull.

Dove had keys hanging from her belt and one by one she chained the children. She locked the iron shackles around those thin little ankles, and most of the children didn't even wake up while she was doing it.

"Well?" Dove then said to the three pirates. "Won't Bragder be waiting for you?"

Looking stupid, they nodded and prepared to leave. The one with the tattooed face muttered that a word of thanks wouldn't be out of place since they'd slaved all day guarding the children.

"And you can tell Bragder to send someone who doesn't talk so damn much tomorrow," was the answer he received from Dove.

Once the pirates had gone she locked the door and went to the end of the room where her own bed stood. I watched her sit down to take off her boots. She was ugly, no doubt about that, but she wasn't old. She was worn and wasted in the way a piece of driftwood is scoured dry and white and brittle by the sea. She put her gun on the bed, doused the lamp on a small table beside her, and lay down. She gave several deep sighs. There was sadness in those sighs, a sadness without end.

Fear sleeps with a gun in its bed, I thought. Who would have thought that Whitehead's jailer was the sort to sleep with her gun?

I lay for a while blinking at the roof and trying to comprehend the incomprehensible. That this was my home now, that this was where I would live and where I would die. Possibly quite soon. Or in a few years. I wondered which was preferable.

"Siri?" Miki said.

"Yes?"

"Do you think Dad is missing us?"

"Ssh!" Dove hissed in the darkness. "Go to sleep so you can get through tomorrow."

We said no more, but after a while I began singing very quietly a song I used to sing to Miki in the pull-out bed at home. I didn't know if she was too far away to hear, but this is what I sang:

Mistress Plump fished with her toes,
How she did it no one knows,
But her plate was always full
With cod and ling and mackerel.

Lines and nets and suchlike gear
She did without for many a year,
Until a sailor floating by
Happened to catch her watchful eye.

Tripping over nets and ropes
He'd tumbled from his fishing boat.
Now drifting past and losing hope
He hung on tight to her small toe.

Mistress Plump was more than pleased
To drag him from the chilly seas
And take him home and get him dry
And let him stay, till by and by

She became a fisher wife
With nets and floats and fishing line.
And children two she had as well,
Two pretty girls with the fisherman.

◆ ◆ ◇ ◆ ◆

38

The Coal Seam

We were wakened early by Dove handing out bread and water. My shackle was hurting me and I tried to move it as I ate. But the shackles were tight, tight enough to prevent children slipping free no matter how thin they became on a bread and water diet.

Dove wore the bunch of keys on her hip like an iron bouquet. There weren't many flowers on Little Bluesay where Miki and I lived, but sometimes in spring we'd find dog roses. We'd give them to Dad and he'd put them in a cup on the kitchen table. We felt really fancy when we did that.

I looked at Miki. She was happy and waved a black hand at me. She thought everything was going to work out now we were together again. But how? This wasn't just a tangled net or an awkward trouser button or a rose thorn in the finger. This wasn't the kind of thing I could sort out just by being her big sister.

Once everyone had eaten and used their pots we had to wait for Bragder's pirates to arrive. They came striding through the door with the sour faces of men who'd just been woken. They weren't the same men as the day before. One had evil eyes, almost no teeth and a nasty scar right across his throat; the second wore a cloak of speckled fur, which I think was hooded seal—the others called him Punchfirst; the third was hardly taller than me and the most sullen of the three, probably because he was the one who'd be cooking peas and emptying chamber pots.

Dove unchained us from our beds, and with the shackle off my ankle I felt a little more hopeful. Things were going to work out, even if that only meant a slight improvement. One thing I knew for sure as we lined up to be marched to the mine: I'd help Miki fill her basket so she wouldn't be the last to come up.

Dove walked at the front, Punchfirst and the man with the scar brought up the rear. All three had guns, of course. Two new uglies were posted at the door to the mine and the man by the lift had a skipper's beard and several gold teeth, which I saw when he yawned.

I did as all the others did: unhooked a basket and picked up a lantern and a pick. Dove gave one of the boys a spill, which he lit from the lantern on the wall, then lit his own lantern and passed the spill on.

We were sent down the deep mineshaft three by three. I went into the lift with Miki and a girl with a squint.

My heart turned over as we began to move. The lift dropped quickly and endless lengths of blackness flashed past my eyes. It seemed we would never reach the bottom. The air became poor and I gazed up at the speck of light in the distant opening above. I was frightened by how far away it was and the darkness seemed choking.

When the lift eventually reached the bottom it landed so hard I toppled over. I stood up quickly and stepped out. How could anyone work in this oppressive darkness? I tried to turn up the flame of my lamp but it was already as high as it would go.

Miki's eyes gleamed like two moving points of light in the gloom. Suddenly she threw her arms round my neck. "I'm so glad that…" she said, but her voice broke before she could say the rest.

How awful it must have been for her all alone down here.

"Let's get to work," I said, taking her arms from my neck. "You'll have to show me where to go and then you and I will share everything we dig."

Miki nodded. She raised her lantern to show the different tunnels.

"I usually take that one, the smallest one," she said.

I looked at the small tunnel and the thought of

crawling in there was terrifying. With my basket on my back I was sure I'd get jammed.

"Why don't you take one of the bigger ones?" I asked.

"Because she'd just get chased away, of course," said the girl who'd been with us in the lift. I held up my lamp to take a better look at her.

"Chased away?" I said. "By who?"

"By someone older than her. That's how it works down here. The smaller you are the less say you have. Your sister has been in that little gallery ever since she arrived."

"Couldn't you try to get along instead of chasing one another away?" I pulled myself up to my full height. I wasn't afraid of this girl even though I could tell from her rags that she'd been here a long time.

The girl spat on the ground and bared her teeth in a scornful grin.

"There's no point in that sort of thing down here." She attached her pick to her basket, dropped to her knees and set off into one of the tunnels. She couldn't use her lamp hand for crawling, of course, so she disappeared into the darkness limping like a three-legged animal.

I looked at Miki and thought how small and brave she was. Day after day she had crawled around here and been chased away and bullied by the other children. It was so unfair it made me want to scream.

But I didn't. I nodded towards one of the galleries that gave us plenty of room and no risk of getting stuck.

"We'll take that one," I said. "As from now, no one will be chasing you away."

Miki straightened up and looked pleased. Then my little sister and I went together to hew coal from the great black seam.

We worked and worked until pain echoed through our bodies. I would never have believed that coal was so hard. I swung the pick with all my strength and if I was lucky a lump of coal fell out, but mostly the pick bounced back and gave us nothing to put in the basket.

Miki was even worse. She scarcely had the strength to raise the pick above her head and sometimes it slipped from her grasp and fell at her feet instead of striking where she aimed.

"Why does the coal have to be sorted?" I asked.

"It's because Whitehead only wants one piece every day. The hardest piece," Miki answered. "Once you've picked out that piece, you have to take it to him."

"So you've met him?" I said. "The captain?"

"Yes." Miki nodded. "He's nasty."

"What does he want the hard piece for?"

Miki paused and tried to rub the coal dust from her eyes. "He puts it in a binnacle," she said.

"A what?"

"I've seen it myself." She raised her pick and brought it down. "He puts the hardest piece into his binnacle. Sometimes there's a cracking noise inside."

"That can't be right," I said. A binnacle is a kind of cupboard for the compass on big ships. The reason Miki knew about such a thing was that right beneath the mermaid souvenir on the kitchen wall at home was a small painting of a ship. Dad used to point out all the different parts and tell us their names. But I couldn't think what anyone on shore would use a binnacle for.

"It's true, though," Miki said. "And do you know what else he has? A beast!"

"A beast?"

"Yes, a wolf beast, tied to the binnacle."

I shook my head. It sounded so strange I wondered if she'd imagined it. "Do the other children say it's a binnacle?"

They did, according to Miki. But then she added that they didn't actually *say* it, and then she said she didn't really know because she hadn't asked and no one talked to her. The children weren't allowed to speak to each other at night. Dove had decided that; she wanted the children to sleep and gather strength for the following day's work.

"Do you think it's really true that she's Whitehead's child?" I asked.

Miki nodded. "She is. I heard the pirates talking about it when I was in the hold of the *Snow Raven*."

"Really?"

"Yes. They said I reminded them of her."

"Reminded them? In what way?"

"They said I screamed as loudly as Dove did when she was a child. That she'd been a real little screamer."

"Are you sure?"

"Mm. They like her," Miki went on. "They said that when Whitehead dies she'll be the one to take over the captain's ring. They hope she'll sail with them." She raised her pick again and swung it with all her might at the coal seam. The pick connected with a crack.

Swing the pick, hew coal and work, work, work. That was all we did down in the underworld. I got blisters on my hands and my eyes ached from the dust and darkness. You had no choice but to get on with it if you wanted to return to the light.

A couple of hours later when our baskets were half full three children suddenly appeared in our gallery, two boys and a girl of eleven or twelve.

"Get out of here," one of the boys said.

Miki began to obey, but I held up my hand to stop her.

"No," I said.

The boy exchanged looks with the other two.

"This is our place," he said. "You're smaller so you have to go somewhere else."

"Dove didn't say small children have to go to small galleries," I said.

"Dove isn't the boss down here," the boy replied.

"There's enough coal for everyone," I said.

"Enough coal. But not enough air. Push off now."

"Push off yourself!" I said. "We were here first and we're not leaving."

The boy hesitated and looked as if he wanted to say something, but he turned and disappeared into the darkness, followed by the others. I raised my pick and slammed it into the seam so hard that a great pile of coal came loose and Miki and I shared the lumps between us. Our winnings were starting to look pretty good.

"We'll soon be able to go up!" I told Miki, feeling pleased in spite of everything.

Miki nodded and began singing those verses about Mistress Plump. Sometimes she changed it to Mistress Plump doing things with her toes other than fishing—picking her nose or hewing coal— and that made us laugh. Strange that we could stand here in all our misery and laugh!

But then something happened, something so sad and vile it made me more sick at heart than all the other sad and vile things at Whitehead's mine. The three children suddenly reappeared, sneaking in this time. I was startled to see them but tried to put a good face on it.

"What do you want this time?" was all I had time to say before the two boys seized my arms. The girl picked up Miki's basket and Miki was too scared to lift a finger to stop her when she emptied all Miki's coal into her and the boys' baskets. Then all three picked up their baskets and ran.

"Give it back!" I shouted, running after them.

But the girl raised her pick and said, "Get away or I'll chop you!" And they disappeared, ready to go up to the light and the fresh air because their baskets were full and they had no need to hew more coal.

"That'll teach you to stay away from this place!" were the girl's last words in the darkness.

◆ ◆ ◇ ◆ ◆

39

Captain Whitehead

When I think about it now, I don't know how we found the energy to fill Miki's basket again. She told me it wasn't the first time bigger children had stolen her coal. I remembered the stories I used to tell Miki when we lay in the pull-out bed at home, stories about a man who used children as if they were animals. What I didn't know then was that Whitehead's mine *transformed* children into animals. We were no longer children, but animals that moved on three legs, ate from bowls and looked out for ourselves and no one else.

When we eventually finished that day I was so tired that my limbs hardly seemed to belong to my body. They felt like dull, heavy lumps I was dragging behind me along the gallery all the way to the lift. The darkness made my head throb and I might as well have been blind. There was no sound of other picks still working. We were the last.

We tugged the rope and when the wooden cage landed with a crash I shooed Miki in.

"Up you go," I said. "I'll see you when I've finished the sorting."

Miki nodded and looked at me with anxious eyes.

"I'll be fine," I said, and smiled so she wouldn't see how frightened I was about what lay ahead. Meeting the captain!

The lift started without delay. Miki pressed her face to a crack between two boards and watched me for a short time before we were both swallowed up in darkness.

Once Miki was at the top the lift came back and it was my turn. During my journey up to the light I greedily sucked in the air as it grew fresher; it felt as though life was flowing back into my lungs. The headache eased and my eyes seemed to grow bigger as we went up.

By the time I reached the top, the other children had been marched off by Punchfirst and the other fellow, and only Dove and the pirate with gold teeth remained.

Dove stood by the heap of that day's coal. "When you've found the hardest piece, you have to take it to Whitehead," she said. "Only then may you eat and sleep."

"How can I tell which is the hardest?" I asked.

"You take two pieces and scratch them against

each other. You discard the piece with the deepest scratch and keep the other, which you then scratch against another piece. Once again you discard the one with the deepest scratch. And you go on like that until you've worked your way through the lot."

She sat down at her small table, which had been laid with things presumably brought over from the *Raven*: smoked seal, porridge and a red apple on a plate.

I looked at the enormous heap of coal in front of me. It was crazy. We hewed coal from morning to night without a break and all this coal was brought up in the lift from underground. And Whitehead wanted one single piece. The hardest piece! Crazy! What did he want it for? For the life of me I couldn't work it out as I sat there hour after hour scratching one piece against another.

It was hard work. The room was lit only by a couple of lamps and I had to screw up my eyes to compare the scratches. As my head grew more and more weary there were times when I had to start again. Time after time I imagined I'd made a mistake and discarded the harder piece.

At last, my hands shaking and bleeding with the effort, I had one piece left. The hardest piece.

"I've finished," I said in a hoarse voice.

Dove stood up and drank the last mouthful from her mug. She slung her gun over her shoulder. She had ordered the pirate with gold teeth to refill all the oil lamps, but now she nodded to him and then at the coal on the floor.

"See about clearing this away," she said. "After that you can go back to Bragder."

The fellow marched off to fetch a two-wheeled handcart and a shovel and as Dove and I went out through the door I heard him scraping up the coal we had worked so hard to dig. It would be tipped out in the snow.

Side by side we stepped out into the black night. My breath became glittering steam in the cold air. Waves of green light billowed across the sky and shifted to white and blue and then back to green. They were the northern lights, which I'd seen many times before and always thought were beautiful. But nothing could be beautiful at that moment because I was about to meet Whitehead.

What if the piece of coal I was carrying wasn't the hardest? What if I was mistaken and Whitehead knew it? What would he do? *And why did he need the hardest piece?*

We stopped at the cottage with the lit-up windows. Confused, I looked at Dove and she nodded at the door.

"Go on," she said.

I knocked very quietly on the door. It was amazing that anyone could hear it, but the door opened and there he was, in the doorway. The captain. He looked old and young at the same time, an elderly man and a youngster in the same body. His eyes were light as water, but so sharp I could almost feel them pierce my skin and see the cold, wet, swelling fear that lay within.

He wasn't wearing a hat and his hair was tied up in a bun. Hair as white as Dove's.

"The new child?" he said.

I didn't know whether to answer, whether it was actually a question, or directed at me. I gave a slight nod.

Whitehead gave me a look that was impossible to interpret. Perhaps it was just indifferent.

"Do you have something for me?" he asked.

I nodded again and handed him the piece of coal.

"Thank you," he said in a light voice, as if we were two friends at the dinner table and I'd just passed him the butter dish.

"That's us finished for the day." Dove gave me a nudge.

I don't know how I found the courage at that moment. Perhaps because I believed I'd spend the rest of my life hewing coal for Whitehead, in which case I needed to know why. And if my question made him angry, if it made him order my death, it was all the same to me. It really was!

"Why do you need the hardest pieces?"

Dove spluttered. One of Whitehead's mine children had dared speak to him.

But Whitehead looked at me with more interest. There was a long silence and then he said, "Bragder told me that you were looking for me. Is that true? Did you come here of your own free will?"

"Yes," I answered, even though it felt wrong. He'd made it sound as if I'd come out of longing. As if he, Whitehead, rather than my sister, had drawn me there.

Whitehead studied me a little longer, then he looked at Dove and said, "Wait here. The girl can come with me for a moment." He stepped to one side and gestured for me to enter.

I didn't want to. Every ounce of my being objected to going with him, but there was little I could do about it. Whitehead had invited me in as a guest and while Dove leaned on the cottage wall to wait, as she'd been told to, I stepped nervously over the threshold.

Once inside I stared. I'd never seen a room like it. There were many lamps and the light they gave was good and warm and beautiful. Everywhere, high and low, on shelves and on tables, lay papers with drawings that looked like plans. And there were mechanical parts everywhere: screws, springs, objects of iron and brass, inkwells and dried-up

quill pens. But that wasn't all. In the middle of the room stood a weird contraption that actually did remind me of a binnacle. A big binnacle with a long wooden arm attached. And harnessed between two shafts on this arm—and this is no word of a lie— was a wolf. A real white wolf with patches over its eyes. It was in an awful condition, under-nourished and its fur dull. In fact, its fur was rubbed away in places and there were sores on its skin. There it stood, quite still and silent. I could easily have taken it for a stuffed animal if I hadn't seen the rise and fall of its belly as it breathed.

Whitehead closed the door and we were alone. Him, me and the wolf.

* * ◇ * *

40

Pressure and Heat

Whitehead didn't say anything for a long time. He studied me as I looked wide-eyed at the papers, books and mechanical bits and pieces, at the white wolf and the contraption it was harnessed to.

Then I glimpsed my own face reflected in the globe on top of the contraption. I was frightened at how black it had become, just like the other children's faces. How quickly I'd become one of them! How quickly all traces of the old world had been erased. I spat on my hand and rubbed away as much of the coal dust as I could. I looked at my reflection again. That was better. I was myself again. The old Siri, not just a mine child.

Whitehead smiled. He took a couple of long strides into the room and picked up a paper on which was some sort of calculation.

"You were wondering what I use the hardest pieces of coal for," he said.

I nodded but wasn't brave enough to meet his eye.

Whitehead sat down on an armchair and studied the calculation as if he were reading a map. I could see he was tired. Tired and careworn to the core of his being.

He looked up from the paper as if suddenly remembering I was there. "Do you know how diamonds are born?" he asked.

"No," I answered, for I knew nothing about diamonds. I knew how to set nets and how to crack the skull of a herring with my thumb. I knew how to make a keep box for fish and how to tar a boat, but I knew nothing at all about diamonds.

"They're born in heat and pressure," Whitehead said. "Far, far down in the earth. Down there, in the very marrow of the earth, there is enormous heat and the pressure is so great that the coal down there is melted and compressed into diamonds."

He stood up, let the calculation fall to the floor and he didn't seem bothered when he stepped on it. Suddenly it was no more important than any of the other papers that lay in their hundreds, scribbled on, crossed out and ink-blotched.

He walked over to the contraption and now, for the first time, the wolf showed signs of life. It gave a start and tried to walk, but the harness pegs were locked in some way and the wolf couldn't move from the spot. At once it became both angry and frightened, trampling with its enormous paws, twisting this way and that and making stifled growls.

Whitehead stroked his contraption as if it were a living thing. He wore a ring on his right hand, the captain's gold ring, decorated with a pattern of small, graceful bones that was both beautiful and horrible.

"I built this machine," he said. "And it's going to create diamonds for me."

He opened the globe at the top of the machine and brushed away some ash.

"People say..." he said, studying his hand, which was gray with the ash, "...that I am an evil man. But it's not true."

I couldn't answer, but Whitehead surely knew that I would have contradicted him if I'd dared. Which was why he looked me in the eye and said:

"I grew up on the *Snow Raven*, you know. My father was the pirate captain and his crew was feared across all the Ice Sea."

"I see," I mumbled.

"I hated the pirate life," Whitehead went on. "I hated the sorrow and misery we caused. I used to flee to the captain's cabin when we boarded a cargo vessel. I would hide from the screams and the killing. My father had an encyclopedia—he'd stolen it, of course, and he never read it. But I did."

Whitehead sat in the armchair again. He looked at a point far, far away, and when he continued it was in an almost mechanical voice. In his father's encyclopedia he read about diamonds and how they were formed and that was when he decided to build a machine to create them. He wanted to show his father that it was possible to become rich without stealing from others.

The old captain had no time for Whitehead's ideas. He said they were arrogant and when Whitehead was only sixteen they parted as enemies. Year after year he dug for coal, seeking a piece that could survive the pressure and heat produced by the machine he'd built. Every piece he tested either burned to ash or was crushed to dust—or both. But the idea of diamonds had taken such a hold of him that he couldn't give up the search. When his father died in a sea battle, Whitehead was so busy digging for coal he couldn't find time to attend the funeral.

But the pirates on the *Snow Raven* came looking for him and gave him his father's ring, since it was an ancient custom in our waters that the child of a dead captain took over the captain's ring. For anyone else to take it would lead to bad luck: that's what was said, anyway, and pirates were superstitious people. After receiving the ring Whitehead had a dream. A dream that would change everything.

There are times when we wake after dreaming

and know that the dream has been special. We know it has been trying to say something, that it will come true. The dream that came to Whitehead on that occasion was about a child. The dream told him it was a child who would find the Right Piece, the piece of coal that at long last would enable his contraption to create a diamond.

Whitehead then gave an order to his crew: Get me children. Anything else you lay hands on when ramming, boarding, burning and killing, you may keep. But give me the children.

He looked at me with his tired, pale eyes. "I've often dreamt of the child who will find that piece for me. My dreams cannot be wrong. That's why you must go on digging."

Once again I stood there with nothing to say. What was so strange was that he didn't know he was evil. He believed that the mine and the children toiling in it was all for a good cause. Well, it was possibly good at the start, but somewhere along the way it had become evil. And Whitehead didn't understand that, which made it all the more terrifying.

Telling me about his work seemed to have lifted Whitehead's spirits and he rose quickly and went back to his machine. He put the lump of coal I'd given him into the globe, closed it and turned numerous knobs and screws. Then he fetched a spill, lit it from one of the lamps and went to the machine. The wolf was trampling uneasily on the spot and tossing its head back, but it was tied too tightly to move properly. Whitehead opened a hatch in the cupboard where the globe was resting. Inside the cupboard he lit a special burner with a much fiercer flame than an ordinary lamp. He took a cane from against the wall, and removed a split pin from the harness, allowing the wolf to walk in circles. As the wolf walked Whitehead beat it with the cane to make it go faster. He struck blow after blow until the wolf's hide was flayed open, and then he struck even harder. The idea was that the wolf's strength would build up pressure in the machine and the pressure, together with the heat from the burner, would create a diamond for Whitehead.

Watching this made me feel ill and I wept to see the wounds on the wolf's hide deepen and bleed. At long last, there was an explosion inside the globe. The wolf came to a halt and the beating stopped.

Whitehead replaced the split pin. The wolf was breathing heavily from its efforts and the mistreatment. I couldn't stop crying. I hated the man in front of me, hated him for using children as though they were animals and animals as though they were things.

Whitehead opened the globe and studied the dust, which was all that was left of the coal. Then he looked at me, strangely unconcerned. "Not this time, either," he said.

He went to the door. "The girl can leave now."

Dove gestured for me to come and I went without a word. In the doorway I stopped and turned round. "My friend, is he…what I mean is, can you tell me what will happen to him?" I asked.

Whitehead had collected the dust in one hand. In his other he was holding one of his many papers and studying it. He gave me the briefest of looks.

"Your friend?" he said. "Bragder has made him an offer on my behalf. But he's obviously stubborn." He sighed. "It's a pity, because Bragder says he'd make a good pirate. Strong. Brave. Not all are made of the right stuff these days. He has until morning to make up his mind."

He hesitated for a moment and appeared to be thinking about something else while he looked at me. Then his face lit up. "It was nice to talk to you," he said.

. . ◇ . .

True Dreams

All I could think about the following day was Fredrik. Worry gnawed at me like a rat, hour after hour, as I hewed coal deep underground. What would he do? Would he accept their offer and become one of them? Or would they kill him?

Of course it would be awful if he became a pirate, went to sea, abducted children and imprisoned them in the *Snow Raven*'s hold ready for the mine.

But I'd rather he be a pirate than dead. Because in his heart he'd always be good, kind Fredrik.

Miki and I stayed away from the larger galleries. I wanted to be the last in the lift so I could see Whitehead again and hear Fredrik's decision. That would only be possible if I did the sorting.

When the time came I didn't have the patience to sort properly. I scratched the pieces against each other as fast as possible and chose more or less randomly which lump to put aside and which to keep. At last, with my heart racing, I had only one piece left.

"Finished already?" Dove said, looking up from her supper.

I nodded and stood up. The pirate who'd hauled up the lift that day was called Porkchops. She was tall and gangly, with big fleshy lips and a flea-bitten fur cap on her head.

"You're a smart girl, quick too," she said, pleased that she'd soon be allowed back to the ship.

Dove gave me and the coal in my hand a suspicious look, but she said nothing. She swallowed her last piece of salmon and stood up. Porkchops went to fetch the cart and Dove and I stepped out into the starlit night.

The moment I knocked on Whitehead's door it flew open as if he'd been standing inside waiting. When he saw me, he became eager, and almost anxious. He chucked me under the chin.

"Is it you?" he said.

I was so surprised and frightened that I couldn't say a word. He went to fetch a damp rag and used it to scrub my face clean of coal dust. When he'd finished he took me under the chin again and gave such a big smile that cold shivers ran up and down my spine.

"Come," he said, pointing into the cottage.

I stepped into the light and warmth. Just as she'd done the evening before, Dove leaned back against the outside wall in spite of its coating of frost. Whitehead closed the door and went over to some plans. He looked at them closely, then went to his machine. The wolf jumped and growled, but Whitehead paid no attention. He picked up several papers from the floor.

"I'd like to ask about Fredrik," I said. "My friend. Has he given you an answer?"

Whitehead went on studying his papers. "It's about time," he muttered. "But have we thought of everything?"

He bent and inspected several screws on the machine and checked the shafts attached to the wolf. Suddenly the wolf attacked, struck with its jaws and I thought it would bite his hand off. But it couldn't reach.

Whitehead looked at me, smiled and shook his head. "Stupid beast."

"Mm, Fredrik…" I said, but Whitehead cut me off in sudden, extreme irritation.

"Shh!" He eyed me with a piercingly cold stare. "Stop talking rubbish now. Don't you understand that we have to concentrate?"

"On what?" I was baffled and wondered why he'd seemed pleased to see me. "What's happened?"

Whitehead stared at me for some time with a

look of something like bliss in his eyes.

"What's happened?" he said. He shook his head and laughed at the same time. "What has happened is a miracle. I've had another dream. About the child who'll bring me the Right Piece. And you know…"

He pulled up a stool, sat down beside me and put his hand under my chin again. "For the first time in all these years I saw the child's face. And the face…was yours!"

He stood up and walked over to the machine. Moving rapidly, he checked the parts once more, polished the inside of the globe with his thumb, took a few steps back and looked at me and the piece of coal in my hand.

"M–my face?" I said.

He nodded.

"But if it was only a dream…"

"No." Now he sounded stern. I realized that his mood could change in the blink of an eye and that he could become dangerous if anyone said the wrong thing.

"I explained it all to you yesterday. *Weren't you listening?*"

"Yes, but…"

"Some dreams are more than just ordinary dreams," Whitehead said. "And when you wake you know they were trying to tell you something true. I have dreamt of a child for many years. A small child who'll come to me with the Right Piece in its hand. But since the child's face has been black with coal dust I've never been able to see it. But last night, last night I had the dream again and the child had washed its face. Just as you did yesterday!"

I didn't say anything. I didn't dare. That I was the one destined to find the Right Piece for Whitehead seemed an impossible thought. I'd been here the shortest length of time and I wasn't in the least familiar with the mine.

Whitehead was so sure the dream had told him the truth that he seemed not the least worried about improbabilities. He took the lump of coal from my hand and went to his machine. The hairs on the wolf's back bristled and it began stamping on the spot and showing its teeth.

"Are you going to beat it?" I asked.

"Beat what?" Whitehead asked.

"Surely you don't have to beat it?" I said. "Please, please, don't beat it."

When Whitehead understood I was talking about the wolf—he had long since stopped thinking of it as an animal and used it as a thing—he put his head to one side and smiled. He had the expression of a mother about to tell her child it must take its medicine even though it tastes bad.

"Don't think about that," he said. "We're going to create a diamond."

He solemnly placed the piece of coal in the globe and closed it properly, tightening all the screws. With a spill, he lit the burner in the compartment beneath the globe, then he fetched the cane—the horrible cane that was leaning on the wall. The wolf seemed to recognize the smell of the cane and grew even more uneasy. When Whitehead removed the split pin from the wolf's harness, it began its journey round and round, and as it circled round and round Whitehead struck it blow after blow.

I pressed my hands to my ears, shut my eyes and screamed so as not to hear or see what was going on. But when the explosion came at last, I heard it and opened my eyes.

The wolf stopped. Exhausted and bleeding, it rested while Whitehead replaced the split pin, undid the screws and lifted the top of the globe. He studied the gray dust and it was impossible to read the expression on his face. Then he picked up the dust and threw it at me.

"What's wrong?" he snarled. "Why did you bring me such useless rubbish?"

"I'm sorry," I said.

"Were you careless with the sorting?"

"No, I wasn't."

He sat down, suddenly looking extremely old. He looked as tired and worn as he had yesterday, before his new dream brought a spark back to his eyes. After a while he said, "From now on you must be very, very careful when you sort the coal. Do you understand? You mustn't let the Right Piece slip through by being careless."

"Of course not," I said. There was something uncanny about the way he knew I'd been slapdash with the day's sorting.

He stood up and went to the door. "Dove!" he snapped.

"What, Dad?" Dove said.

"As of now, this girl and this girl alone is to do the sorting. Understood? She is to stay on the surface and rest while the other children are digging coal." He looked at me and his eyes were mild again. "That way you'll have all the energy you need to find it." He thought for a while and then he said: "And she's to have better food too. I'll get Bragder to send up salmon and fowl and…other tasty things. I'll have a word with him about it."

"Yes, Dad," Dove said.

"Right." Whitehead gave me a pat on the head and shooed me out of the door.

"Has Fredrik given his answer yet?" I asked.

"Who?" Whitehead said.

"My friend. The one who's a prisoner on the *Snow Raven*."

Whitehead was so taken up with his new ideas

that it took him some time to understand who I meant.

"No, no…he doesn't want to."

I felt as if the ground beneath my feet was falling away and for a moment I blacked out.

"So what will happen to him? Will he be shot?"

Whitehead nodded, his mind on other things. "Yes. Early tomorrow morning. Now I need to be left in peace."

* * ◇ * *

Dove

That night I lay in bed and wept. When morning came the pirates were going to shoot Fredrik. My good, kind Fredrik. Why had he said no?

The answer was actually very simple. Fredrik knew that it was impossible to be one thing in your heart and another in reality. All those years of trying to sail away from the memories of his little sister had taught him that.

But it wasn't only Fredrik; I was crying for Miki too. Whitehead had decided I shouldn't do any digging and that meant that Miki would be down the mine on her own. It would be the end of her. Mine children didn't last long, particularly those who were robbed of their coal and often of their pea soup too. Miki would grow thinner and more crooked before my eyes and I wouldn't be allowed to do anything to help her.

All around me the other children were sleeping.

They were breathing deeply and some were sniffling with colds. After a little while I heard someone talking to me in the darkness.

"Try to sleep."

It was Dove. I couldn't see her, but I recognized the voice.

I didn't answer, just went on crying, and I heard her leave her bed. She lit her lamp and came over to mine.

"You must get some sleep," she whispered. "There's nothing to be gained by lying awake crying."

"I can't sleep," I said. "I'm so sad."

"It will pass," Dove said.

"It will never pass. They're going to shoot my friend at dawn and my sister will die in the mine."

Dove sighed. The shadows gave her face an eerie look—hard and staring, like an eel.

"Do you believe I'm the one who'll find the Right Piece?" I asked.

"I don't believe the Right Piece exists except in Whitehead's dreams," Dove answered. "He can go on feeding coal into that machine until his dying day and all he'll get back is ash."

She raised her lamp. "If you don't have to work the pick and you have better food you'll survive this," she said. "There are times when you have to help yourself and no one else."

I shook my head. "If I do that I won't be able to live with myself."

"Yes, you will." Dove looked me in the eye. "It's always possible. People find a way."

She said nothing for a little while and seemed to be having difficult thoughts. Then she took the bunch of keys from her belt and unlocked the shackle on my ankle.

"Come with me. I'll show you something."

We stepped out into the ice-cold, creaking night. Dove had her gun on her shoulder and a lamp in her hand. We halted outside the cottage where Whitehead kept his machine. The lights were out and Dove opened the door as she pointed to the smaller cottage.

"That's where he sleeps," she said in a low voice. "But don't worry, he won't wake up. His work with the machine exhausts him."

We went in and Dove lit all the lamps from her own. The big white wolf was still harnessed to the machine but our arrival didn't seem to excite it.

When Dove went over and stroked its head it didn't bite her. She took the patches off its eyes and what big, fine, gray eyes they were, and they looked so calm. The wolf licked Dove's hand and she freed it from the harness.

The wolf walked a few steps, stretched, shook itself and then pressed its head against Dove's hip.

She scratched it and took a bone from her jacket pocket. The wolf devoured it in a trice, splintering the bone in its strong jaws.

Dove looked at me as I stood there dumb with amazement.

"Whitehead bought this wolf many years ago on the Wolf Islands," she said. "And I've come here at night ever since she was young. Whitehead doesn't know."

The wolf was so content it almost fell asleep with its head against Dove's hip. After a while, however, it stirred itself and walked around the room several times, sniffing at things and sneezing when it got ash in its nose.

When the wolf approached me I backed away in fear. I hadn't forgotten that day outside Nanni's hut when I'd stood eye to eye with a white wolf, its teeth bared and the fur bristling on its neck.

"Just stand still," Dove said.

I held out my hand cautiously. The wolf's fur was thick and rather dirty. It let me scratch it for a short time before going back to Dove, who threw her arms around the beast as if it were her best friend in all the world. When she looked up from the embrace her eyes were shining.

"I was supposed to be a mine child too, you know," she said.

"Really?"

She nodded. "I was captured by Whitehead's pirates. I was just a girl at the time."

"I thought you were Whitehead's daughter."

She shook her head.

"No, well, perhaps I became his daughter. Before that, I was the daughter of other people."

She gave the wolf another piece of meat and while the wolf chewed on it Dove told me how she had become Whitehead's daughter.

She told me that when she was small she was very frightened of everything. She was frightened of spiders, frightened of the dark and frightened of people she didn't know. And whenever she had to step into her father's boat he had to make the boat fast with double ropes because she was afraid she might fall in. She wept whenever it was time for her to scrub the floor for her mother because she was afraid the hot water would burn her feet. In fact, she was afraid of absolutely everything it was possible to be afraid of.

But on the day the pirates captured her she was more terrified than she'd ever been. She screamed when they hurled her into the *Raven*'s hold and she kept on screaming all night. By the time the pirates came to give her bread and water in the morning, terror had turned her hair white. When Whitehead saw her long white hair he was more than delighted and said she could well be his own flesh and blood!

He decided there and then that she could become his daughter if she wanted to. That way she wouldn't have to crawl and creep, hew and carry, eat rotten peas and dry bread, and instead she'd learn to be a warden for the mine children.

Dove looked at me and stroked the white wolf's head. "I said yes. I chose to become his daughter. I did it because I was afraid—afraid of the toil, of being broken by work in the mine, of dying and being no more."

They held three days and three nights of celebrations for her on board the *Snow Raven*. She was given good things to eat and drink and they tossed her in the air to loud cheers. Whitehead changed her name to Dove, because that—he said— was just what he needed to make his enterprise successful: a raven that stole the children and a dove that cared for them.

The days became months and the months became years. Dove carried out her role and Whitehead was pleased with her. Although there were occasions when she might have been able to escape, she chose not to. In fact there was nowhere for someone like her to go, because she'd bought her freedom at the expense of her soul.

She looked at me again. "You think it's impossible to live knowing that you've helped no one but yourself. But I've found a way. On nights when my anguish is too great to bear, I come here. I release the wolf from her harness so she can move and I take the patches off her eyes so she's no longer blind. A wolf doesn't care that you've sold your soul—she likes me, loves me even. That's what makes it possible for me to live."

She let go of the wolf, walked over to me and took me by the shoulders.

"You can be like me," she said. "You'd be able to eat well and dress properly. And when you can't sleep you can come here with me if you want to. Sometimes when I'm here I'm happy!"

I looked at her, looked into those eyes that were like water mixed with milk.

"I don't believe that," I said.

Dove took her hands away and sat down on a stool. "Would you rather lie in bed weeping then?"

"No," I said. "I want to save the lives of my friend and my sister. And the rest of the children too, even though I don't like them. It's not their fault they behave like animals."

She sighed. "You can't save them. Can't you see that?"

"Yes, I can! If you lend me your gun!"

She laughed, but it was an empty, frightened laugh. "I can't do that. Come on, we must go back now."

"No." I stood in front of the door and blocked her.

She raised her voice. "Bringing you here was a mistake!" she said. "I thought you might understand."

"I'll never understand how you can keep children as prisoners even though you know it's wrong."

"I made my choice."

"You can change your mind."

"No, it's too late for that. It became too late when I agreed to be Whitehead's daughter."

"You were never his real daughter. You're not like him. Who you are has nothing to do with your hair!"

Dove started to cry and sank to the floor. She touched her hair—the hair that terror had turned white and ugly.

"You have beautiful hair," she said. "Coal black."

"There's nothing beautiful about coal," I answered. "Please help me."

She smiled, still stroking her hair. "My hair was beautiful too, though you may not believe it. But it wasn't black."

"Was it brown?" I asked.

"It was red," Dove said. "Thick and red like molten gold."

I studied her carefully for a long time. Then I said, "I know someone with hair like that."

* * ◇ * *

The Right Piece

The white wolf padded around the room, sniffing at this and that. Now and again it licked the floor; perhaps Whitehead had spilled food when he was busy with his calculations.

While the wolf was occupied I sat down beside Dove. "My friend, the one they're going to shoot at dawn, has exactly the hair you had when you were little. He told me he had a sister once and that pirates took her. They'd been crab fishing together."

Dove swallowed and began to tremble.

I went on: "He's spent twelve years sailing the seas trying to forget, but he can't. That's why he decided to help by coming with me and trying to free my sister. But they discovered us, which is why I'm Whitehead's prisoner and why my friend is to be shot in the morning. He's called Fredrik, and I guess your real name is Hanna, isn't it?"

The moment I said "Hanna" it was as if a dam burst within Dove and she began to weep. The wolf went to her at once and nuzzled her, but she carried on.

"Please, please lend me your gun," I said.

She hid her face in her hands and shook her head. "He left me," she said. "He left me alone on that skerry when I didn't want him to."

"He's come to make up for it. Don't you understand? It's never too late to make amends for something you've done!"

Dove sat for a long time with her face in her hands. The first gray shades of dawn light seeped in through the window.

In the end I cleared my throat and asked, "So, what do you say?"

She dried her cheeks and stuck her nose in the air. "We won't be helping anyone if we run down to the *Raven* with one gun between us," she said. "All the pirates on board are armed. We'll have to use our heads."

"We?" I said. "Do you mean you'll help me?"

She nodded. "Yes, I'll help you."

I felt a rush of emotion. I don't know if it was relief or joy or fear, but it made me leap up from the floor.

"So then?" I said. "How do we go about it?"

Dove thought hard. "One gun is enough to shoot one captain," she said.

"Sh-shoot him? Would you really do that?"

She shook her head. "All we need is for him to *believe* I'll shoot him. Come with me!"

The wolf didn't look at us as we locked it in and hurried from the cottage. It was light outside now, lighter than I'd realized, and my heart missed a beat. We had to reach the *Raven* before it was too late!

In a low, breathless voice Dove explained what we should do.

"We'll wake him in his bed and order him to come down to the ship and pardon Fredrik. The pirates love their captain so they won't try anything as long as I'm holding a gun to his head. Once they've..." She paused and swallowed hard. "Once they've freed Fredrik, you and he must go and release all the children. And then..."

"Yes?" I said. "What do we do then?"

"You run for all you're worth!" Dove said. "And I'll keep Whitehead in my sights as long as possible."

"Aren't you going to run too?" I asked.

"We'll have to see what becomes of me. The important thing is to give you as much of a start as possible. Take my keys."

I took the bunch from her belt. As I was putting them in my jacket pocket I noticed something already there. The stone Einar had given me back in Seglen. I put the keys in the other pocket and we set off across the black snow. I was truly glad that Dove had a gun and that I wasn't going to have to fight the coldest and most evil man in the Ice Sea with nothing but a stone.

When we stopped outside Whitehead's sleeping quarters Dove turned to me. "Siri," she said.

"Yes?"

"My wolf. Please set her free, will you? She won't hurt you. Whitehead is the only one she hates."

I nodded and then, when we'd both taken a deep breath, I opened the door as quietly as I could.

Dove crept forward with the gun and I followed. The cottage was simple. A fire, almost out, in the fireplace, a table polished by wear, and a curtained bed. Everything was clean and almost austere. It might have been the home of any fishing family.

I cautiously drew aside the bed curtains. He looked so peaceful lying there, his white hair like a flower on the pillow, his eyes gently closed. An old man and a young one asleep in the same body.

"Wake up!" Dove said. She must have heard how frightened she sounded because she cleared her throat and said in a louder voice, "Get up!"

He opened his eyes, those pale eyes with pupils like needle points. He looked at Dove. He looked at me. It was impossible to read anything in his face.

"Get up!" Dove said again.

Whitehead sat up and put his feet on the floor. He wore white linen night clothes. He sat like that for a while with his big hands resting on his knees. He said nothing, just looked again at Dove and then again at me.

"Y-you must let Fredrik go," Dove said.

Whitehead didn't answer.

"Siri's friend," Dove went on. "Siri's friend. The one who's being held in the hold of the *Raven*. Let him go."

Whitehead still did not answer. He sat there, silent, looking from one to the other of us, and thinking. And when he'd finished thinking he said calmly: "Treachery."

Dove swallowed. She was afraid of him, no doubt about that, and it didn't escape Whitehead, of course. She was the one holding the gun, but he knew, as a father would, which of them was trembling like prey.

"You have betrayed me," Whitehead said. "Now, at last, after all these years…you want to deprive me of the glory."

"No," said Dove. "You're mistaken."

But Whitehead was convinced of Dove's motives. Spurred on by my arrival at the mine— the Right Child—she'd decided, so he thought, to make the machine her own and thus become the creator of the first diamond. The invention would bring her fame and would also put an end to misery and piracy.

"You involved this girl in your plans," he said. "You tempted her with the promise of her friend's life. Was there anything besides that? Are you two planning to share the glory when the first diamond is born?"

"Release Fredrik!" Dove was becoming desperate. "Go to Bragder and order him to do so!"

"No."

"What do you mean 'No'?"

"I won't do it," Whitehead said calmly. "I'd rather die."

"You'd rather die?"

"Yes, I would."

"But why?"

"I've given my life to the machine and now you're going to take it from me. I might as well die." He gave a weak smile. "Let's see which shot rings out first: you shooting me or the one that kills your friend on the ship." He glanced at the thin glass of the window where the threat of dawn was revealing itself.

Dove was crying, her finger trembling on the trigger of the gun. Whitehead's merciless eyes pierced her to the core. His face was rigid, its muscles tensed by what I believe was hatred. And then, all at once, he shot forward and grabbed the gun from her hand. It was easy, almost as if she gave it to him.

She covered her face. "I don't want your machine, Father. There's no glory in it."

"You know there is," Whitehead said.

"But the children…"

"The children are working for a good cause."

"No! You've let it all turn your head. The children are dying!"

Whitehead said nothing for a moment.

"Things have turned *your* head." He cocked the gun and aimed at her.

There are times when your body does things without you giving the orders. Sometimes, when it really matters and you're faced with two choices, one black, the other white, actions happen of their own accord, even though you're so off balance that your will seems frozen. When I saw Whitehead preparing to shoot Dove, I felt how close the end was.

My hand slipped into my pocket and I heard myself say, "I have something for you."

Whitehead's eyes shifted from Dove to me. He looked at what I was holding: an angular piece of stone about the size of a cod's head. In the hours I'd spent down the mine it had turned as black as coal.

His eyes narrowed. "What have you got there?"

"You're right," I said. "We wanted to steal your glory. When I brought you a piece of coal yesterday I hadn't chosen it out of carelessness. I gave you the wrong piece on purpose and I kept the Right Piece for myself. Take it. Spare Dove and take it."

Slowly, very slowly he approached me. Slowly, very slowly he bent to look at the black stone. Slowly, very slowly he took it in his hand and I watched him turning it, watched his trembling fingers close around it to feel its hardness, and all the time I was silently praying that the coal dust wouldn't rub off.

"The Right Piece," Whitehead said in a whisper. "So hard!" He shook his head and his eyes glistened. "I've never felt such a hard piece of coal."

He looked quickly at Dove and at me, but suddenly we were no more important than the furniture in front of him. He rushed out to the cottage where he kept his machine—where the wolf was.

And the wolf was not harnessed.

He had no time to shoot. The only thing we heard was a short, harrowing roar and then silence. Whitehead was no more.

For the things we do in this life leave a trail. One such trail might be a cormorant that taps on your window one day and begs for a piece of fish. There were many young creatures that could have been

Whitehead's cormorant. Dove, perhaps, or me. But the wolf cub that was born in a snowy lair on the Wolf Islands and grew up to drive Whitehead's machine—that, in the end, was the one.

♦ ♦ ◇ ♦ ♦

The Ring

I looked at Dove and Dove looked at me, but it was only for a second and then we ran. We'd heard no shot from down on the ice. There might still be time to save Fredrik.

We'd gone only a short distance when Dove stopped. "Wait," she said, and her eyes flashed.

"Come on!" I pulled at her arm. "Don't waste time."

But Dove shook her head and turned back. "I have to fetch something."

"What?"

"Something important. You run on and delay them!" she yelled.

I ran. I ran as I'd never run before, through the coal-black snow that became lighter as I went. First the shade of the steel used to sharpen knives, then the skin of a gurry shark, then like our weather-beaten houses in Blue Bay, then the pale gray of dried fish, then like the most washed-out pebbles in the sea. And then, at last, white. As I ran a shot rang out and the hairs on my neck rose in horror. They had already shot him.

But then came another shot, and another.

When I finally reached the ice I heard laughter and cheering and more shots. What was going on?

As soon as I arrived I understood. The ice around the *Snow Raven* was alive with pirates. It appeared that every man and woman of them had got up bright and early and the source of their great amusement was the two people with guns who stood a short distance away. Another target-shooting competition was under way.

The men taking turns to shoot were Baldy and Beardy, the two uglies with whom I'd sailed in *Cuttlefish*, but they weren't firing at a snowman this time. Today's target was a flesh and blood human— Fredrik! He was standing straight as a fir tree, hands and feet tied, waiting for Baldy or Beardy to manage to hit him. Each time one of them missed, the other pirates cheered, slapped their thighs and laughed until the tears ran. They hurled snowballs at the two marksmen and it was obvious that both men were fuming with rage and shame.

"Stop!" I shouted.

They all turned around.

"A runaway!" someone yelled.

"Hands up, girl!" another shouted, at which every one of the ruffians aimed their gun at me.

My eyes searched for Bragder, the mate. There he was, standing with a couple of others, pipe in mouth and staring at me in amazement. It clearly wasn't every day that a child from the mine came down to the bay.

I walked towards him with my hands in the air. Some of the pirates made a move to grab me but Bragder shooed them away.

"Let's hear what she has to say." He looked at me, his black teeth chewing slowly on the mouthpiece of his pipe. "Well?"

"Please…" I tried to speak in a steady voice. "Please don't shoot Fredrik."

That set all the pirates laughing again. I didn't know why, until I realized that what I'd said sounded ridiculous.

Bragder took the pipe from his mouth and smiled. "I wish I could do what you want, because you certainly know how to ask nicely. But it's like this, you see: I've announced a competition to find which of these two is the better shot. So why don't you just stand here beside me and watch rather than spoil our fun."

Fun? Well, I could see they liked their fun, the *Raven's* pirates, so I said loudly, "Which is better? You mean which is less bad."

Bragder laughed and the other pirates joined in, except for Baldy and Beardy, of course.

"Watching those two shoot reminds me of a story," I went on. "You may have heard it already. Do you know the story about Stupid and No-one? If you don't know it I'll be happy to tell you, and I promise you'll find it amusing."

Bragder looked at the pirate rabble as if to ask whether anyone knew the story. None of them spoke up so he shrugged and gave me an amused nod. "Let's hear it then," he said.

And I told them the story exactly as Nanni had told me back on the Wolf Islands. About how Stupid and No-one bought a gun and wanted to learn to shoot. No-one went first and the bullet ricocheted and hit him in the forehead, so Stupid ran to the village for help. But the hunters there thought he was behaving so strangely they asked him if he was stupid.

The pirates laughed so hard it sounded like thunder.

"Stupid and No-one," Bragder said, nodding towards Baldy and Beardy. "I think we've got their crew names now! What do you all think?"

The pirates all laughed again and voiced their agreement. The longer they laughed the more time I was gaining—and time was what I needed.

Suddenly, however, Baldy raised his voice and

roared: "Enough! Let me take aim properly and I'll show you a bull's-eye!"

He took hold of the medallion round his neck, his oarfish, which he had taken back. He held it in his hand for a long time before shouldering his gun and taking aim.

I looked at my friend, my good kind friend, who stood bravely on the ice. He smiled at me as if to say, don't take it too hard, Shrimp. Baldy cocked his gun and then…

"Stop!"

Someone was coming from the direction of the mine. This time, however, none of the pirates shouted out and none of them took aim; in fact most of them smiled and Bragder said: "Good morning, little Dove." He raised his cap and several of the others did the same.

Dove didn't respond to their ugly smiles and she spoke in a loud, clear voice: "Release the prisoner."

Some of the pirates smiled again and a couple muttered in amusement, the way people mutter when a child says something stupid.

"Can't be done, little Dove," Bragder answered. "Orders from Captain Whitehead."

"I am no longer little Dove. And Whitehead is no longer captain."

She held up her right hand. She'd had to put the ring on her thumb because it was made to fit a man's finger. But on her thumb or not, it was still a ring, and not any old ring but Whitehead's captain's ring.

"My father is dead," she said. "Bitten to death by his wolf because he harnessed it carelessly. I am the new captain of the *Snow Raven* and no one is to shoot that prisoner."

45

A Triple Salute

Bragder sent eight pirates to go and check that Whitehead was dead. They returned in double file using their guns as a stretcher. On the stretcher lay Whitehead.

They laid their captain on the ground and they all gathered around him. Later Dove told me their names and I thought I'd tell you them now.

They were Bragder and Iron, Sheepskull and Punchfirst, Porkchops and Faithful, Noisy and Noggin, Hairybelly and At-them, Young and Foxyfur, Frozen and Pretty, Poison and Fairwind, Trouble and Crabby, Knife and Tom Thumb, Healthy and Willing, Thumper and Rudder, Sober and Foresail, Danger and Goldteeth, Chopper and Smiler, Shot and Last Minute. And then there were the two who'd just been given their names by Bragder—Stupid and No-one. Every one of them took off his cap to Whitehead.

Dove joined them. She crouched beside her dad and looked at him for a long time, stroking his cheek with an expression impossible to read. I had to crane my neck to see and I studied his pale, staring face. His long white hair was bloodstained and the wolf's teeth marks were on his neck.

The men and women gathered around their captain wept silently. It was a strange sight: scarred, hunched, one-eyed pirates with tears running down their cheeks. I hadn't believed that pirates had souls, but at that moment I thought perhaps everyone has one; it's just that the soul finds a better home in some people than in others. If the soul is offered nothing but a harsh and frozen home it has no choice but to take it.

Bragder cleared his throat and spoke in a loud, clear voice. "Whitehead is dead! Fire a salute to our dead captain."

All those with guns pointed them in the air and fired salutes to Whitehead. Some reloaded and fired several times, shouting and yelling, "To Whitehead! To our dear captain! He was the terror of the Ice Sea!"

As the echo of the last shot died away Dove turned to me. "Go and release the prisoner," she said, for there was no one to stand against her now. She was the one giving the orders.

I ran over to Fredrik, so eager to untie the ropes

on his hands and feet that I tugged at the knots and made things worse.

"You'll have me in such a tangle I'll never get loose," Fredrik said.

"Ugh, what a blimming mess!" I said.

Once I'd managed to untie him I flew into his arms and held him so tight that my own arms ached.

"I'm sorry I haven't been much use on this expedition!" he said.

"You most certainly have. If it wasn't for you I'd never have dared."

He put me down on the ice and looked at me with his shining blue eyes. "It was a wolf, I heard."

I nodded. "It had scores to settle with Whitehead."

"Like that, was it? And you didn't have a finger in the pie?"

"Well," I mumbled. "Perhaps I helped things along a bit."

I felt my cheeks blushing. Was I a little afraid of what I'd done? After all, I was guilty of the death of a human being. And even though my actions saved many other people from death, I'd always carry a trace of that guilt with me.

Fredrik seemed to understand, for he ruffled my hair with his huge fist and said, "It's always easy to make cowardly choices. But every so often someone comes along who makes a brave choice.

And that is very fortunate for everyone else."

He looked at the gang of pirates and he looked at their new captain. "So that's Whitehead's daughter, is it?" he asked. "The prison warden?"

It's hardly surprising that he didn't recognize her. She'd changed a great deal in her twelve years on the island, becoming haggard, ugly and white-haired. But still…I could see he was wondering.

"Yes," I said. "She became his daughter. But before that she was the daughter of other people. Perhaps you'd like to meet her?"

With some reluctance he walked towards the shore. Dove was surrounded by men and women wanting to pat her on the back and talk about her dead father, whom they'd loved so much. When she saw Fredrik approaching she left the others and went to meet him.

They stood looking at one another. Fredrik shyly removed his cap and said, almost as a question, "I should thank you for sparing me, I believe."

She nodded. "Hello, Fredrik. Do you know if our mother and father are still alive?"

The air went out of him like a balloon, his eyes became shiny and his mouth sought the right words. The only thing he could think of came out as a whisper: "No. I haven't been home for a while."

She could see how sad he was and she understood how much he regretted the day he'd left her on the skerry. She realized, too, that it was because of her he'd sailed the seas for so long and, in a way, it was because of her that he was there now. Even though he'd never dared believe she was still alive. She wrapped her arms around him, big as he was, and embraced him. For a long time they stood like that and at last he couldn't help putting his arms around her. In that embrace they said things to one another that I couldn't hear and that, of course, was as it should be.

The pirates had saluted their dead captain and now they thought it was time to celebrate their new captain too. Chopper pointed out that the proper way was the grand way, for the crowning of a new pirate captain is not an everyday occurrence.

They all agreed on that and Dove gave them permission to ready the *Snow Raven*'s cannons. The crew swarmed aboard like manic beavers; the chance to fire the cannon really put a spring in their steps. Bragder went to the ship, but halfway there he turned around.

"Well, captain?"

Dove looked at him and then at Fredrik. "They're going to fire it for me now, big brother. You won't be afraid, will you?"

She followed Bragder across the ice and climbed the rope ladder to the ship, which was now hers to command as she wished.

Fredrik and I were left standing alone on the snow-covered shore. A short distance away lay Whitehead with his bloodstained hair. We saw the lids of the gunports being opened and heard the heavy gun carriages being turned to face the right direction. Someone was berated for dropping a cannon ball on the deck. Then, one by one, the cold, merciless, evil iron eyes poked out of the gunports.

After a few more preparations Foxyfur came hurrying up from below decks, tapped Bragder on the back and said something. At the same time he bowed to Dove a number of times.

Bragder nodded, raised his head and yelled, "Fire!" Smiler was standing by the hatch on deck and he repeated the order for the gun crews below decks to hear.

One after another the iron eyes flashed and thundered, a dense wreath of white smoke billowed around the *Raven*'s tubby belly, and the balls whined across the ice, making big, smoking holes where they landed.

When the last ball had been fired Bragder shouted, "Hurrah for Captain Dove!"

"Hurrah for Captain Dove!" The pirates at the rail took off their caps and waved them above their verminous heads.

At that moment, just when it seemed peace and quiet would return, there came a crash from out at sea. A muffled but tremendous sound that made the cannon sound trivial.

"What's happening?" I said.

"Don't you know?" Fredrik smiled. "It's the ice. It's cracking."

So that was it! The ice that made a thick, shining floor over the sea was suddenly breaking up. Perhaps the cannon balls had roused it, perhaps it would have stirred anyway. But the ice was waking up with crashes like thunder. Soon we saw water washing up over the big white ice-floes, but that didn't stop the noise. Crack followed crack, each louder than the last, and this put the pirates in such a solemn mood that they took their caps off again.

"Who's that salute for?" I jokingly asked Fredrik.

He looked at me. "Shrimp, that salute is for you."

◆ ◆ ◇ ◆ ◆

46

Free

With Fredrik at my side I walked through the snow that gradually changed from white to black. The crack and thunder of the sea had finally eased. In my pocket were Dove's keys and she'd ordered the children to be freed and prepared for their journey. *Snow Raven* was to take its prey back home.

The cottages by the mine lay strangely still, as if already they were no more than memories. No longer was there the ring of picks from underground. The doors to the machine cottage and to Whitehead's stood ajar, and the next storm would fill them with snow and make a tomb for his papers and devices. The wolf had run away, presumably out onto the ice; I hoped it would reach land safely.

We opened the door to the large building that resembled a jerry-built storehouse. The fire in the hearth had died long before and twenty children sat chained to their beds and trembling with cold.

"Siri!" one of them said, her face splitting in a smile.

I ran over and threw my arms around her.

"I was getting worried." Miki buried her face in my chest. "We heard bangs and crashes."

I laughed and squeezed her even tighter. "You don't have to worry about anything any more. We're going home." I raised my voice so that all of the coal-black mine children could hear my words: "All of us are going home!"

I threw the bunch of keys to Fredrik. It took him a long time to find the right keys and while he went around removing shackles, the children cautiously turned to one another and whispered. I had imagined joy, happiness and loud rejoicing when they heard the news, but I realized that what was happening was too great and difficult for them to take in all at once. They were free!

"Whitehead is dead," I said. "He died a couple of hours ago and no longer needs coal for his machine."

They were still whispering to one another, whispering and whispering that grew into something like bubbling and boiling.

"Are you the one who killed him?" one of them asked.

"No," I said.

"Who did it then?"

"It was the wolf."

There was more whispering and they rattled and tugged at their chains. The more impatient, those who'd begun to understand that this was real and they were no longer Whitehead's prisoners, rocked and pulled at their beds.

"And Dove?"

"Dove is the new captain of the *Snow Raven* and she's the one who's going to sail you home. I hope you can all remember the names of the islands you came from."

"I can remember!" one boy shouted. Fredrik hadn't unchained him yet, but he was so excited he couldn't keep still and stood up on his bed. "I come from Pale Isle!"

Another child immediately stood up and shouted, "I'm from Anchorsay!"

"I'm from Axholm!" a third child shouted.

"From Cliffholm!" yelled a fourth.

Child after child shouted the island they came from, and from which they'd been carried off to work in the mine. Not a single one had forgotten the name, because with every day that passed in the mine they'd yearned to go home.

Once they were all unchained we went outside. No longer herded by pirates with loaded guns, the children looked around as if the place were new to them.

"We're going down to the ship now," I said. "Follow me!"

And all of us, the children who'd worked in Whitehead's mine, set off together through the snow that changed from black to gray to white. Our names and our islands went like this: Ivar and Edla from Outersay, Saga from Fat Holm, Snar from Axholm, Vala from Valay, Sven and Ingmar from Dark Isle, Nils and Elis from Stocksay, Hella from Hornholm, Astrid from No Man's Isle, Unni from Underholm, Ymer from Pale Isle, Olaf from Weary Isle, Tora from Anchorsay, Daga from Saltholm, Agna from Cliffholm, Bror from Northwick, Brisa from Grayholm and then Miki and Siri from Little Bluesay.

Right at the back, whistling to himself, walked a big, red-haired man with a belly like a barrel. He laughed when Miki began nagging me about the new boots I really had to find for her now. And he remarked how strange it was that this whole adventure had started in order to help someone he'd never met before but somehow felt he knew so well.

As we approached the shore I noticed that the children were growing reluctant. Astrid, the girl who stole Miki's coal that day, suddenly said, "I'm scared. What if the pirates beat us?"

"They won't," I said.

Several others were having the same thought.

Olaf from Weary Isle came to a halt and said, "Wouldn't it be better to take the timber from the lift at the mine and build our own boat? Then we wouldn't have to sail with those swine."

"You'd starve to death a dozen times over in the time it took to build your own boat," I said. "They may be swine but they'll obey orders, and Dove has promised we're going home. And that we'll be safe and well."

Olaf mumbled about me having no idea how quickly he could build a boat, but the other children went along with me and walked the short distance remaining.

Dove was waiting on the shore. She had two oarsmen with her, Sober and Punchfirst, who had pulled the *Raven*'s rowboat up to the water's edge. The gray sea, newly woken from the winter freeze, was being whipped up by the wind, and ice-floes were dancing a dangerous dance on the waves. Clouds rolled rapidly across the sky like smoke from *Raven*'s cannon.

Dove stood erect, hair flying in the wind. She studied the children without showing any sign of what she felt, face to face with those who'd been her prisoners. She simply said, "Time for you to go aboard."

It was a big rowboat, an eighteen-footer at least, but there were many children to be fitted in. Small children squeezed together on the thwarts and bottom boards, arms wound around knees. It was pitiful to see the rags they were wearing; they must have been freezing.

Fredrik sat at the stern and Dove stood with one foot up on the forethwart. Sober and Punchfirst mustered all their strength to push the boat out into the waves, causing those on board to rock and sway. But not Dove!

Then the two oarsmen leapt in over the rail and the children ducked in fright to avoid the ice-cold water that followed them, which made Punchfirst roar with laughter. He took one oar and Sober took the other and we were off.

It was a choppy crossing of the bay. The children sat with chattering teeth and stared at the waves. Some glanced anxiously at the *Snow Raven* as we approached. None said anything.

Or, rather, there was one who spoke up. Miki had crawled forward and was tugging at Dove's trouser leg. Dove turned to look.

"I need new boots," Miki said.

"Shh!" I said. How could she possibly be so stupid? A dozen or more children had nothing but rags on their feet and she was whining!

But Dove gave her a quick nod and said, "We'll find better clothes for everyone."

The rowboat gave the hull of the *Snow Raven* a

gentle kiss as we came alongside. The rope ladders were dropped and one by one the children climbed aboard. Loyal and Foxyfur helped them with the last bit over the rail. Being the kind of men they were, they didn't miss the chance to poke as much fun as they could at anyone small and frightened.

"We can't take filthy kids like these with us," Foxyfur said. "It might be an idea to keelhaul the lot of them to tidy them up a bit."

"Nope, why not tie them all in a bundle and tow them behind the ship?" Loyal said. "We don't have time to keelhaul every one of the little rats."

Dove was climbing aboard just then and she told them to stop.

Once all the children, followed by Fredrik, had climbed up from the rowboat, Dove called out, "Porkchops and Noggin, warm up some water for washing! Healthy and Willing, find coats and shoes for all the children! Sober and Punchfirst, row back to shore and fetch my dad! Quick about it!"

The children climbed down to the deck below, accompanied by Porkchops, Noggin, Healthy and Willing. I stayed with Fredrik. My clothes had their share of holes but they would do until we were home in Blue Bay. I had no intention of putting on pirate clothes anyway.

Fredrik leaned his elbows on the rail and looked towards the narrows which was our gateway to the open sea. He looked good with the wind tugging at his hair, which shone as red as molten gold. I stood alongside and neither of us said anything for a long time. Sober and Punchfirst arrived back with Whitehead's body on the bottom boards of the rowboat.

"Do you think the porridge is any good on this vessel?" I asked Fredrik.

"Damned if I know," Fredrik answered. "Perhaps I should give them a hand in the galley."

"Yes. But we won't pick out the maggots for the pirates."

"No," Fredrik said. "They're welcome to them."

Neither Fredrik nor I could help smiling when Bror from Northwick came back up on deck. Bror had washed and put on new clothes. The jacket he'd been given was far too big and the sheepskin cap kept falling over his eyes so he had to push it up to see out. The next boy up was Ivar from Outersay who'd been given a pair of sealskin trousers so big he could have pulled them up to his nose.

One by one the mine children came up on deck dressed in warm pirate coats and trousers, caps and shoes. Everyone looked funny, but the funniest of all was Miki, for when she eventually appeared she was wearing boots so big it was a wonder she'd managed to climb the ladder. They all laughed at her but I went over, took her by the arm and said firmly, "Go back down and put on your old boots."

"But my old boots hurt!" Miki said.

"They'll do for now. Can't you see you're making a fool of yourself?"

"Why can all the others do it?" Miki pointed at the other children in too-big boots.

"They're not as small as you," I said. "Off you go."

But Miki cried and said that never, never, ever would she put her old boots on again. They were too small for her now and I should know that.

I had to give her another cuddle.

"Don't blame me," I said, "if you go head over heels every five minutes."

Miki assured me she'd do no such thing.

＊ ＊ ◇ ＊ ＊

Between Wet Holm
and Cat Skerry

If anyone asks me where Whitehead lies I'll say he's somewhere between Wet Holm and Cat Skerry, cradled in the long arms of the seaweed. And I was there when they put him over the side.

The weather wasn't pleasant that day, but then nor was the man they were sending down to the deep. He lay gray and cold on the boards of the half deck. His face, which had looked like that of an old man and a young man at the same time, now seemed carved in stone, and the bloodstains on his neck had gone black.

The crew had gathered around him. Fredrik and I stood a little to the side. Unni from Underholm, Olaf from Weary Isle and Daga from Saltholm wanted to witness the proceedings, but Miki and the others were huddled in the sleeping quarters below deck.

Wet snow had made the boards slippery. Loyal brought a bodybag and when he and Willing were about to lift the corpse, Loyal fell over. I can't decide whether that made the whole business ridiculous rather than horrific—or perhaps it was the other way around.

Anyway, once they'd put him in the bag they gave him twelve cannon balls to keep him company—he was a pirate captain, after all—and Loyal sewed it up tightly with many stitches. Porkchops, Dangerous, Foresail and Chopper, the four strongest pirates, picked up the white bag and walked to the stern, swung it three times and, on the count of three, in it went. It sank out of sight in seconds. One or two large bubbles rose to the surface as a sort of last greeting from the man who'd sunk his claws into my little sister and would never sink his claws into anyone again. Smiler sounded the ship's bell.

In the silence that followed I looked at Dove. She'd put her hair up in a bun and over her fur jacket she wore a sealskin cape, which I think had come from Punchfirst. There was a knife at her belt. Bragder could often be seen standing close to her, talking in a low voice. He seemed to be offering a good deal of advice and helping her make plans. The plans of a pirate captain.

I believe Fredrik was thinking the same as me because as Dove walked past he said, "Are you planning to be the terror of the Ice Sea now?"

She stopped. She looked offended, as if Fredrik was accusing her of something he had no right to bring up. She gazed out over the gray waters on which a thin, dull layer of snow had settled before turning to him.

"What did you think I intend to do? Go home to Fell Holm and eat cod roe?"

"There's nothing wrong with cod roe," Fredrik muttered.

"That's not what I'm talking about," Dove snorted.

She sighed, perhaps regretting her harsh tone. She nodded towards the small ladder that led down to the main deck. "Come with me a moment," she said. "Both of you."

We followed her down the ladder and Dove opened the door to the captain's cabin. It was exciting to see what it was like in there. There were woven rugs and beautiful oil lamps with elegant glass globes; there were books and candelabras; there were guns, some of which looked ancient, and on one wall was the stuffed head of a ringed seal with eyes of black glass and its sharp, white hunter's teeth visible in its open mouth.

Dove took off her knife belt and sat down in an armchair. She looked at Fredrik for some time. All these fine things and his sister with her hair done up in a bun seemed to have made him shy. She was a very different creature from Urstrom, who'd also had a lovely cabin with rugs and precious objects, though Fredrik had called him a worm. I couldn't put my finger on exactly what the difference was.

"There's nowhere for someone like me to go," Dove said.

"What do you mean by someone like you?" Fredrik asked.

"Someone like me? Someone who sold their soul to buy their freedom."

Fredrik threw his head back in a gesture I took to mean, what rubbish—that's hardly the end of the world!

But Dove said, "What do you think they'll say about me back on Fell Holm when they hear about it? When they hear I became Whitehead's daughter? That I became the prison guard who sent the others underground? Our parents weren't the only people whose children were abducted by the pirates. Two children from Fell Holm died before my eyes while I was on Whitehead's island. Of lung disease and exhaustion. And the boys the pirates took from Wolverine Isle were killed when a shaft caved in. Their father knows our father and they've fished together. What's their father going to say if I return home and feast on cod roe as if nothing had happened?"

Fredrik shrugged and looked as if he wanted to say something but couldn't find the words.

Dove shook her head and said again, "So there's nowhere for someone like me to go. Nowhere but the sea." She sighed and seemed to search for something to cheer him up. "I might possibly steal a sack or two of corn but I won't go near children. I don't want to see another child as long as I live."

Fredrik lowered his eyes. "It's just that...well, I dislike pirates so much," he said quietly.

Dove nodded. "Me too."

"So is that how it has to be?" he asked. "You go through the rest of your life disliking yourself?"

She didn't answer at first, but then a bitter expression came to her face, as if she'd tasted bile. "Perhaps," she said.

That's when I joined in. I felt sorry for Fredrik, who was looking more and more bent and miserable because, of course, he blamed himself for his sister's decision to become the terror of the Ice Sea.

"You say you've sold your soul," I said to Dove. "But it's not true. For the last twelve years your soul has had some pretty harsh treatment and so it's had to toughen up. It might take a while to coax it out of its wintry lair."

Fredrik looked at his sister and gave a little smile as if to say, what about that? "I think Siri is right," he said. "You're not the stuff pirates are made of."

Dove said nothing. I don't know if we'd annoyed her or if she simply thought we were stupid.

At last she fixed Fredrik with a piercing look and said, "Let's see what you can do to convert me."

She stood up, buckled on her knife belt and went out, leaving Fredrik and me alone. The ringed seal on the wall gazed at us and the ship rolled in the swell.

"Do you think you can?" I said. "Convert her?"

He scratched his big red beard and narrowed his eyes. "We'll see what can be done. I am her big brother, after all."

Through the small, leaded, bottle-glass panes I could see Dove's silhouette as she supervised the crewmen working at the stern windlass, hauling in the chains so we could leave the burial site and sail on. I understood then the difference between Dove and Urstrom, why he'd been afraid and why she would never be afraid again. It was because she had nothing in the world left to lose.

◆ ◆ ◇ ◆ ◆

Young Things

We made our voyage home at breakneck speed. Dove, who had once been frightened of every possible thing, was now utterly fearless. We sailed night and day across the raging Ice Sea, newly awakened from its frozen winter sleep. The pirates hung over the rail praying for their lives and when we struck unbroken ice, Dove didn't slow down as other captains would have. She ordered full sail ahead and *Snow Raven* flew as if on wings, its evil beak slicing through all hindrances. The pirates were terrified of Dove, but they also loved her, perhaps more than they'd loved Whitehead.

We encountered no other vessels. No one was mad enough to sail on a sea that resembled thick soup, a broth of water and ice-floes as big as our sails. Even if they had put to sea they would have turned tail at the sight of *Snow Raven*, the most feared pirate ship of all.

Three days after we buried Whitehead I was standing at the stern watching the waves. All those who could be in the sleeping quarters were down there. Snow was still falling, coating the deck with sludge and putting white whiskers on the stays. The only people on deck were the helmsman and me.

I stroked my hand along the wet rail, scooping up snow. I don't know why I'd left the others. I suppose I wanted to be alone for a while. It was many weeks since I'd set out from home and almost everyone I met on my journey had told me it would end in failure. But they'd been wrong.

I can't say, though, that the journey had a perfectly happy ending. Out on the Ice Sea I'd seen much I'd rather not have seen, things I was unlikely to be able to wipe from my mind. The wolf cub on the Wolf Islands, for instance, trying to cling to its dead mother's body. The chick whose life would be spent catching fish for Einar. And the purse I'd seen in Seglen. The one made of skin so soft and pale. I would never forget that purse.

The world that starts in the east at the island of Little Bluesay and ends in the west at the island of Outersay is like a table. That was my thought, anyway. And on this table, people sit and count their money. But the table is supported by legs, and those legs are young creatures. They're the ones we harness to our sleds, the ones we cut with knives, the ones whose throats we constrict and whom we send down beneath the earth with baskets and picks.

That's what the world is like and that, I thought, is evil. But then I saw a little snow bunting on the rail twitching its tail and I felt so happy that the heavy thoughts fell away. Perhaps it was just our age that was evil in that way, and perhaps there were better times to come.

The snow bunting sang for a while and then flew away as if something had frightened it. I turned to go back down to the warmth and found someone behind me. It was Baldy, the one the pirates had named Stupid.

His eyes were narrow slits and his mouth was pulled in an ugly grin, showing the cramped yellow teeth in his lower jaw. "Are you looking at the sea?" he asked.

"Yes." I tried to leave, but he elbowed me back against the rail, knocking the breath out of me as he did so.

His friend, now called No-one, stood a short distance away, acting as look-out in case anyone came or the helmsman turned around. He pulled his cap down over his ears and said, "Get a move on. I'm getting soaked."

Stupid grinned again and studied the gray waves, which were rising as high as the roofs of houses. Their foaming jaws seemed keen to swallow us.

"I'd like to thank you," he said, "for the names you gave us."

"It was Bragder who did that, not me," I said quietly.

"With plenty of help from you," Stupid snapped. "I'd have much preferred some other name."

In his eyes there was something like shame, or perhaps sorrow. Or both. I suppose the name Stupid was like a dunce's cap, reminding him of all his failures and disasters. It would always call to mind the shots that missed their target and hit the snow. And I was the one he blamed for branding him.

He moved in very close. "Perhaps you'd like a closer look at the sea."

"Leave me alone," I answered. "It's Dove who gives the orders and you have no say at all."

"Dove isn't here right now," Stupid said. "What if one of the children accidentally tripped and fell overboard? Her orders couldn't do much about that, could they?"

He looked at me scornfully and sucked on his foul yellow teeth. "Drowning you is unfinished business for me. You should've been dead long ago and there's only one explanation why you aren't: you took my oarfish into the water and that's what saved your life."

He held up the oarfish so I could see it properly. "But it's mine again now, tied on with a new thong that's good and strong and won't break whatever happens."

I was about to scream for help when Stupid grabbed me by the hair and clapped a hand over my mouth. He pressed me against the rail so hard I thought my back would break. In a moment I'd be over the side and into the sea.

I was going to die. I thought of the little snow bunting I'd just seen and of something Dad used to say: the snow bunting is the only bird in the Ice Sea that can sing. That made me so terribly sad, because the only thing I wanted in life at that moment was to be sitting on the steps with Dad hearing him tell me about snow buntings. And we'd be watching Miki run around playing by the sheds as she used to. Those were the things I most wanted and couldn't have because I was about to die.

All at once, there was a roar, followed by a yelp. Stupid turned to see No-one kicking and jerking as he skidded far across the wet deck. Fredrik had thrown him and now, enormous and raging, he was storming our way. Stupid released me and tried to run, but Fredrik caught him.

"Trying to kill my friend Shrimp, are you?" he growled. "Now it's your turn!"

"Don't throw me over!" Stupid stared in terror at the waves. "Please, whatever you do, don't throw me in!"

Fredrik screwed up his eyes. "No, I won't do that. You're so ugly the chances are the sea'd spit you back again. I'm going to kill you with my own hands."

He grasped the leather thong around Stupid's neck and twisted it until the pirate couldn't breathe.

"Let go!" Stupid gurgled, but Fredrik put another turn on the thong, and then another. Stupid had been right: the thong was good and strong and nothing was going to snap it.

Stupid hung there going bluer and bluer in the face. His eyes looked ready to pop out of their sockets and I was worried that Fredrik was really going to kill him.

No, Fredrik just meant to give him a real fright. When he put Stupid down on the deck the pirate collapsed, but then he was back on his feet like a shot. Coughing and hacking he ran away so fast he almost tumbled like a wounded animal down the ladder.

Fredrik looked at me. "I wondered where you'd gone. So it was lucky I came looking. I let a rat put you off the ship once before—and once is enough!"

I could only nod in reply.

"I'm off to have a word with the captain," Fredrik said. "I think it would be wise to put that pair of ruffians in the hold for a while. Teach them not to come up with so many stupid ideas."

I watched him go. Fredrik had told me he thought he'd been more trouble than help on this expedition. It's true that I had taken care of Captain Whitehead without him, but at this moment I knew I was fortunate to have had him along on my adventure. I was happy to have a friend like Fredrik!

* * ◇ * *

49

Blue Bay

Our ship now proceeded to call at every conceivable island, to return the children the pirates had kidnapped. We sailed to Outersay and No Man's Isle, to Fat Holm and Saltholm, to Axholm and Valay, to Stocksay and Northwick, to Hornholm and Underholm, to Pale Isle and Weary Isle, to Anchorsay and Dark Isle, to Cliffholm and Grayholm. And last of all to a small, insignificant island called Little Bluesay.

It lay on the eastern edge of Fredrik's map, so far east that if you went any farther you'd fall off the edge. Miki and I had to be more patient than all the others. Every time a boy or girl climbed down into the boat to be rowed ashore by the pirates, my heart ached. How I longed for it to be our turn.

The last to be dropped off before Miki and me was the girl called Brisa. She took it into her head to shake my hand when we said goodbye.

"I'm grateful to you," she said.

I didn't know what to answer and felt slightly ridiculous. I mumbled something inaudible, then Brisa in her fox-fur coat went to the rope ladder and climbed down. It was a good sign, though, that she shook my hand and said what she said. It showed that the animals from Whitehead's mine were becoming human again.

By the time the smoke of the houses at Blue Bay was finally sighted on the horizon I was so longing to get home to Dad that I was in turmoil. Would he be waiting for us? Or had he given up and told himself there was no point in hoping any longer? Our poor, poor father, what pain he must be feeling.

It was a beautiful day with the first signs of spring when *Snow Raven* hove to and the pirates lowered the rowboat.

Dove put her arms around me and said, "Take care now, and watch out for pirates."

"I will," I said. "Good sailing!"

Her broad smile showed almost every one of her yellow teeth. "Get away!" she said.

I went over to Fredrik, my big, wonderful friend with the red beard. I couldn't say goodbye to him as if we were parting forever. So instead I said, "See you!"

He nodded and said, "Yes, you will."

Then he picked me up, held me at arm's length and laughed as if he was the happiest person in all the world. And I laughed too; I couldn't help it.

Miki and I were helped down the rope ladder, which was just as well in Miki's case since her boots were big enough to sail in. Shot and Last Minute were already down in the boat, hands on the oars and ready to go.

"Right, girls," said Shot, who was bald and had a hump. "Let's be off!"

And we were.

They were both fine oarsmen and the boat seemed to cross the shining water in leaps and bounds. I felt a smile coming to my face at the sight of the skerries and reefs I knew like the palm of my hand, the skerries of *home*. There's something special about home skerries. They're somehow more beautiful than other skerries and they make your soul rejoice. Although when I saw Iron Apple I couldn't help thinking of the fateful foggy day that had started my adventure. And I felt I had to question Shot and Last Minute.

"What were you actually doing here?"

"How do you mean?"

"When you kidnapped Miki." I nodded at my sister, who was sitting by the rail trailing her forefinger in the water as she always did. "What made you go ashore on Iron Apple?"

Last Minute jerked his head and said they'd gone to pick snowberries.

"Is that true?"

Both of them nodded. They remembered it well because they'd managed to fill two baskets.

I hardly knew whether to laugh or cry. Pirates being fond of snowberries, just like all the Blue Bay children. It was the strangest thing I'd heard for a long time.

Miki didn't think it the least bit strange. She said it explained why she and I had barely found a single berry that day. Then she babbled on and said that was the worst day of her life and she'd never ever *ever* eat snowberries again.

"What will you eat instead?" I asked.

"Fish, of course."

"Lucky you've got me, in that case," I said. "Because I can catch fish."

"I can catch fish too," Miki said.

"No, you can't," I said.

"Yes, I can!"

"Rubbish! You've never pulled in a fish in your life. You can't even pull up a net without getting it in a tangle."

Shot and Last Minute giggled and gave each other looks. They were enjoying our bickering.

Miki glared at me. "I'll go fishing with *my toes*! Ha ha ha! What can you say about that?"

"I'm sure that'll be fine," I said, and Shot and Last Minute laughed again.

Later, though, when Miki was bigger, she actually was a wizard at fishing with her toes. She'd go down to the quay, take off her boots and socks and return in an hour with enough for dinner in our little gray cottage. And whenever I took another helping, she'd smile and say, "You're lucky you've got me, Siri, aren't you?"

I couldn't know that while we were in the rowboat, which is why I only said, "I'm sure that'll be fine."

The bay came into sight, with people scuttling here and there like frightened chickens. They'd no doubt learnt that the ship out in the roads was *Snow Raven* and that a rowing boat was approaching. They were all in a hurry—a frantic hurry—to get indoors, lock themselves in and shove the heaviest cupboards in front of the doors.

But one person stayed out. One person wasn't afraid. It was a man, small and gray like a twig, even smaller and grayer than when I'd last seen him. He looked almost as if he'd been snapped in half. He stretched up to see the boat better, and that's when I lifted my hand and waved.

* * ◇ * *

FRIDA NILSSON is a leading Swedish children's writer. She has published eleven books, translated into multiple languages, winning awards both in Sweden and internationally. In 2017 she was chosen by the Hay Festival as one of the best emerging children's writers in Europe for their "Aarhus 39" celebration of children's and YA authors. Nilsson received the Astrid Lindgren Prize in 2014, has been nominated for the August Prize three times, was nominated for the prestigious Deutscher Jugendliteraturpreis in Germany and several literary awards in France, including the Les Olympiades and Prix Tam-Tam.

The Ice Sea Pirates is Nilsson's first book published in English. It has won the Nils Holgersson Plaque, the Heffaklumpen Award and the BMF Plaque, was selected for the White Raven Award and nominated for the Nordic Council Prize for best children's book.

Frida Nilsson was born in January 1979. She lives in Mörkö, in the countryside outside Stockholm, with her family and two basset hounds.

The Travelling Restaurant
by Barbara Else

In the reign of Lady Gall (Provisional Monarch of Fontania), the word "magic" is forbidden. When 12-year-old Jasper Ludlow's parents flee the city, he gets left behind and finds refuge on *The Travelling Restaurant*, a sailing ship captained by old Dr Rocket and crewed by the feisty Polly.

Jasper faces challenges, adventures, storms and hungry pirates. Should he go in search of his parents, or his lost baby sister? Who should he trust? And why is Lady Gall hunting him?

"A heaping plateful of adventure, spiced to perfection with dangers, deft humor and silly bits."
Starred review, Kirkus Reviews

"This absorbing fantasy-adventure features an engaging, everyday protagonist who discovers courage, resourcefulness, and confidence in the face of familiar and fantastical events."
Booklist

"Constant action, lively language, and a Mahy-esque sense of whimsy carry the narrative as the mysteries unfold."
Horn Book Review

"An enchantment ... this is one of the best fantasy books I've read in several years"
Kate De Goldi, author of *The 10PM Question*

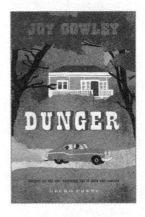

Dunger
by Joy Cowley

William and Melissa have been
roped into helping their old hippie
grandparents fix up their holiday home
in the middle of the Marlborough
Sounds. They'll have no electricity,
no cellphone reception, and only each
other for company. As far as they're
concerned, this is *not* a holiday.

"Utterly charming and engaging ... A great holiday read to
share, read aloud, or pass around."
The Alligator's Mouth

Winner, NZ Post Book Award for Children and Young Adults:
"Dry, droll and never dull ... rich and deep."
Judges' Report